DUST DEVILS

THE DESERT IS A GOOD PLACE FOR A VENDETTA

DUST DEVILS

A NOVEL BY

DOUGLAS BUCKLAND

Good Friends Are Hard To Come By
Vigilantes, Payback and Poetic Justice
Creative Retribution
The Jackrabbit Boogie
The Counterfeit Express
Catfish Alley

A 'dust devil' is a phenomenon that occurs in dry regions, usually on hot calm afternoons.

The dust devil is characterized as a small atmospheric vortex made visible by swirling dust picked up from the ground.

Dust devils typically do not cause injuries, but on occasion severe dust devils have been known to cause damage and even death.

CHAPTER 1

THE CHIHUAHUAN DESERT EXTENDS FROM the southeastern portion of Ariz
ona, the southern part of New Mexico, and much of West Texas down across
the Rio Grande River into the northern and central Mexican Plateau. Its
largest, continual expanse is located in Mexico, covering a large part of the
state of Chihuahua, hence the name.

There are several mountain ranges in the Chihuahuan Desert, including
the Sierra Madre, the Sierra del Carmen, the Organ Mountains, the Franklin
Mountains, the Sacramento Mountains, the Chisos Mountains, the Guadalupe
Mountains and the Davis Mountains. These mountain ranges create 'sky
islands' of cooler, wetter, climates alongside or within the desert and the
mountains may contain both coniferous, broadleaf woodlands and decent
grazing for cattle or sheep.

Wildlife in the region includes: coyotes, mountain lions, pronghorn
antelope, bighorn sheep, javelina, desert cottontails and kangaroo rats.
Western Diamondback rattlesnakes are also plentiful.

The desert itself is classified as a rain-shadow desert due to the presence
of the bordering mountain ranges. These ranges bordering the desert prevent
most of the precipitation in the region from reaching the area, creating an arid
and dusty desert climate. Some seasonal rainfall does occur within the desert
itself, usually between late June and early October. On average the mean

annual precipitation is 235mm or about 9.25". Summer temperatures in the desert range from around 90 to 104 degrees Fahrenheit during the day. The evenings, like in most deserts, can be chilly. The winters can be downright cold.

The floor of the desert consists of broad basins and valleys bordered by sloping alluvial fans and terraces, along with isolated mesas and mountains. The floor of the desert is generally considered to be desert shrubland, which is dictated by the harsh conditions and lack of water. Plant life has adapted to the unpredictable and scarce water supply and tends to be smaller, with the agave plant being the exception. Cacti, sage, yucca and buckbrush are common.

The Chihuahuan Desert is a hot, dusty, arid, dangerous sweat box of a place which most people would avoid at all costs, but to some hearty souls it is a brutally beautiful place to live in and call home. Dust devils are common occurrences.

CHAPTER 2

THE PORTION OF THE CHIHUAHUAN Desert located in Texas, just below the state line with New Mexico to the north and bordered by the Rio Grande River to the south, is particularly inhospitable, yet still contains a number of small towns. Large towns would be impossible due to their water requirements. These small towns are generally in locations to support local industry, such as it is. There are cattle and sheep concerns in and around the 'sky island' ecosystems created by the various mountain ranges, as well as many small mines eking out a living by bringing various minerals to the surface. Pecans and onions are the main agricultural crops. There is some oil and gas to be found under the desert, and the railroads connecting the small towns with the outside world need to be operated and maintained.

Grady Allison was born in the old Gibson Hospital located in Fort Stockton, Texas on the second day of May 1960. He was to be the only child born to Amelia and Sam Allison and he was their pride and joy. Sam Allison worked a variety of jobs in the oilfields around Fort Stockton, while Amelia worked as a secretary in the CCC rail yard there.

Grady was not overly disappointed with being born in the Chihuahuan Desert, he didn't know any better and had no idea that there was a world beyond the Davis Mountains to the west, the Glass Mountains to the south, the Stockton Plateau to the east or the Pecos River to the north. This all came to an abrupt end while he was attending Fort Stockton High School. While playing middle linebacker for the Fort Stockton Panthers, which at 6'1" and 200 pounds he was well suited for, chasing cheerleaders and hot rodding a '65 Ford pickup, he was required to take geography. This revealed to him that there were in fact other places worth visiting and perhaps other girls to chase. The question was, how was he going to get there? The United States Marine Corp provided the answer shortly after he graduated from high school in 1978.

Young Grady enlisted in the Marine Corps after graduation and was summoned to Camp Pendleton near San Diego, California for his indoctrination into the USMC and boot camp. Boot camp was a walk in the park for a kid who had grown up in the Chihuahuan Desert, and before he knew it young Grady was a PFC, private first class, with a Military Occupational Specialty (MOS) of 0300 which is a Basic Infantry Marine. After several years and several deployments with the fleet or overseas, Grady found himself as a Master Sergeant with the MOS of 0369, or Infantry Unit Leader.

It was while serving as an Infantry Unit Leader in the First Gulf War that Grady got shot in the butt, which left him with a permanent limp afterwards. While with the 1st Marine Division and in the rush to liberate Kuwait City back in 1991, Grady found himself leading a squad of Marines against the Iraqi's who had dug in at the Kuwait International Airport. Although the battle at the airport was mostly a field day for the Marine's armor and attack helicopters, there were still pockets of Iraqi soldiers embedded in the demolished airport that required the attention of the infantry Marines.

After Grady and his men had rooted out several machine gun nests burrowed into the rubble at the airport and things had died down for a while, Grady had just stood up to walk over to one of the LAV's (light armored vehicles) to figure out what to do next when an Iraqi sniper shot him in his right butt cheek and shattered his hip.

After being flown to Ramstein Air Base in Germany for his hip to be attended to, Grady was flown back to the Walter Reed National Military

Medical Center in Washington, D.C. for two more surgeries before he was medically discharged from the USMC.

With no real plan in mind, Master Sergeant (retired) Grady returned to the Chihuahuan Desert and took over the range and ranch management for the McKenzie Land and Livestock operation in the Davis Mountains just to the north and west of Fort Davis, Texas, just a hop, skip and a jump, or around 65 miles west-southwest of Fort Stockton.

It was while working as a cowboy for McKenzie Land and Livestock that Grady met, and married Mary Wassermann of the huge Wassermann Ranch located just west of Alpine. Mary was four years younger than Grady and was considered quite a catch. Of German stock, she was blonde, tall, willowy and attractive. She also didn't take any nonsense from Grady. It was a match made in heaven, they both agreed. Grady built Mary a nice 2,500 square foot ranch house at Bridge Springs in the shadow of Mount Livermore, an 8,378-foot-high mountain located in the Davis Mountains west of Fort Davis. Bridge Springs just happened to be located on a satellite ranch from the main Wassermann ranch outside Alpine, and it was bequeathed to Mary as a wedding present on the day she got married. Grady quit his job with the McKenzie Land and Livestock operation and began managing Mary's ranch at Bridge Springs.

Mary gave birth to Deacon Clay Allison in September of 1993. Like his father, Deacon was not overly disappointed being born in the Chihuahuan Desert because, like Grady in his youth, he didn't know what was beyond the mountains ringing the desert.

Although both of his parents were tall and his father had a husky, brawny build, Deacon developed a lean, rangy build and topped out around 5'10" tall. Oddly enough, he inherited his mother's blonde hair and ice blue eyes, which made him an oddity in a community that was around 75 per cent Hispanic. Unlike his father, Deacon played defensive halfback, not linebacker, for the Fort Davis Indians. Like his father, he decided to enlist to get out of the desert and see the world, but much to USMC Master Sergeant (retired) Grady's chagrin, Deacon enlisted in the Army.

Deacon finished his Basic Combat Training and Advanced Infantry Training at Fort Benning, near Columbus, Georgia. Over the years young Deacon moved up in rank and after attending and passing the U.S. Army Sniper School and the Ranger School, both again at Fort Benning, Deacon was invited to join the 75th Ranger Regiment and was eventually promoted to Sergeant First Class which was the rank he held when he finally left the military.

With nowhere else to go Deacon, like his father, also headed back to Texas after serving his country and settled in with his father until he could develop a plan for his future. Mary had passed away five years before Deacon came home and Grady was now by himself on the big ranch house at Bridge Springs. Mary had gone out to the woodshed one afternoon to get some wood for the fireplace in the living room that they used to knock the chill out of the air in the evening, when she was bit by a large Western Diamondback rattlesnake that had taken up residence in the woodpile. Grady was out checking livestock at the time and when he arrived home that evening, he found that Mary had made it to the front porch swing before she had passed away from the snakebite. Her funeral was a well-attended event and she was laid to rest in Hillcrest Cemetery located at the eastern end of Cemetery Road outside of town.

Grady and Deacon reconnected during this time and Deacon would often ride along with Grady on his daily rounds, either in a truck or on a horse, just to pass the time and relax. Eventually, Grady recognized the signs and knew that his son was getting restless and needed an outlet for his energy.

"Son, I know you don't want to chase cows with me all day, every day and you need something else to keep you occupied. I heard that that new lady sheriff in Fort Davis is looking for a deputy, maybe you could do that while you figure out what you really want to do."

Deacon had heard about the new sheriff in Fort Davis. She was young for the job but had brought new blood to the Sheriff's Department and a new way of doing things. She was also supposed to be damn attractive as well.

"Sounds interesting and I am a getting a little bored with chasing these cows. Maybe I'll run over there and check out the job and the new sheriff tomorrow."

CHAPTER 3

SHERIFF LORNA STIMS WAS NOT your typical west Texas county sheriff. First of all, she was a woman, which was not that common at the time she was elected to the job. Secondly, she was not a Texan by birth. Lorna had grown up in Chicago and after high school she had followed in her father's footsteps and gotten a Bachelor's Degree in Criminal Justice and Law Enforcement Administration at the Calumet College of St. Joseph in Whiting, Indiana. After graduation she moved back in with her mother and father in Chicago and applied for, and was accepted into, the Basic Metropolitan Recruit Program, just as her father had done decades earlier. After 600 hours of instruction with the BMRP, Lorna passed the Illinois State Peace Officer's Certification Exam and became a patrolman, or to be politically correct, a patrolwoman, on the mean streets of Chicago.

The only difficulty that Lorna had as a police officer, was the other police officers. Lorna was a very attractive auburn haired, hazel eyed young woman and it seemed that every unattached, and some attached, police officers in Chicago, regardless of which of the 25 precincts they were assigned to, had to make a run at Lorna. She didn't want the attention, but she loved the job, so she tried to be polite as she deflected their advances.

Even when she married Adrian Stims, an English professor at Wheaton College, whom she had known since high school, the unwanted attention did not ease up. She wanted to stay in law enforcement, but she needed to get out of the Chicago cesspool. Her father had watched this situation evolve over the years and was not happy about it either. One Sunday after church, when Jeff and Lorna were at her parent's house for dinner, her father casually threw out that he had heard that there was an opening for a sheriff in Jeff Davis County, Texas as the present sheriff was resigning due to health issues. Lorna picked up on this and her and Jeff did their research. Granted, the county seat for Jeff Davis County was Fort Davis, a small town of no more than 1,200 residents located in a desert, but Lorna and Jeff were still young enough to appreciate a good adventure, so they both took some vacation time and travelled to Fort Davis to have a take a look at the place. They fell in love with the wide-open spaces and after Jeff was offered a job as an English professor at Sul Ross State University in Alpine, a town about 25 miles southeast of Fort Davis, he put in his notice at Wheaton College and Lorna resigned from the Chicago Police Department. After they had a looked around a bit, they bought a small house at the corner of Catclaw Street and Court Avenue in Fort Davis and Lorna threw her hat in the ring for the sheriff's job.

While Jeff went back to Chicago to pack up their belongings and have them shipped to Fort Davis, they were very optimistic of Lorna's chances and decided to play the odds, Lorna hit the campaign trail, and she was a natural. She did not politic so much as just explained her background and education in law enforcement and then actually listened to what the residents of the county had to say. She won the election by a landslide.

Once Lorna was sheriff, she began to make some 'not so subtle' changes in the Jeff Davis County Sheriff's Office located at the northeast corner of Court Avenue and South Front Street, a mere three blocks from her and Jeff's new home. The first thing she did was to divide her county up into quadrants.

Jeff Davis County is an irregularly diamond shaped county with the long axis being east to west. The western point of the diamond was where Presidio County to the south ran into Culberson County to the west and the three counties all met at a point. The northern point was where Culberson County ran into Reeves County. The eastern point was the intersection of Pecos and Brewster Counties and the southern point was the intersection of Brewster and Presidio Counties to the south. Jeff Davis County was sandwiched between five other counties since both Pecos and Reeves Counties formed the northwest county line.

Lorna simply drew a line from the eastern to the western point and another from the northern to the southern point creating four triangular shaped zones. She assigned one zone to each of her three deputies, which left her a deputy short.

Enter Deacon.

CHAPTER 4

DEACON GOT HIMSELF CLEANED UP the morning after his father had mentioned that the Fort Davis Sheriff's Department was looking for a deputy, then jumped into the '70 Chevy short bed stepside pickup he'd been bringing back to life before going down the driveway and getting onto Madera Canyon Road and taking it the seven miles northwest until it hit County Road 118. Hanging a right onto 118, Deacon followed it into Fort Davis from the north. Taking a right on Court Avenue brought Deacon to the parking lot in front of the Sheriff's office.

Checking his look in the side mirror, he ran his fingers through his shoulder length blond hair, squared his shoulders and walked into the office. Pushing through the glass front doors, Deacon found himself facing a reception desk manned by an older grey-haired gentleman in jeans and a tan snap-button western shirt.

"Good morning! What can I help you with, young man?"

"My father mentioned to me that you may be looking to hire a deputy, and I thought I'd check into it," replied Deacon.

"Well, we are a deputy short at the moment. Who's your father?"

"That would be Grady Allison out by Mount Livermore."

"I guess that would make you Gunny's son, Deacon," said the guy behind the desk as he stood up to shake Deacon's hand. "You can call me Chuck;

your dad and I go way back. I'm an old deputy just filling in to help until Sheriff Stims gets her feet on the ground. Have a seat while I go let Sheriff Stims know you're here and what you're here for."

While Chuck went down the hall to the right of the desk, Deacon took a seat on the couch located to the right of the entry door and just settled down to wait for the Sheriff. Eventually Chuck came back and sat behind the reception desk and let Deacon know that the Sheriff would be with him shortly.

A few minutes later a very attractive auburn haired, hazel eyed woman in her early 30's, dressed in the uniform of the Fort Davis County Sheriff, approached Deacon and put out her hand. Deacon jumped to his feet and shook her hand. Sheriff Stims was not at all what he had pictured she would be like. The uniform failed to hide a very fine figure and her relative youth and the fact that she was wearing a Fort Davis sheriff's baseball cap with her long auburn ponytail pulled through the hole above the adjustment strap in the back did nothing to diminish her professional demeanor.

"Mr. Allison, I am Sheriff Lorna Stims. Chuck has told me that you may be interested in applying for the position of Deputy Sheriff. Would you mind following me back to my office so that we could have a chat?"

"I'd be happy to, Sheriff Stims." Any red-blooded male wouldn't have minded following Sheriff Stims to her office, the view from behind was just as good as the view from in front. Once they were in her office, Sheriff Stims walked behind her desk and indicated that Deacon should have a seat in the oddly out of place brown leather Chesterfield chair placed directly in front of the sheriff on the other side of the desk.

"So, Mr. Allison, Chuck has told me that your family has been in the area for quite a few years and that you grew up in and around Fort Davis. Other than that, what makes you think that you'd make a good deputy for me?" Sheriff Stims was direct and to the point. Deacon took a few seconds to collect his thoughts before answering.

"Sheriff Stims, I did grow up around here and I know the country from Van Horn to the Rio Grande River like the back of my hand. While this knowledge would no doubt be handy in the role of deputy, I think that it is my military training and experience which would be of more value to you and the Sheriff's office," replied Deacon.

"If I do consider you for the job, you'll need to provide me with a copy of your DD214, but perhaps you can give me the CliffsNotes version now," suggested Lorna.

"After graduating from high school here in Fort Davis I enlisted in the Army and did my Basic Combat Training and Advanced Infantry Training at Fort Benning. I was in the Army for 11 years and left the service with the rank of Sergeant First Class. I have attended and successfully completed both the U.S. Army Sniper School, the Ranger School and the Ranger Assessment and Selection Program," Deacon informed Lorna.

"So, you served with the Rangers?"

"Yes, with 1st Platoon Company A, Second Battalion, 75th Ranger Regiment."

"Impressive. Would you say that you are good at taking orders, even from a woman?" queried the Sheriff.

"Ma'am, if I was not good at taking orders I would never have been promoted beyond Private, let alone been allowed to serve as a Ranger. The military is built on the idea that legal orders will be followed without question. As for taking orders from a woman, I would have thought that even asking me that question was beneath you. No offense, but you are the Sheriff here and all of your deputies are men. In the military the gender of the person giving the order is immaterial."

Lorna hadn't expected that answer and sat back in her swivel chair behind her desk and contemplated the man in front of her. "Have you ever been deployed overseas?"

"I was deployed to Syria in 2019 when Hezbollah activity flared up, but I obviously cannot relate the specifics to you."

"Fair enough. Did you fire your weapon in anger while you were there?" asked Lorna.

"I never fired my weapon in anger, I only fired my weapon when it was necessary to complete the mission. That said, the Kateeb Hezbollah bunch would probably like to have a few words with me," said Deacon with a grin.

Lorna sat back again and gave the issue some thought. "Okay, Mr. Allison, I'll give your application, once you have completed all the paperwork, some consideration. Chuck will have an application packet ready for you when you leave, and I'll need a copy of your DD214 Army discharge form as well. I'll start the background check process today. Dismissed," Lorna said with a smile.

Deacon stood up, snapped to attention and saluted, which got a laugh out of Lorna. "Get out of my office, Top, I'll be in touch."

As Deacon was heading toward her door, Lorna advised him, "Mr. Allison, I noticed in the reflections from the other glass doors in the hallway on the way to my office that you seemed inordinately interested in my posterior. We will not be playing that game in this department. I am a very happily married woman, and I intend to remain so. Apparently, I am an attractive woman, but this caused problems for me back in Chicago and I do not intend to go through that again. Is this understood?"

Deacon turned around and faced Lorna. "First, I think that you underestimate yourself. I'd bet that you must have passed 'attractive' somewhere during your high school days. How about we meet in the middle and you just allow me to read the menu, and I promise I will not try to order?" he said with a grin.

Lorna was trying not to laugh as she pointed at the door and shouted, "Out!"

CHAPTER 5

THE APPLICATION PACKET CHUCK HELD out to Deacon as he left was pretty thin, about a dozen pages detailing the application process, which needed to be submitted electronically. Since the internet was not very strong out at his father's place, Deacon spent a lot of time over the following week at the Jeff Davis County Library, three blocks from the Sheriff's Office, using the library's internet connection and his own MacBook Pro to complete the application and submit it.

Keep in mind that Fort Davis only has a population of around 1,200 souls on a good day. That being the case, there really wasn't much in the way of amenities in town. During the week that Deacon was preparing his application for the deputy's job, he'd walk over to the Blue Mountain Bar & Grill to grab lunch. The Blue Mountain Bar & Grill was only a short 75-yard walk from the library to their front door on Texas Mountain Trail, which is what State Highway 118 was called as it passed through town.

Usually, Lorna just walked the three blocks from the sheriff's office to her home for lunch, but on the Wednesday after her interview with Deacon she must have felt the need for a change of pace and went to the Blue Mountain Grill for lunch. Deacon had already ordered and had taken a table by the front window when Lorna walked in. She said hello to some folks before going to the bar and taking a seat to order her lunch. If you are alone, it is generally considered bad manners to take up a table by yourself and you sit at the bar, unless like Deacon you were working on your computer and needed the space.

Deacon watched her come into the bar and had to admit she was one fine-looking sheriff but keeping in mind Lorna's admonition about fraternizing among the ranks, he didn't bring attention to himself. Lorna, in seemingly total disregard for her own rules, finally noticed Deacon sitting by the front window and strolled over to his table.

"Do you mind if I have a seat?" she asked.

"You'd better not, the sheriff will kick our asses for fraternizing," Deacon replied with a straight face as he moved his paperwork and computer out of the way to make room.

Pulling out a seat, Lorna replied, "You let me worry about that old hag of a sheriff." She was grinning as she said it.

"How's the application coming along?" asked Lorna.

"Typical government paperwork, just like in the army. I'm used to it. We don't have good internet at dad's place so I'm spending my days at the library getting it done."

Their meals came, a grilled chicken sandwich for Lorna and a chicken fried steak for Deacon, so they just chatted while they ate their lunches.

"So, you had some problems with unwanted attention back in Chicago?" asked Deacon, not knowing if this was an off-limit topic or not.

"Yeah, I did. I suppose it was to be expected in a male dominated job like a cop, but I thought that I could handle it. I figured it would stop when I married Adrian, but it seemed to make it worse, like I was now forbidden fruit that needed to be taken."

"I have the exact same problem!" Deacon exclaimed. "I can't go anywhere without women just throwing themselves at me! It does get to be annoying, doesn't it?"

Lorna looked at Deacon for a second before she realized he was just pulling her chain and laughed. "I'm serious Mr. Allison, the advances got to be very old and very bold. My dad was a cop in Chicago, which is likely why

I became one. He warned me that this might happen, but I didn't realize just how bad it could be. Anyhow, my dad told me about the sheriff's job here and Adrian and I came down to take a look. It's a whole different planet than Chicago, but we like the people and the country is beautiful, in its own way. When the university down in Alpine offered Adrian a job, I stayed here and began campaigning while Adrian went back to pack up our things in Chicago."

"That was taking a risk, what would you have done if you hadn't been elected?"

"I never lose, Mr. Allison, never. You should write that down," suggested Lorna.

"I haven't had a chance to read your DD214 yet so excuse my ignorance but tell me some things about yourself, Deacon. How old are you, have you ever been married, what are your plans now that you are out of the military? You know, some personal stuff."

"I'm 29 years of age. No woman in her right mind has had or would have me. I plan to rectify that in the future, but no rush. As far as the future goes, I'll play it by ear. It's kind of nice just hanging out with my dad at the moment."

By the time they had finished their lunches they were just relaxing and enjoying each other's company over a coffee, but eventually it was time for them both to get back to work. As they stood up, Lorna looked over at Deacon and let him know that as far as she was concerned, he had the job, but the paperwork still needed to be processed correctly. The quicker he got it done, the quicker he could start earning a paycheck.

"By the way, we are a vehicle short since Tito wrecked the Ford Explorer cop wagon that you would have gotten. Do you happen to have a truck or SUV that you can use until I can afford another one?"

"No problem. I'm in the process of rebuilding my old '70 stepside Chevy. I'll get the new engine and suspension in it while you process my application. It should be ready to go in a week or so."

"Fine. See you soon, Mr. Allison," said Lorna as she sauntered across

Texas Mountain Trail on her way back to work while Deacon headed back to the library to get his application sorted out.

By Friday Deacon had collected and collated all of the information necessary to apply for the job as deputy sheriff in Jeff Davis County, Texas, and had submitted the application electronically to Lorna. He now just had to wait for the call.

Since Lorna had essentially said that the job was in the bag, he spent his time getting his truck together so that he would have something to drive when he eventually got put on the payroll.

He'd bought his stepside from a rancher over in Van Horn before he'd gone into the military back in 2011. It had sat under an old tarp since that time. The dry desert climate had ensured that the body and frame had not rusted during its time under cover, but the engine would need to be rebuilt, and the suspension upgraded, especially if he was required to do any off-road stuff in his new job.

Grady had a few outbuildings around the ranch house that formed sort of a courtyard in front of it. Deacon was using the garage directly across the courtyard from the ranch house to rebuild his truck in. Rigging up a chain fall to a rafter in the roof, Deacon removed the hood and pulled the 350 cubic inch motor out of the old stepside. Getting it onto an engine stand, he got to work. Taking off the original intake manifold and carburetor, he pitched them to one side before removing the valve covers and the heads. The water pump, timing chain cover and timing gear came out next along with the distributor. Turning the motor upside down on the stand, he pulled off the oil pan and pulled out the crankshaft and pistons before rolling it back over and taking off anything else that wasn't needed before he took it to the machine shop in Fort Stockton to have the old block acid dipped and checked out to make sure nothing was cracked and that everything was within tolerance.

While the block was getting cleaned up and acid dipped, the crate arrived from Summit Racing with just about everything else he'd need to put his engine back together. This included a set of cast-aluminum flat-top pistons to go along with the Summit Racing Vortec 67cc-chamber heads. This would kick up the compression ratio at least one full point from the original set up. A slightly more performance-oriented hydraulic roller cam was also in the crate along with the correct hydraulic roller lifters, push rods, bearings, gaskets and other jewelry to put the thing together. Once it was finished, Deacon reckoned it would be good for at least 400 horsepower.

A few days after the crate arrived, Deacon took his dad's old Ford F-100 pickup to Fort Stockton to collect the block and bring it back home. Getting it back on the engine stand he took his time and rebuilt the engine before putting it back in the old stepside. The original transmission was the 4-speed manual Saginaw. Since this was essentially bombproof, it went back in as well. A new carburetor and intake manifold were needed to feed the new heads and cam set-up, and Deacon had gone with an Edelbrock Super Victor 23-degree intake topped off by the Edelbrock 750 cfm Performer carburetor with an electric choke. The exhaust system needed an upgrade as well, so a set of black Hedman headers were installed. Each header tied into a Summit 2-chamber performance muffler before exiting via dual exhaust at the back of the truck.

Suspension was now the issue. Deacon essentially needed a scaled down version of a suspension suitable for the Baja 1000 race. This took some research. Eventually he settled on the Ridetech front and rear coil over conversion specifically for older Chevy trucks. Lifting the body 2" allowed for the installation of 31" General Grabber AT/X tires on a set of 16" black Daytona (Series 84) wheels from the U.S. Wheel Corporation.

The truck still had the original Medium Blue paint job, and it cleaned up well after a wash, polish and wax. The interior was the grey motif and it was still in good shape as well. As far as a set of wheels was concerned, Deacon was now good to go whenever he got the call.

CHAPTER 6

THE CALL CAME THE FOLLOWING Friday. Deacon was sitting out on the porch with Grady after they had just finished cleaning up after a dinner of spicy homemade chili and cornbread when Deacon's cellphone rang.

"Deacon here," answered Deacon.

"Funny, that's the number I called, how convenient," was Lorna's smart-assed reply. Continuing in this vein Lorna asked, "If it is not too much trouble, and if you can fend off all of those women throwing themselves at you, do you think you can manage to come by the office on Monday and start performing the duties generally expected of a new sheriff's deputy?"

"Let me check my schedule," replied Deacon as he looked over at his dad and winked. "Since it appears that I have no conflicting appointments or any trysts scheduled at that time, I should be free Monday morning to come by and begin my penance as a sheriff's deputy. Have you given any more thought to the idea of my reading the menu while refraining from ordering?"

"Good, I'll see you on Monday at 0800. Please remember to bring your truck as I don't have a spare one at the moment. In regard to the menu and ordering issue, I have not given it any further thought as I believe that I have explained the situation to you sufficiently. If you would attempt to place an order, I would attempt to shoot you. Besides, where would you find the time with all those hussies throwing themselves at you?" replied Lorna just before she hung up.

Putting his phone back in his shirt pocket, Deacon informed his father that he was now looking at the newest deputy sheriff for Jeff Davis County. His father congratulated him on his new job before suggesting that he may be acting a little flippant with his new boss.

"Dad, Lorna is definitely an eyeful whether in these parts or any other parts. She has made it abundantly clear that she does not want any unwarranted attention, and she will not put up with it. It seems that this unwanted attention had a lot to do with her and her husband leaving Chicago. That said, she's only a couple of years older than I am, she's a hoot to be around and she gives as good as she gets when it comes to our banter. She has made it abundantly clear that she is very happily married, and I have no intention of trying to horn in on Adrian's, that her husband, action. That is a line I will not cross," explained Deacon.

"Well, it's good to know I raised a kid with a good moral compass. Most guys in your shoes would be trying to get into her pants from the get-go. In fact, you may be able to help her out by casually letting other folks know that the sheriff is not interested in any unwanted attention. What goes around comes around, she may return the favor later when you need it most."

Monday morning rolled around, and Deacon fired up his old stepside and drove it to the Sheriff's office. He didn't push it as he was going to take his time breaking in the new engine properly. That said, the engine seemed to be a beast, and the suspension was tight and firm, but not uncomfortable.

Pulling into a parking spot in front of the Sheriff's office on Court Avenue as quietly as his new exhaust system would allow, Deacon shut down his truck and made his way into the office only to find Chuck waiting for him.

"They're waiting for you in the conference room on the other side of the hall from the sheriff's office. Don't let them rattle you, they'll try."

"Thanks for the heads-up, Chuck. Better folks than they have tried to rattle me during my time in the army, we'll just have to see how it goes," replied Deacon with a grin.

Sure enough, when Deacon opened the door to the conference room there were three men, two Latinos and one Anglo, on the far side of the conference table with Lorna at the head of the table to the right and another girl, who looked just out of high school, at the opposite end of the table from Lorna. There was a single chair on the side of the table opposite the three men and it was obvious that Deacon was supposed to park his butt there.

"Take a seat," commanded the Latino man sitting in the middle of the other two.

Deacon had spotted a coffee urn and a tray of cups on a counter running the width of the room behind the young girl sitting at the other end of the table from Lorna. "I'll grab a coffee first, if you don't mind."

"I do mind, I told you to take a seat."

Deacon went and got a coffee anyhow before returning to the empty chair and sitting down. Looking directly at the man who had told him to take a seat, he took a sip of coffee then began to set the stage for his new role as deputy sheriff. It was obvious that the three men across the table were the other Jeff Davis County deputies, and he needed to put his cards on the table before they took a run at him.

"Gentlemen, perhaps you can correct me if I'm wrong, but I believe that I have been hired as the new deputy. If that is the case, then I take orders from Sheriff Stims and only from Sheriff Stims. I'm obviously a few years younger than you guys, and I am a huge fan of experience and learning from that experience. That said, I spent 11 years in the service, much of that time with the 75th Ranger Regiment. I left the service with the rank of First Sergeant after getting shot in Syria in 2019. I may not be an experienced law enforcement officer at this time, and I would greatly appreciate any assistance you can give me in becoming one, but I seriously doubt that you have the tactical training or the experience taking orders that I have. If you have any questions concerning my background or abilities, I would be more than happy to answer them, but I will not be treated as a junior member of this team. Let's get this over with."

The conference room got deathly silent after Deacon's monologue, but eventually the Latino deputy that had told Deacon to take a seat stood up and reached his hand across the table. "The names Tito Maldonado, very glad to make your acquaintance Mr. Allison. No hard feelings, the sheriff wanted to see if I could rattle you."

By this time, the other Latino deputy and the Anglo one had stood up to shake his hand as well.

"I'm John Carter," said the Anglo." Pleased to meet you."

"I'm the smart one," said the last deputy, "Armando Ruiz at your service."

By this time, the girl at the end of the table had come over by Deacon to introduce herself as well.

"I'm Macy. I'm the dispatcher here and I have seniority over you by a little less than a month. I think we'll be learning the ropes together," she said with a smile.

After this, they all got down to business. Lorna explained how she had divided up the county into quadrants and assigned a quadrant to each deputy. Since the deputy Deacon was replacing had been responsible for the southwest quadrant of the country, basically an irregular triangle with the northern point located at the McDonald Observatory on Mount Locke and the eastern leg extending from there down to the point where Jeff Davis County met with Brewster and Presidio County. The western leg stretched from the observatory to where Jeff Davis County touched both Culberson and Presidio County, which just happened to be a point on the Rio Grande River. The entire base of the triangle bordered Presidio County to the south.

Lorna was in the process of persuading the county that they needed to budget for additional deputies, but even if she was successful, it would take months to work the budget through the county and state bureaucracies so they would have to make do with the four present deputies, Macy the recent high school graduate dispatcher and Chuck, the retired deputy, and of course Lorna providing support as necessary.

Jeff Davis County consisted of 2,265 square miles of essentially desert scrub, the Davis Mountains, and 0.08 square miles of water in various basins within the county. The population of the entire county was 1,996 according to the 2020 census. It was a very desolate piece of real estate and was a perfect place to hide out and do bad things such as cook meth and traffic people among other things. With only four full-time deputies all that the Jeff Davis County Sheriff's Office could reasonably be expected to do was 'put out fires', that is, to react to situations as they arose.

Although each deputy would be assigned a quadrant, they would be on-call to assist any deputy in any other quadrant. The key to this strategy would be communications. All the deputies' vehicles, 2020 Ford Explorers including the replacement for the one Tito trashed in an arroyo chasing a group of illegal aliens, would be equipped with Motorola MW810 mobile workstations with the base station being installed in Macy's office. Everybody would be issued a Motorola MOTOTRBO Ion personal handheld radio and would be required to have it on or near them at all times. Everybody would be on-call 24/7 until Lorna could hire more deputies to relieve the pressure. All radios would be able to communicate with the other sheriff departments of the five counties surrounding Jeff Davis County.

They would all be working 12-hour shifts until new blood could be brought into the office. Lorna realized that this would wear down her officers and crew and if anyone felt that they were burning out and needed some down time to recuperate and get their head back in the game, that she would take over shifts as required.

The sheriffs in the surrounding counties were well aware of the personnel shortage in Jeff Davis County at the moment due to health issues, resignations and retirements and they were all willing to help out in any way they could.

Lorna told the crew that if they had any issues or problems due to the workload until they could get crewed up, that they needed to bring them to her sooner rather than later before they could negatively impact the performance of the department.

At this point Lorna shooed everyone out of the conference room and laughingly told them to quit slacking off and to get back to work.

"Deputy Allison, may I have a word with you?" asked Lorna before Deacon could get out the door.

"Sure, what's up?"

"I never knew that you got shot! Where were you shot?"

"I think they still call it Syria, but place names seem to change regularly over there so I may be wrong," Deacon informed Lorna.

"No, you idiot, where on your person did you get shot. It could affect your performance."

"I'd have to drop my pants to show you the scar. I guarantee you that it will not affect my performance in any way, but once I drop my pants to show you the scar you may not be able to restrain yourself," retorted Deacon with a lecherous grin.

"I'd likely laugh myself silly, Mr. Allison. Let's forget that I asked."

"Hold on Sheriff, I was just joking with you." Pulling his uniform shirt out of his jeans he showed her the puckered scar of an entry wound on the right side of his abdomen at the same level as his navel. Twisting around he showed her the larger puckered scar of an exit wound.

"The day before I was supposed to go home, I got careless and stood up when I should have stayed down and some jihadi popped me with an AK-74. Those wicked little 5.45mm rounds can do some damage," said Deacon as he tucked his shirt back in.

Lorna was thinking about the incredible six-pack abdomen she's just been exposed to as she asked, "Did it hurt?"

"Of course not, I'm a Ranger!", declared Deacon in mock annoyance.

"Bullshit!", asserted Lorna.

"Okay, it actually hurt like a bastard, but it was a through-and-through, and we had a medic with us, so I was in good hands as soon as I got hit."

Sheriff Stims looked like she was pondering something for a moment, then said, "Too bad you weren't shot in the leg, then you really would have had to drop your pants," she said with a grin.

"Lucky for you I wasn't. I'm going commando today and it would have taken you weeks to recover from the exposure to my toxic masculinity, for lack of a better term."

"Dream on, soldier," laughed Lorna.

Getting back to business, she said, "Okay, since we've got that out of the way, I think that since you will be driving an unofficial sheriff's vehicle, I thought that I should take the time to inspect it and make sure it is suitable for the job."

Walking out to the parking area in front of the office where Deacon had parked the old '70 Chevy stepside, Lorna asked Deacon to give her a brief summary of the truck and it's running gear.

"Well, Sheriff Stims, she started out as your typical 1970 Chevy C10 short bed stepside truck. I bought her while I was in high school, and she's sat under cover at my dad's place until I got out of the service. Since I've been home, I've rebuilt the engine and upgraded the suspension to coil-overs on all four corners. The rear axle is a heavy duty 12-bolt unit with stout Global West tubular upper and lower control arms to set the pinion angle. She's only rear wheel drive, but with the old Saginaw manual four-speed transmission I've got a 'Granny low' first gear to get me through any rough spots," Deacon informed her with pride.

'Okay, pop the hood, I want to see what's under there," demanded Lorna.

Deacon opened the hood then stepped back to let Lorna take a look.

"That does not appear to be the original motor. What is it and how much grunt does it have?" asked the sheriff.

"It's not a race motor per se, just an upgraded 350 that breathes a bit better than the stock motor. I'm still breaking it in, but I think if I could get it on a dyno it would run about 400 horsepower. I'll build a rollbar for it and get a toolbox up against the cab in the bed to store my kit. So, Sheriff Stims, what do you think? Does she pass inspection?"

"It's a pretty impressive truck, but she lacks one more piece of equipment before you can put her on the road. Hold on a minute, I'll be back."

Lorna walked back into the office and came back with a flat cardboard box about 3' square. After opening the tailgate, she laid the box on in the bed before pulling out two magnetic vehicle signs showing the Jeff Davis County Sheriff's Office logo embossed on them.

"You'll need these on your truck before you go gallivanting around the county on duty, you can take them off when you are on personal business. I'll get you one of those Kojak lights you can plug into the cigarette lighter and stick on the roof later. This is just until we can get a replacement Explorer for the one Tito wrecked."

Putting the signs back into the box, shoving the box into the bed and closing the tailgate, Lorna informed Deacon that he could now take her to lunch so that she could take a ride in the newest addition to the Sheriff's Department motor pool.

"Lorna, it's just after breakfast, where did you have in mind for lunch, Fort Stockton?"

"No, we'll take a run down to Alpine and pick up Adrian after his morning classes and have lunch at Magoo's Place."

"Do you really think it is a good idea for the recently elected, incredibly good-looking Sheriff to be seen driving around with the recently hired and also incredibly good-looking county deputy. I thought you were trying to avoid unwanted attention? The neighbors will talk, and this will be all over town before sundown," informed Deacon with a smirk.

"First off, it is an order. You do remember our discussion regarding following orders, don't you? Second, Alpine is in Brewster County so we should be safe from nosy neighbors. Third, I want to touch base with Sheriff Gutersohn regarding reports of people trafficking in the area and for him to meet my new deputy and lastly, I want you to meet Adrian. It's good to meet new people and let's face it there aren't too many Anglos our age in the area. Now drive, we'll stop by the Brewster County Sheriff's Office on the way to pick up Adrian."

"Yes ma'am," was all that Deacon could come up with as a reply.

CHAPTER 7

ON THE WAY TO ALPINE they just made small talk and told each other a little more about themselves. Deacon hadn't had time to put in a sound system yet to listen to his preferred '70's and '80's rock and roll, so they really had to either make conversation or drive in an uncomfortable silence.

Somewhat to Deacon's chagrin, it became obvious that Lorna was deeply in love with Adrian and vice versa. That said, he thought it was actually nice since in this day and age marriages tended to be looked at as temporary or limited duration contracts. He envied them and wondered if he'd ever be in the same place as they were.

When they hit the long straightaway on 118, the North Davis Highway, north of Alpine, Deacon opened up the old stepside for about a mile, and was doing well over 100 miles per hour before Lorna grabbed his arm and told him to shut it down before she wrote him a ticket. She was laughing as she said it and actually seemed to enjoy the rush.

The North Davis Highway became North 5th Street as you pulled into Alpine, and they followed this until they came to West Sul Ross Avenue before Lorna indicated that they should take a right on Sul Ross. They drove two blocks before coming to the Sheriff's Office on the left, at the corner of West Sul Ross and 7th Street. Pulling into the parking lot, Deacon shut down the truck and they got out and walked into the building.

At the reception desk on the ground floor, the receptionist had them wait until she'd called and cleared the visit with the Sheriff. Once that hurdle had been jumped, Lorna and Deacon took the stairs to the second floor and walked down the hall to the northwest corner of the building where the sheriff's office was located. Even though they were expected, they walked to the sheriff's door and knocked before being told to come in.

Sheriff Gutersohn was in his mid-60's, had his hair cut flattop style, and a neatly trimmed moustache that was turning grey. He was also slightly overweight and had a cheery disposition. He got up from behind his desk and came over to give Lorna a professional handshake.

"Sheriff Stims, good to see you again. What brings you down to my neck of the woods, and who is the riff raff with you?" he asked.

"Always a pleasure to see you, Sheriff Gutersohn. I'm breaking in a new deputy and thought I'd get him used to the chauffeuring part of the job and had him drive me down here to discuss the issue you phoned me about the other day. Sheriff Gutersohn, let me introduce Deputy Deacon Allison."

As the sheriff shook Deacon's hand he asked, "You're not by chance related to that old coot Grady Allison who hangs out in the Davis hills are you?"

"Guilty as charged, sir. The old coot is my father."

"Well, tell the old codger that Hank Gutersohn said to say hello and to come down to Alpine for a beer someday, I'll buy."

"You know my dad?"

"I know him well. We went to high school together, played football together, and when he went to join up with the Marines our paths went different ways; he went into the military, and I started a career in law enforcement. Since he's come back, we've gotten together a few times, and we stay in touch when we can."

Turning to Lorna he said, "If the apple didn't fall too far from the tree, you've likely got yourself a good deputy there. Now let's sit down over at the coffee table there in the corner and have a chat about what's going on down here."

After everyone had a seat and coffee had been poured, Hank began to discuss recent events which had him worried.

"As you know, the southern boundary of my county is the Rio Grande River, right up against Old Mexico, about half of that is in Big Bend National Park and Big Bend Ranch State Park. I've always had a problem with illegal immigrants coming across the border in my county and it has gotten worse with Biden and his policies, or lack thereof. This I understand. Sheriff Cabrera over in Presidio County, whose southern boundary is also the Rio Grande, has also seen an increase in activity, mostly between the official border crossings at Presidio and Candelaria, which is again expected with these open border policies. What has Sheriff Cabrera and myself concerned is that there seems to be more activity than usual right at the point on the border where Jeff Davis, Brewster and Presidio counties come together at the border near Lomas de Arena. This part of the border has always been uncommonly quiet and we have always thought that this was due in part to the inhospitable terrain, although it is only about 20 miles from the border to the town of Lobo, and the actions of the Mexican law enforcement officers on the other side of the border, for some reason they seem to be more active in that area than anywhere else."

Taking a sip of coffee, Hank continued. "The thing that really concerns both Sheriff Cabrera and myself, is that there is a significant uptick in the number of women and children being trafficked through this corridor. The drug busts have dropped to almost nothing, but the apprehensions of young women and children being herded by the 'coyotes' or guides assisted by cartel gunmen is rising quickly.

"Intelligence from the Drug Enforcement Agency indicates that a new cartel, a splinter group of the Juárez Cartel and with their blessing, has begun to operate out of a base in San Juan del Hueso, about 30 miles into Old Mexico, west of where our three counties meet at the border.

"This splinter group is referred to as the 'Roosters' or the Gallo cartel, for no apparent reason. I just wanted to give you a head's up so that maybe you can be on the lookout for these jackasses as well as keep your eyes and ears open for anything to do with the Roosters."

After finishing their coffee, Hank walked them down to the front door and asked them to let him know if anything came up on their radar concerning this new bunch.

"I assume that you are now going to go grab that incredible lucky husband of yours at the university and take him to lunch. Please tell Adrian I said hello," Sheriff Gutersohn instructed as they walked out the front doors.

With that, Lorna and Deacon got back in the truck, which had been sitting out in the sun and was now broiling inside. Lucky for Lorna, Deacon had reinstalled the factory air conditioning when he rebuilt the truck, so after firing up the truck he kicked on the air conditioning and they just stood outside the truck with the doors closed for a few minutes before getting in to go roust Adrian.

Lorna had called ahead so Adrian was waiting just outside the front entrance of the Briscoe Administration Building on the East Ross Avenue roundabout. He jumped in sandwiching Lorna in the middle, which caused Deacon some discomfort. This was not due solely to the fact that she was an extremely fit and attractive women in close proximity, but also to the fact that she was an extremely fit and attractive woman whose husband just happened to be in the same truck with them.

Magoo's Place was just off the campus on East Avenue East, which Deacon thought was a silly name for a street and showed a certain lack of creativity and initiative by the city planners, between North Walker Street and North Harrison Street. Once inside and seated, they perused the menu; Lorna had the beef tacos, Adrian ordered the hamburger steak with sauteed onions, brown gravy and home fries, while Deacon had the asado plate. Everyone ordered iced tea for a beverage.

While waiting for their meals, Lorna asked Adrian about his morning. He then returned the favor.

"Well, to start with I had Tito try to rattle Deputy Deacon here when he first walked into the conference room. That didn't go anywhere, and Deputy Deacon ended up giving us a lecture on who takes orders from whom. We then examined his truck for suitability as a law enforcement vehicle and it passed with flying colors. After that we went to see Sheriff Gutersohn to discuss some law enforcement issues, and then I decided to talk my husband into buying me lunch. That's about it at the moment."

It got awkward at this point as Deacon couldn't think of anything worthwhile to say, which didn't seem to faze Adrian in the least. "So, did Lorna give you the speech about unwanted attention? She practiced it on me for days so I'm hoping it wasn't time wasted."

The directness of the question actually relaxed Deacon so that he could get comfortable enough to chat. "Yes, I got the lecture along with the back story of what occurred back in Chicago."

"Do you think anyone will hit on her and cause us the same problem here?" Adrian said sort of in jest, but Deacon got the impression that he really wanted to know.

"Well, not unless they want shot. The Sheriff made it perfectly clear that this is what awaits those who fail to heed her warning. I've been shot once, and once is enough. I'll definitely be toeing the line. How many admirers did she shoot in Chicago?"

Lorna piped in at this point. "You realize that we cannot comment on ongoing investigations but suffice it to say that for the bodies they actually found I was never convicted of any wrongdoing. Hopefully, the other bodies will never be found."

"But if you had to take a guess, in total how many unwanted admirers never showed up for breakfast the next morning?", pressed Deacon.

Lorna looked over at Adrian and said, "Seven?" Adrian disagreed and thought it was eight. Looking back at Deacon she said, "We're pretty sure it was eight unwanted admirers who didn't make it to breakfast," she said with a smile. Deacon thought she was probably the best-looking mass murderer he'd ever seen.

At this point their meals came and they all dug in. When they finished, Lorna paid the bill and made sure to keep the receipt for expenses before they ran Adrian back over to the university so that he could prepare for his next lecture. Deacon and Adrian shook hands before Adrian got out of the truck and they agreed to get together back in Fort Davis for a beer in the future.

On the way back to Fort Davis, Deacon got the question that he knew he'd get. "So, what do you think about Adrian, Deputy Allison?"

"Well, he seems fairly normal for a guy married to an exceptionally attractive mass murderer. He also seemed in fairly good health for a guy that you'd expect to be overstressed from the constant worry hanging over his head that someone would inadvertently hit on his wife and start a new crime spree here in Texas."

"You're really not trying to make points with the boss today, are you?"

"Not really my style. I do envy you and Adrian's relationship though. It seems like you are friends as well as husband and wife, which doesn't appear to be that common anymore. I may need to keep my eye out for a hot, unattached, female serial killer, although I'm sure I'd be fishing in a very shallow pond. There just can't be that many of your type out there running wild."

"So true. Seriously though, we seem to have been lucky. We fit together like a hand in a glove. Keep the faith Deacon, there's somebody out there for you. Believe it or not, the trick is to stop looking and just let it happen."

"Oh well, one can only hope. What am I doing the rest of today, boss?"

"Get your handheld radio and check with Macy that it's set up and works correctly. Put the magnetic sheriff's signs on your doors and get that toolbox for your truck, you'll need it. Just so you know, they are having a sale on Weather Guard cross bed aluminum toolboxes at Higginbotham Brothers hardware store on Douglas Drive this week. I'll see you tomorrow at 0800 deputy." She might have been married, but it was Art Appreciation Week somewhere, so he just sat in the truck and watched as Lorna walked into the office before heading over to the hardware store to get a toolbox and then going home to mount it and maybe even get the rollbar he was welding together mounted as well.

CHAPTER 8

DEACON WAS IN UNIFORM AND in the deputy's bullpen at 7:50 the next morning to start his first full shift riding solo. Tito, John and Armando strolled in before 8:00 and they just sat around and jacked their jaws before Lorna walked in at 8:00 sharp to give them an informal briefing before sending them out on their separate ways.

At the door she stopped suddenly and took a closer look at her deputies. "I sense a disturbance in the Force this morning, gentlemen," paraphrasing a quote from the first Star Wars movie.

"What do you mean, Sheriff? We haven't had time to wind up Deacon yet, so the Force should still be composed and untroubled," replied Armando.

"If you look closely, Señor Ruiz, you will notice that the Anglos seem to prefer the Sheriff's departmental baseball caps as headgear, as opposed to the Latino contingent who seem to favor the unadorned straw cowboy hats. I hope that this is not the beginning of a segregation issue within the Sheriff's Department here in Fort Davis?"

"It has nothing to do with segregation, Sheriff. The Anglos simply do not have any fashion sense," Tito informed Lorna before she began the morning's briefing. Deacon had the feeling that even though both he and Lorna were relatively new, that the crew was an informal, well-knit group.

After everyone had stopped by Macy's office to trade in their handheld

Motorola radio batteries for freshly charged ones, they walked out to their respective vehicles, three Ford Explorers and one old Chevy pickup, and took off to patrol their assigned sectors.

The duties of a deputy sheriff are fairly well defined. They are to assist at accident scenes and secure disaster areas. They are to detect, investigate and deter criminal activities, and they are to apprehend criminal and traffic law offenders. Along with this they are to transport and escort detainees to and from court or healthcare facilities as required. Since the Fort Davis County Sheriff's Office was so severely understaffed, Gordon, Macy and Lorna handled anything required from the sheriff's office in town while the deputies rode out to maintain law and order in the sticks.

Deacon had grown up in the area and knew the roads and general layout well, but he decided to spend the day reconnoitering the southwestern zone of the county, which is the one that Lorna had assigned him, to re-familiarize himself with the area. There were not many paved roads in his area of concern, or in the entire county for that matter, so he left Fort Davis headed south on State Road 17 and took a leisurely drive to Marfa before heading west on State Highway 90 up to Valentine. Topping off his tanks in Valentine, he got back on 90 and took it through the one-horse town of Lobo before he got off the highway and just meandered on the dirt roads across the badland ridges and mountains of the Sierra Viejo until he came to the extreme tip of Jeff Davis County, where it touched the Rio Grande River just across the border from Lomas de Arena.

Getting out of his truck, he took a bottle of water and walked the 50 yards to the river and looked across at Old Mexico while he slowly drank his water. He found it hard to believe that he could simply wade ten yards across this stream, it was more of a stream than a river at this point, and he'd be in another country. There was nothing here to prevent him from doing just that; no buildings, no people, no checkpoint, nothing. Which was the whole problem from a law enforcement perspective.

Getting back in his truck, he backtracked to Highway 90 before continuing on to Van Horn where he stopped and had lunch at Mom's

Kitchen on Laurel Street and called in to touch base with Macy. After eating a large, homecooked beef burrito with green chili, Deacon got back on the road, east this time on Interstate 10, until he came to the intersection with 118 and took it south through the Davis Mountains and on into Fort Davis.

Arriving at the sheriff's office around 4:00 that afternoon, Deacon walked in and went to his assigned desk and typed out his first patrol report and emailed it to Sheriff Stims. Neither Lorna or the other deputies were in the office so he just stopped by to shoot the breeze with Macy before getting back in his truck and driving back to Grady's place in the hills. Deacon's first day as a deputy had been completed with no hits and no runs, but no errors either.

Getting back to Grady's place, Deacon got out a couple of steaks to thaw and made a green salad after he'd loaded the grill with charcoal and fired it up. When Grady pulled into the courtyard in front of the porch in his old Ford F-100 pickup, Deacon was just putting the steaks on the grill.

During dinner, Deacon passed on the message from Sheriff Gutersohn about coming down to Alpine for a beer.

"I need to do that; I haven't seen John in a few months now. We had some fun back in the day, and an adventure or two while you were still in the Army," Grady reminisced with a faraway look in his eye.

"Want to tell me about these adventures?" asked Deacon. It seemed like there was more to this than some mid-life crisis, middle-aged adventures.

"In this case, son, I think it might be better to let sleeping dogs lie. Not so much for me, but John can't really afford for our little adventures coming to light in his line of work, if you know what I mean."

"You mean some of these adventures may have been skating on thin ice, legally speaking?"

"I always said you were a clever lad," Grady said with a wink.

CHAPTER 9

OVER THE NEXT FEW WEEKS Deacon drove every road in his quadrant just to familiarize himself with where they went as well as to let people become familiar with the odd sheriff's vehicle with the magnetic signs on the side as opposed to the proper departmental Explorer with an official paint job.

He also fabricated a pretty cool dual-tube rollbar for his truck instead of the usual 'quick & dirty' single-tube variety. He'd mounted his properly by cutting holes in the bed behind the cab and about two thirds of the way down the bed so that he could actually weld the rollbar and support tubing to the frame preventing it from just punching through the sheet metal of the bed if he did manage to roll the thing.

He'd been assigned a Rock River AR platform rifle chambered in 5.56 x 45 and a Glock 17 service pistol, but after wearing Lorna down with his constant whining, she agreed that he could carry his Springfield Armory M1A chambered in 7.62 x 51 NATO with a composite stock and the 20" barrel. He wanted the more powerful round so that he could reach out and touch someone at a distance if he had to. Unlike the budget conscious Sig Sauer Romeo 5 red dot optical sights provided on the departments Rock River rifles, Deacon had installed a Nightforce SHV 3 x 10 power scope on the M1A, which made it very similar to the M25 Sniper Weapon System which he had become familiar with from his time in the Army.

Deacon hated the feel and balance of the polymer framed Glocks, so he also got dispensation to carry his personal Beretta 92FS, also in 9mm like the Glock. Again, he was familiar with this handgun, which had been adopted by the US military as the M9 in 1985, and was really just a re-packaged Beretta 92FS.

The days rolled by and after a few months Deacon had reacquainted himself with the area and people in it. He'd done the gamut from getting cats out of trees, to securing the occasional accident scene he'd been called to on the few paved roads in his sector, to helping out Sheriff Gutersohn with the increasing number of illegal aliens crossing the long border between Mexico and Presidio County.

On a few occasions he'd gotten a call on the radio handset beside his bed and had to get up in the middle of the night to investigate suspected prowlers in Fort Davis, break up drunken brawls at the Blue Mountain Bar and Grill, or to consider and resolve the other occasional misadventures in his area of responsibility, usually alcohol or drug related.

The job really didn't pay much, a little over $3,000 per month, but the work was interesting, he was meeting new people, and Grady wasn't charging him rent so it was a good way to pass the time until he figured out what he really wanted to do with his life.

After a few weeks of 'riding the range' together, the other deputies figured out that Deacon could handle the job, but more importantly he'd listen to them and try to learn from their experience. Although due to the shortage of deputies, and the fact that they were all on call 24/7, the whole crew; Lorna, Macy, Chuck, Tito, John, Armando and Deacon would occasionally walk over to the Blue Mountain and have a beer to unwind after work. Now and then, Adrian would stop by as well. He was accepted as a member of the team, and by far the most educated one.

One Sunday afternoon, after the day's patrolling was finished, the entire Fort

Davis County Sheriff's Department was invited out to Grady's place for a good old-fashioned barbeque. This was really Grady's idea. Although he liked having company, he rarely received any since he lived out of town in the Davis Mountains, he also figured it couldn't do Deacon's newfound career any harm as well.

While the sheriff's department were going about its business that Sunday, Grady dragged a couple of old barbeque pits out of the barn and cleaned them up, then loaded them with charcoal and mesquite chips so that they were ready to fire up when the time was right. In Grady's line of work, he had easy access to fresh beef and kept a freezer full of it in the garage. He'd also visited an old Hispanic butcher in Marfa and loaded up on authentic chorizo sausages.

Half an hour before the crew was due to arrive, Grady fired up the old barbeque pits, made up a green salad in a huge bowl in the kitchen, and wrapped up 10 potatoes in foil and tossed them in the coals. The beer would be self-served out of a pony keg of Tecate which was iced down in a tub on the front porch.

Around 5:00, the deputies, Macy and Chuck rolled up to the front of the house in convoy, followed shortly thereafter by Lorna and Adrian. Deacon introduced everyone to his father before telling everyone to grab a seat on the porch, either on the porch swing, the old, battered couches, or on any of the chairs which Grady had brought out of the house to accommodate everyone.

Grady and Deacon took care of the cooking duties while everyone else just got comfortable on the porch. While doing duty at the pits, Grady took the opportunity to enlighten Deacon.

"Son, I've been around the Horn a few times and I have never, ever seen such a good-looking law enforcement officer as the one over there in the black Carhartt polo shirt. You could do a whole lot worse than a woman like that."

"Dad, it's good to know that your eyesight is still good and that your cull factor concerning the ladies hasn't suffered over the years, but your memory seems to be slipping. That woman is definitely an eye-catcher, but she does have a downside."

"Yeah, what would that be?" asked Grady.

"Well, you didn't see this crew drive up, but that woman was accompanied by the gentleman she is now sitting next to on the couch."

"So, a little competition never hurt anyone."

"Well, in this case the game is over, done and dusted. That woman is Mrs. Stims, the elected sheriff of Jeff Davis County. You seem to have forgotten that Sheriff Stims is married. The gentleman she is sitting next to is Mr. Stims, who is a professor of English down at the Sul Ross University in Alpine. They appear to be very happily married, and I don't chase married women."

"Damn, that's a shame, she's quite a little stunner. That said, Allisons do not plow in another man's field. It shows character and it may keep you from getting shot. Oh well, someone else will show up that turns your crank, you just gotta to keep the faith."

The steaks, sausages and potatoes didn't last long as everyone seemed to be hungry after a day's work. The Tecate was slowly being consumed, but since everyone was still on 24/7 call, nobody was over-serving themselves.

As the sun went down to the west, everyone just sat around on the porch gossiping and enjoying themselves. Eventually Lorna asked a question of Grady that had been bothering her.

"Mr. Allison, Deacon and I were down in Alpine a few weeks ago to meet with Sheriff Gutersohn and he said that you and he were old high school buddies and palled around together before you went into the Marines, and he went off to pursue a career in law enforcement. Care to tell us some stories?" she asked with a grin.

"First, just call me Grady, everyone else does. Second, I hesitate to tell you any stories about Hank and I on the grounds that they could incriminate us. Suffice it to say that Hank and I cut a pretty wide swath through Culberson, Reeves, Pecos, Brewster, Presidio and Jeff Davis counties in our youth and it's a wonder we never ended up in jail. I think Hank became a cop simply so that he could avoid arresting himself! Once we both settled back here, we decided to behave ourselves and now we've slowed down a bit with age. We've had a few adventures since we've been back, but they are the exception, not the rule."

"Care to tell us about them?" probed Deacon.

"No, I do not. These were not the sort of adventures that you regale law enforcement personnel with, if you know what I mean.

Eventually, everybody went back to their own abodes after helping Deacon and Grady clean up. It was a very relaxing evening for all concerned.

About five months after the barbeque, Deacon got the call that would change his life in ways he never would have imagined.

CHAPTER 10

IT ALL STARTED ON A Wednesday morning. Deacon had gotten two calls that morning: one was to check out a possible 'breaking & entering' at the Girl Scout camp down by Mitre Peak on 118 and the other was to check out some vandalism of heavy equipment at The High Frontier, a full-service event venue that was under construction in the middle of nowhere and just happened to be off 118 as well.

Technically the Girl Scout camp was in Tito's quadrant just before the county line with Brewster County, but Tito had asked Deacon to look into the issue as he had his hands full with a domestic violence situation up near Toyahvale, almost in Reeves County to the north.

Pulling into the Girl Scout camp around 9:00, Deacon had to wait about half an hour for the caretaker of the camp to show up. The caretaker was an old rancher that looked like he'd spent a lot of time on the back of a horse as his legs were so bowed that you could probably fit a pony keg between his knees sideways. After shaking hands, they took a walk around the buildings in the camp and found a broken window in one of them. The caretaker let them inside, but nothing appeared to have been vandalized and nothing seemed to be missing so they just chalked it up to windblown debris and the old guy said he'd have the window replaced before he left that day.

The High Frontier was an old ranch property that the same team that had reinvigorated the Hotel Saint George in Marfa was fixing up as a deluxe cabin-style accommodation event venue complete with hiking trails, a wellness center, a farm-to-table restaurant and bar, a tranquil outdoor pool and lounge, and leisurely hiking trails complete with rattlesnakes. The perfect spot to host weddings, celebrations and gatherings of all types and sizes. The joint was supposed to open in a year or so, but there was still a lot of construction happening onsite.

The High Frontier was about halfway back to Fort Davis on 118, so Deacon was looking forward to a burrito for lunch at Cuervo de Leon on State Street after looking into the issue at the High Frontier.

The 'vandalism' at the High Frontier was a storm in a teacup. Some of the local kids had obviously built a fire in the bucket of a skid steer loader and had a party judging by the trash and empty beer cans around the bucket. There was some singed paint and the hoses and hydraulic connections would need to be inspected for damage, but there was no indication of any real criminal intent. Deacon would write up his report and asked the foreman at the site to send him a summary detailing any damage to the skid steer and what was required to put it back in service.

With that done, Deacon was heading back to town when Macy broadcast a call to all the deputies. Sheriff Cabrera down in Presidio County had put out a BOLO, a 'be on the lookout' for a white, late model Toyota Vellfire people carrier. The vehicle was last seen an hour ago headed north on Highway 17 towards Fort Davis. The occupants were likely illegal aliens, and the van was to be approached with caution.

Since the road Deacon was on, Highway 118 led directly into Fort Davis and intersected with Highway 17 on the south side of town, Deacon informed Macy that he was just coming into town on 118 and would just head south on Highway 17 as soon as he got to the intersection.

Deacon had just made a left on State Street, which is what Highway 17 was named as it went through town and was about to pass the entrance to the McMillen RV Park when he noticed a white Toyota Vellfire parked at the very back of the lot in the southeast corner.

Deacon slowed down and turned into the RV park and was approaching the Vellfire when it suddenly came to life and threw gravel as it passed Deacon on his passenger side.

Not to be outdone, Deacon put the pedal to the metal and spun 180 degrees in the gravel before getting it under control again. At the entrance to the RV park, the Vellfire hung a left and headed back down Highway 17 with Deacon in hot pursuit.

Now you would think that an old Chevy stepside pickup running a 400 horsepower 350 V8 against essentially a soccer mom's van would be no contest, and generally speaking you'd be right, but some of those Vellfires came equipped with a 275 horsepower V6 and were pretty quick in their own right. The thing was, Deacon couldn't consider shooting out the tires or performing a PIT (Precision Immobilization Technique) where he 'bumps' a rear corner of the van to send it out of control due to the fact that there were innocent illegal aliens, an oxymoron if there ever was one, in the van. He'd just have to chase them until they either decided to call it quits, stopped the van and escaped into the desert on foot, or they just ran out of gas. Deacon had two 21-gallon fuel tanks, one mounted on either side of the driveline, so he wasn't really concerned about running out of gas.

The Vellfire people carrier went balls to the wall for about a mile and a half before slowing down and making a hard right onto Highway 166 heading southwest into the desert. Highway 116 was a well maintained two-lane paved road without any serious twists or turns in it for miles. The traffickers obviously knew this and were back up to speed shortly after they turned off Highway 17. Deacon was hanging about 50 yards back since there was really nothing else that he could do. If he tried to pass the van and the driver got silly, he'd be putting the illegals at risk.

After about 20 miles of this foolishness, the Toyota slowed back down to take a left onto Barrel Springs Ranch Road, which was an entirely different kettle of fish. The Barrel Springs Ranch Road was simply a two-lane dirt road with soft sand shoulders. If either the van or Deacon's pickup got onto the shoulder the game would be up as they'd lose control in the soft sand.

Due to the dust being kicked up by the van, Deacon had to back off about 100 yards behind it so that he could see the road without being enveloped in the dust cloud kicked up by the van.

They blew right through the middle of the Barrel Springs ranch, which straddled the road about a mile after they left Highway 166, at about 50 miles an hour and kept right on going.

At this point the traffickers must have realized that they couldn't outrun or lose Deacon before they came to Highway 90, which would give Deacon's pickup an unfair advantage on a paved road and where other law enforcement vehicles could be waiting. They needed a Plan B.

Deacon had kept Macy informed of where he was at and what he was doing. She let the other deputies know what was happening and also called Sheriff Cabrera in Marfa, in Presidio County, to let him know what was happening as well. Sheriff Cabrera knew the area much better than Lorna or Macy and he had sent some his people out on Highway 90 to block the highway above and below where the van would come off of Barrel Springs Ranch Road and onto the highway.

The traffickers' Plan B was both brutal and effective. About five and a half miles past the Barrel Springs Ranch is a cutoff to an unnamed dirt road to the south. As the van slowed down and made the turn onto the unnamed road, the sliding door on the driver's side of the van slid open and a body was tossed out. The body appeared to be dressed in teal green hospital scrubs, but it was difficult to tell if it was male or female as it bounced, cartwheeled, and somersaulted along the shoulder of the unnamed road in the soft sand before it rolled to a stop against a good-sized sage bush on the side of the road.

The traffickers knew that Deacon would have to stop and render aid, which he did as the van continued on its way south trying to reach the border and safety. Deacon locked up the brakes and fishtailed to a stop about 10 yards from where the body had come to rest on the side of the road. Grabbing his first aid kit out of the toolbox behind the cab he ran over to see what he could do for the victim. The victim appeared to be a she, but it was hard to tell with all the blood running into its face from a scalp wound on the left side of head as well as all of the dust and dirt that was on the victim. Deacon was fearful of moving the victim due to the probability of a neck or spine injury after bouncing down the road in such spectacular fashion, but he checked the airway, which was clear and for a pulse which was weak but steady. There was a lot of blood seeping into the pants of the scrubs at the upper right thigh. Deacon ripped down the waistband of the scrub pants to get to the wound and judging by the lack of certain anatomical features and the dainty female undergarments, Deacon concluded that the victim was definitely a woman. Although this subconsciously registered in Deacon's lizard brain, the rest of his brain was focused on the wound. Thankfully, it was not pulsing blood, so he didn't have to worry about arterial bleeding and a tourniquet.

Getting the wound cleaned up and packed with Bleedstop blood clotting powder, he bandaged the wound and taped it up tightly before pulling the woman's pants back up. Running back to his truck, he got Macy on the radio and told her what had happened and that he needed an ambulance at his location as soon as possible, a Flight-For-Life helicopter would be even better. Macy said she was on it and for Deacon to keep his handheld radio with him so that she could update him as necessary.

Deacon got back in his truck and pulled it as close to the woman as possible to give her some shade before grabbing a couple of bottles of water out of a cooler in the back and some clean rags out of the toolbox. He knelt down by the woman and without moving her, cleaned up her face and got as much of the blood and dust off of her as he could. She was actually a very striking Hispanic woman in her late 20's or early 30's.

Macy called and told him that an ambulance and a Presidio deputy were headed his way on Highway 90 and could hopefully get to him in about 30 minutes. Deacon said if that was all she had, he'd take it, but he wasn't sure the woman would last that long in the heat. Five minutes later Macy called back excited and said that a Medivac chopper out of Fort Bliss in El Paso was out on a training run and had heard the radio chatter and would be with him in less than five minutes. Deacon told Macy that she was an angel.

Three minutes after the call, Deacon heard the sound of a chopper and a big, beautiful Sikorsky UH-60 helicopter with big red crosses on the sides landed about 30 yards behind Deacon's truck. Deacon had to cover the woman's body with his own to shield her from the dust and gravel kicked up by the choppers rotor wash before he got out of the way and let the experts do their jobs.

They had the young woman in a neck brace and on a backboard in minutes with all the IV's that she required and were putting her in the chopper less than five minutes after the chopper had touched down. They would fly her to the medical facility at Fort Bliss and would be in touch later with the Fort Davis Sheriff's Office to let them know the outcome. From the time the chopper appeared overhead until it took off again could not have been more than ten minutes. Amazing.

Deacon called back to Macy and told her what had happened and that he was going to stop in at Sheriff Cabrera's office in Marfa to see what the situation was. Marcy called back a few minutes later and told Deacon that Sheriff Stims would also like a word with him when he got back to town.

Driving further along the unnamed dirt road that the woman was thrown out on, Deacon came to Highway 90 about two miles further on. Turning left on 90, Deacon drove to Marfa and found a parking spot in front of the sheriff's office at the corner of North Dean Street and East Lincoln Street, just beside the county courthouse. After identifying who he was and indicating that he'd like a word with the sheriff, the receptionist, who appeared as to be as young as Macy, asked him to have a seat and that she would call him when the sheriff could see him.

About five minutes later Sheriff Cabrera himself walked into the reception area and over to Deacon. Deacon stood up to shake hands with the sheriff, who then asked Deacon to follow him to his office so that they could chat. Once they were in his office, Benito, Sheriff Cabrera's given name, asked if Deacon would like some coffee to which Deacon replied that he'd kill for a cup of coffee right about then.

Benito went to the door and asked his secretary, personal assistant or whatever they are called these days, and asked her if he would bring him and his guest some coffee. While they waited for the coffee, Benito told Deacon that he was aware of what had happened out in the desert earlier that day, but he'd appreciate it if Deacon would run through it again for him.

Sheriff Cabrera was Hispanic, as you'd expect with a name like Benito Cabrera, and he was 5'10" and 170 pounds of lean and rangy sheriff. Deacon guessed he was in his mid-50's with a full head of wavy black hair worn longer than you would normally expect on a law enforcement professional, and dark Latino eyes. He seemed friendly enough, but his attitude seemed to indicate that he didn't suffer fools gladly.

About this time the secretary or personal assistant came in with their coffees. Benito took his and walked back behind his desk and pointed Deacon to one of the two upholstered armchairs in front of the desk.

"Deputy Allison, I've been given the CliffsNotes version of what went on earlier out in the desert, but I wonder if you wouldn't mind running me through it again just to make sure I have the details right."

"Please just call me Deacon, and I'd be more than happy to tell you what I know." Taking a sip of his coffee, Deacon got on with the show.

"I was out this morning to check on a possible B&E at the Girl Scout camp out near Mitre Peak on 118. After that I stopped in at The High Frontier resort to check out a report of vandalism to a piece of heavy equipment. On the way back to town I received a call from dispatch that you had issued a BOLO for a white, late model Toyota Vellfire. I was told that the occupants were likely illegal aliens and that we were supposed to approach with caution. Since the vehicle was last seen an hour before I received the call and I was almost back to Fort Davis by this time, I just turned south at the intersection with 17 and started looking for the vehicle.

"Just as I was approaching the McMillan RV Park, I noticed a white van parked in a back corner of the lot, so I pulled into the RV park to check it out. Just as I got to the van, it took off out of the RV park. I swung around and pursued the van as it headed south again on 17. The van hung a hard right onto 166 and I followed in pursuit. Since there were likely innocent illegal aliens in the van, I couldn't try to PIT it or otherwise interdict the van without putting them at risk. I decided to just follow them until they either put the van in the ditch, ran out of gas, or abandoned the vehicle.

"Eventually they got on Barrel Springs Ranch Road. This is a dirt road and the dust they were kicking up forced me to back off a bit further so that I could see the road. I stayed on their tail until they slowed down to take a left on the unnamed road that they dumped the woman on.

"At this point I had to stop pursuit and render aid to the woman. As luck would have it, an Army medivac chopper was in the area on a training mission and heard the chatter on the radio. Macy, our dispatcher, got in touch with them and they came down and did what they do, then flew the victim to the hospital in Fort Bliss. That's really it in a nutshell, Sheriff."

Benito sat back in his chair and contemplated what Deacon had told him for a few minutes before he sat up again.

"And you have no idea as to who this woman was? She had no identification on her and she never said anything to you?"

"Sheriff, the woman was lucky to be alive. I saw her bouncing down the shoulder of the road and couldn't believe she had a pulse when I got to her. She'd taken a pretty good knock to the head and was out cold. I never had the opportunity to question her."

"Is there something I should know about this incident, Sheriff Cabrera? You seem to be taking a personal interest in it," asked Deacon hesitantly.

"No Deacon, as of now you know as much about this as I do. I suppose Sheriff Stims will ask you to travel to Fort Bliss to question the woman once she is out of surgery and in a condition for questioning. Could you ask Lorna to send me a copy of the results of your questioning of the woman? I have a bad feeling about this."

"Gladly, Sheriff. I'm sure that you and Sheriff Stims will stay in contact concerning this incident, and I'll gladly help out in any way that I can. If you need to ask any further questions once I leave, just give me a call.

Benito stood up, walked around the desk and shook Deacon's hand before walking him back down the hall to reception. "Thank you for your time, Deputy Allison. Please give Sheriff Stims my regards and please do not forget to forward me a copy of your interrogation of the young woman."

CHAPTER 11

DEACON GOT BACK TO THE sheriff's office in Fort Davis about 4:00 that afternoon, and Lorna was waiting at his desk in the bullpen to get the story. He suggested that she wait until he had written up his report, she suggested otherwise.

After he had run through the story almost verbatim to what he had told Sheriff Cabrera, Lorna sat on his desk and wondered out loud if this incident was somehow connected to the splinter group, the 'Roosters' or the Gallo cartel, that Sheriff Gutersohn had mentioned when they had visited him.

"Well, these guys appeared to be trafficking although I couldn't see inside the van due to the dust and there may have been any number of people in it. I don't see why it couldn't be related," offered Deacon.

"The thing is the Presidio County deputies found the van abandoned in an arroyo near the border on the other side of Highway 90. Apparently, they were trying to get back across the border as quickly as they could. The problem is, the forensic team determined that there was only three people in that van: a driver, the person riding shotgun and that woman. Traffickers rarely get out of bed to bring a singleton across. Also, they seemed to be waiting in the RV park to hand her off when you spooked them. Usually, the modus operandi is to get rid of the merchandise as quickly as possible, not to wait for someone to collect the merchandise at a pre-determined location. As Alice in Wonderland said, this is getting curiouser and curiouser.

"I'll have to ponder this and talk it over with Hank and Benito. You, on the other hand, need to write up your report and have it in my departmental inbox by first thing tomorrow morning. When we get word that the woman is up to taking some questions, I want you to go on up to Fort Bliss and see what she has to say. You'd better get busy if you don't want to miss your dinner," suggested Lorna with a grin.

After writing up his report and sending it to Lorna via email, Deacon climbed back in his truck and made his way to Grady's place, it had been a long day.

While at the dinner table with his dad that evening, over a dinner of chicken fried steaks and mashed potatoes, Deacon told his father what had happened that day. Grady didn't seem too interested in his day until they were doing the dishes at the sink later.

"You say that there was only a single illegal in that van?" asked Grady.

"That's what the forensic people in Presidio said."

"And you said the woman was around how old?" queried Grady.

"I'm guessing around late 20's or early 30's."

"And they didn't just keep going on 17 but stopped at the RV park like they were waiting for someone."

"Dad, I've already been over this. I spooked them when they were at the RV park and they took off. Between you, Sheriff Stims and Sheriff Cabrera, I'm starting to get the impression that there is more to this woman than meets the eye."

"There may well be. I'll need to make some phone calls, and I'll need for you to tell me what the girl tells you up at Fort Bliss."

"I really can't discuss any cases with you, Dad, you know that," retorted Deacon.

"In this case, I think it would be wise if you did. I'll bring you up to speed once we actually determine if there is anything that you need to be brought up to speed on. We may just be pissing in the wind if the girl turns out to be just another illegal alien. Until we know better, let's just assume that she is."

A few days later, while out patrolling, Deacon got a call on the radio from Lorna asking him to see her before he went off duty that afternoon. Walking into the sheriff's office around 5:00, Deacon asked Lorna if she had decided to dump Adrian in favor of a certain dashing deputy who would remain nameless.

Lorna leaned back in her desk chair and looked up at the ceiling for a moment as if she were actually contemplating what her deputy had asked before she leaning forward again and said, "Nah, I think I'll stick with the devil I know rather than the one I don't. Nice try though." With that out of the way, Lorna got down to business.

"The Jane Doe that you rescued has sufficiently recovered from her serious concussion and other injuries and is now willing and able to be questioned, although she either still does not remember her name or just refuses to give it. I'd like for you to go up there tomorrow and see what you can get out of her regarding her abduction and the whole situation."

"I'll do that. Who's going to cover my shift tomorrow?"

"I'll do it. I need to get out of the office anyhow."

"Think you still remember how to patrol and chase bad guys?"

Lorna pointed at the door and simply said, "Out!"

The next day, bright and early, Deacon showered, shaved, and brushed his teeth prior to putting on his best pair of Wrangler jeans and an olive colored Carhartt long sleeved work shirt rolled halfway up his forearms. Sliding on his good pair of cowboy boots, the 11" Alamosa square toed ones, he made his way into the kitchen to grab a bowl of cornflakes. Grady was already at the table with his own bowl of cornflakes.

"You going up to question that Mexican girl?"

"Yep, that's what Lorna asked me to do," replied Deacon.

"A word of advice, go easy on her. If she is who I think she is, she needs to be treated with respect."

"Who is this woman and why is everybody treating her with kid gloves?" Deacon was getting exasperated now.

"Son, I think there is more going on here than just trafficking some girl. She may explain it to you, but she doesn't know you. I promise to put you in the picture when you get back as long as you fill me in on what she says or doesn't say. Deal?"

"Deal, but at some point I'll really need to know what is going on here, just to do my job if nothing else."

"Understood, now quit jacking your jaw, eat your cereal and get on the road."

After finishing his cornflakes, washing his bowl and spoon and putting them in the drying rack next to the sink, Deacon walked out to the old stepside and started on his journey. At the end of Grady's long driveway, he took a right onto 166 and took it up to where it intersected with 118. Hanging a left on 118 he had about a 25-mile run before 118 hit Interstate 10. He now had about a 150-mile run to El Paso, passing through the towns of Van Horn, Sierra Blanca and Fort Hancock. Coming into El Paso from the southwest on I-10, Deacon had to get off on Highway 62 heading almost due east out of town to get where he needed to go. The new William Beaumont Army Medical Center was not actually located on Fort Bliss proper, but way outside of El Paso itself and was sited about 2.5 miles from the northeast end of the El Paso International Airport runways. To get there Deacon had to stay on Highway 62 past the Texas Army National Guard Recruiting Station and then get off on Highway 375 heading north then northwest for about three and a quarter miles before he hit the entrance for the medical center.

After figuring out where the front entrance actually was, Deacon walked in and introduced himself to the girl at the front desk and told her why he was there. The girl made a phone call and within a few minutes a doctor of African descent, in a lab coat over his Class B Army Service Uniform, came over to the reception desk and introduced himself.

"Deputy Allison, I'm Major Williams and the doctor in charge of the Jane Doe you're concerned about," said Major Williams as he put out his hand.

"Pleased to meet you Major," said Deacon as he shook the Major's hand.

"You really don't seem fazed by all this military rigmarole Deputy; can I assume you were in the service at some point?"

"Guilty as charged," laughed Deacon.

"Care to share?"

"I spent 11 years in the Army. I ended up in the 75th Ranger Regiment and separated as a First Sergeant."

"If you don't mind my asking, why'd you get out after 11 years?"

"I got shot in Syria and decided I needed to take better care of myself."

"Seems like a logical decision. Let's go meet Jane, she seems somewhat excited to have a visitor."

On the way to the elevators and then on to Jane's room, Major Williams described the extent of Jane's injuries.

"Ms. Doe suffered blunt trauma to the left side of her head which caused a severe concussion. She has also suffered a dislocated right shoulder and left knee as well as several cracked ribs and a deep laceration to the outer right thigh. She was apparently drugged when she was thrown from the vehicle, which likely saved her life. If she had not been as limp as a dishrag when she hit the ground, the damage would probably been much more extensive. Saying that, if you had not stopped the bleeding from the thigh and that chopper hadn't been in the area, she probably would have expired under the conditions you found her in."

"So how is she doing now? Can she be released?" asked Deacon.

Major Williams laughed. "That young woman has the constitution of mule! She thinks she is ready to go now, although I highly do not recommend this course of action. Her shoulder and knee have been reset and are healing nicely as is the laceration on her thigh. It is the head wound that I am worried about. It seems she has recovered from the concussion in fine shape, but I'd like to keep her here under observation for a few more days."

"Has she said anything concerning who she is, or what she was doing in that van?"

"Apparently, she only speaks Spanish, and she has been reticent as far as giving any information to this point. She does not appear to be doing this to be difficult, more like she wants to make sure that she knows exactly what her position is on this side of the border."

"Damn, I may need a translator. My Spanish is not good enough for an interrogation. I should have thought of that."

"Don't worry, we have many people in the building who speak Spanish if you think you need a translator."

"Can you get one of them to meet us at her room? If she only speaks Spanish, I'll need one."

The major pulled out his iPhone and made a call. Just before they entered a private room, the major gave Deacon a word of caution.

"Deputy, a word of advice. In other circumstances this young woman would be an extremely attractive woman. As such, she is somewhat embarrassed about the appearance she projects while in a hospital gown and with the left side of her head shaved. I don't mean to insinuate that she is overly vain, but just a typical young woman who cannot put her best foot forward at the moment. I'd suggest that if you can, let her know that this is all temporary and she'll be back in the saddle in a few weeks. Besides making her feel better about herself and her situation, it will help her to heal."

As they went into the private room, the translator had arrived and followed them in.

"Señorita, this is the deputy that found you on the side of the road and called in the helicopter to bring you here. He may have saved your life. He needs to ask you some questions but doesn't believe he has the Spanish skills to do this, so I have asked an interpreter to assist him. Is this permissible?"

Deacon looked at the doctor in confusion as he translated what he had just told Jane in perfect Spanish.

"Sorry, I should have said something earlier. I speak fluent Spanish, but I have my rounds to make so I could not translate for you, sorry about that," the major informed Deacon as he left the room.

Deacon shut the door for privacy and then asked the interpreter to ask Jane if she required anything before they began. Before the interpreter could translate what Deacon had just said, Jane informed them both that she spoke fluent English, and that an interpreter was not necessary.

Deacon looked at the interpreter, the interpreter looked at Deacon, and then Deacon ushered the interpreter out of the room and pulled a chair up beside the bed. The doctor had been correct, this young woman, in normal circumstances, would have been a knockout in anyone's book. Although the left side of her head above her ear had been shaved so that the doctors could suture up the small, but fairly deep one inch gash at the center of a bad bruise, which was obviously how she had become concussed, the rest of her hair was long, down past her shoulders, and shown like black silk. Considering her bone structure and facial features, from her delicate ears, to her high cheekbones and aquiline nose, to her almond shaped brown, almost black, eyes, to her seductively formed lips, she definitely had a face that could launch a thousand ships, even if it was a bit banged up at the moment.

Although it was hard to get a good idea as to what was under the shapeless hospital gown as she laid back with the bed in a reclined position, she looked to be about 5'8" tall and she did not appear to be as voluptuous, for lack of a better word, as many Mexican women tended to be at her age. She did appear to be well put together and proportioned nicely, built more for speed than comfort. Her skin, what he could see of it, was smooth and a light caramel shade of brown. All in all, she was, in Deacon's humble opinion, and exotic beauty who just happened to be a little worse for the wear at the moment.

"Have you finished examining me, Deputy?" asked the woman.

"Sorry about that, but you look a whole lot different than you did on the side of the road. Please excuse me."

"Perhaps. Are you the one who bandaged my thigh out on the road?"

"Yep, that would have been me."

"I am assuming that to reach the wound in my thigh that you would have had to remove my pants, is that the case?"

"Not at all, I did not remove your pants."

"Then how did you get to the wound?"

"I pulled them down past your knees, I did not remove them."

The woman thought about this for a moment. "Did you see anything that perhaps you should not have seen?"

"I did not. Your naughty bits were well covered by your Calvin Klein Hello Kitty hipster briefs."

"You saw those!" the woman shrieked as she blushed profusely. Well supposing that caramel skinned women can actually blush profusely, glow profusely may be a more accurate description. In any case, she was obviously embarrassed that Deacon had seen her Hello Kitty knickers.

"I did, and just so you know I found them fashionable as well as entertaining."

"You were not supposed to find them to be anything! You were never supposed to see them at all!"

For someone who could only speak Spanish a few minutes earlier, she was doing a fairly good job of expressing herself in English now.

"Well, I did and I'm a better man for it. Can we get on with what we need to do here?" asked Deacon.

"Before we do, I need to borrow your phone and make a call. If you let me do that this interrogation will go much smoother."

"Who are you going to call?" queried Deacon.

"My father. Is that okay with you?"

"Your father doesn't know you are in the hospital?" Deacon asked as he took out his old, battered, but fully functional iPhone 13 and handed it to her.

"Do you speak Spanish, Mr. Deputy?"

"Not really."

"Okay, you may stay while I make my call."

She dialed a number on Deacon's phone and the call was picked up almost instantly. The first words out of her mouth were "Hola, Papá," after that was rapid fire Spanish that Deacon had no chance of deciphering. After about five minutes of this the woman handed the phone to Deacon and said, "Papá would like to speak to you."

"Hello?" was all that Deacon could think of to lead off with as he had no idea as if her father spoke English.

"Is this Deputy Deacon Allison?" asked her papá.

"Yes, it is. To whom am I speaking."

"My name is Diego Navarro. I am Esmeralda's father. That is all that you need to know for the time being. This will all be made much clearer later today. First, I thank you from the bottom of my heart for being there when those bastardos threw my daughter out of their vehicle. I owe you a debt that I can never repay.

"I believe you are the son of Grady Allison, is that correct?"

"Yes, it is, but how could you possibly know that?"

"Your father and I are close friends, Deacon, although we do not get much time to socialize as we did in the past. In any case, I will call Grady after we hang up and clear everything with him. What I need for you to do is to collect Esmeralda from the hospital in three days, which is when I am told is when she will be released and take her back with you to Grady's ranch while she heals. I do not want her coming back to Mexico at this time. Will you do this for me."

"Mr. Navarro, I will gladly do this for you, but you must understand that I am a law enforcement officer, and I will need to report this to my sheriff. Is that acceptable to you?"

"Sheriff Cabrera will be in touch with Sheriff Stims before you get home this evening, I think that everything will be okay with your Sheriff Stims. Your father will explain the situation to you this evening, but I must impress on you that my daughter will be in danger if she comes back to Mexico at this time."

"Okay, Mr. Navarro, I'll do what you ask," but Deacon just had to inject a little levity into the conversation. "If everything works out, can I keep her?", as if he was a kid who'd just found a stray puppy.

Esmeralda gave him the evil eye as Diego told him, "Young man, you have no idea what you would be in for if I said yes. Let's just take this one step at a time," said Diego as he stifled a laugh.

Deacon handed the phone back to Esmeralda, who had a short conversation with Diego before she hung up and handed the phone back to Deacon. "Well, I guess I am at your mercy for the foreseeable future, Deacon Allison."

Deacon just gave her a lecherous grin.

"Don't even think about going where you are thinking about going, gringo. I may be a little beat up at the moment, but I guarantee you that you will look far worse than me if you try anything ungentlemanly."

"The thought never crossed my mind," Deacon announced.

"Liar!" was Esmeralda's somewhat unladylike response, although it was delivered with a smile.

Deacon had her press the button on the bed to summon the nurse, and when she arrived Deacon asked her if he could speak to Major Williams. The nurse went out to find the major, and while she was out looking for him Esmeralda informed Deacon that she would need a few things if she was going to stay with Grady and Deacon for a while. Deacon thought this over and decided Macy would be the one to sort this out, so he told Esmeralda to make a list, and he'd try to get it taken care of before he came back to collect her when she was released.

At about this time Major Williams walked into the room and asked how everything had gone.

"Major Williams, meet Esmeralda. She speaks perfect English, and you should not have any problems with her in the future. Ms. Esmeralda is now a person of interest in a crime, although not a suspect, and I need to know when she will be released from your custody so that I can put her in mine."

"You sneaky little chica descarada! I thought you were holding back on me," said the doctor with a smile.

"I think that Ms. Esmeralda should be able to be released into your custody in three days and I'll start the paperwork for her release tomorrow. I suppose I'll see you again in three days deputy."

Deacon said goodbye to Esmeralda and reminded her to make her list and to give it to the doctor. As Major Williams and Deputy Allison walked back down the hall to the elevators Deacon gave the doctor a redacted version of what he'd learned during his meeting with Esmeralda. He also asked the doctor if he would please email him a copy of the list that Esmeralda was to give him so that he could get her set up in her next place of residence, wherever that may be.

Major Williams said he'd be happy to send the list as they shook hands at the reception desk before Deacon went out to his old truck and started the long ride home with much to think about.

By the time Deacon got back to the Sheriff's Office, written up his report concerning Esmeralda and arrived back at the ranch, it was around half past six in the evening and Grady had already prepared dinner: beef and beans.

While they served themselves and sat down to eat, Grady asked how the interview with the woman had gone?

"Dad, just stop bullshitting me. The woman is Esmeralda Navarro. Her father is Diego Navarro. You know Diego personally and he called you while I was on the way home. Who is Diego Navarro and why would he entrust his daughter to us until some situation is resolved down in Mexico? I need to know the backstory so that I can figure out how this is going to affect my job and my relationship with Sheriff Stims, you know as well as I do that she will smell a rat and will ask me, probably tomorrow, just what the hell is going on."

"Let's finish our dinner, clean things up and go sit on the porch with a couple of beers. It'll take a while to tell you the story."

So, they did.

CHAPTER 12

AFTER GETTING COMFORTABLE ON ONE of the old ratty couches on the porch, they popped the top on their beers and Grady began to tell Deacon a story that up until that day had been relegated to the past.

It all began while Grady was in the Crotch, the Marine Corp, back in 1990, while he was stationed at Camp Pendleton, California. He was by that time an infantry unit leader with the 1st Battalion, 5th Marines and his unit had been tasked with participating in the training of a select group from the Mexican Naval Infantry Corps in desert warfare. The Mexican Marines trained with the US Marines out at the Desert Training Center located in Southern California for three months. During this time, a certain Segundo Maestre Diego Navarro and a certain Master Sergeant Grady Allison formed a bond and became good friends.

When the first Gulf War erupted in February of 1991, both Diego and Grady were involved: Grady with the 1st Battalion, 5th Marines while Diego's group had been attached to the 2nd Marine Division. They managed to get together a few times during the buildup to the ground campaign, but lost track of each other until after the war.

Grady had been shot in the hip and left with a permanent limp and was medically discharged from the Corp in 1992 and returned back to Texas. Diego stayed with the Mexican Marines for a few more years before resigning and taking a job with the Federal Police, the Federales. The Federales were folded into the National Guard when it was created in May of 2019.

The Mexican National Guard is not a military organization as it is in the States, it is a law enforcement organization created by absorbing units from the Federal Police, the Naval Police, and the Military Police, it essentially replaced the Federal Police when they disbanded in 2019.

Needless to say, Diego had the background and the experience to be a shining star in the new National Guard and he transferred over to them with the rank of Inspector. Over the years, the cartels had become a huge problem for Mexico. It was not only the drugs that were a problem, but the immigration issue had now morphed into people trafficking as well as trafficking people for the sex trade. Diego was given the mandate to ignore the drug issue and concentrate on the people trafficking issue. He was assigned the section of the border with the US from Ciudad Juárez to the official border crossing a Ojinaga, and was essentially given carte blanche to get the job done any way that he saw fit.

Diego was ruthless. He handpicked his people well and ensured that they had the skills, equipment, and the experience necessary to beat the cartels at their own game, at least for a while. Eventually the money that the cartels could pump into keeping their ratlines across the border open, as well as the money they could spend to make Diego's life and the life of his organization as dangerous and exhausting as possible, would take its toll. But this would take time, and for the cartels time was money, and they would prefer to spend their time making money as opposed to dealing with Diego and his strategy of 'the death by a thousand cuts', where he and his men would constantly target dozens of 'coyotes', those who actually guided illegals across the border, as well as those business entities which set-up the deals and organized the people being trafficked across the border, while letting the US Drug Enforcement Agency worry about the drugs coming in from Mexico.

Cartel politics also played a part. The majority of the border region that Diego was responsible for was in what was known as a 'disputed zone' that ran all the way from the border down through central Mexico. Diego had the Sinaloa cartel on his western flank and the Zetas to the east, which actually worked in his favor. The Zetas and the Sinaloans spent so much of their time, energy, money and personnel trying to take control of the 'disputed zone' from their rival cartel that it gave Diego and his band of merry men, and some women, the 'wiggle room' to perform their mischief.

Eventually the Zetas and the Sinaloans decided to cut a deal with Inspector Navarro. The cartels would stop harassing and terrorizing his group if he would allow cartels free access to his portion of the border to run their drugs into the US. In return for this, they would stop using his portion of the border to traffic people. Furthermore, if they received intelligence indicating that some other organization was about to sneak people across Diego's stretch of the border, they would let him know in time to stop them.

Inspector Navarro knew that he was making a deal with the devil, but his mandate had been to stop the trafficking of people, not the drugs. He could either accept the deal or he could keep going as he was, wearing out his people, losing some, and eventually losing the war anyhow. He accepted the deal but did not bother to inform his superiors in Mexico City about the arrangement.

During his anti-trafficking campaign, Inspector Navarro had based himself in the in the dusty desert town of Villa Ahumada, about 65 miles from the border and roughly centered between Ojinaga and Ciudad Juárez, since he wanted to be close to the action. After he'd agreed to the deal with the cartels, the threat to him and his crew dropped to a manageable level and Diego asked his daughter to come join him.

Diego's wife had left him when he transferred to the National Guard as she had had enough of moving around and living in fear. The only good thing that Diego could see that came out of his marriage was his daughter, Esmeralda. Diego doted on her and she almost idolized her father. Since Villa Ahumada was not a place to raise a daughter, Esmeralda had been placed in a boarding school in Ensenada in the state of Baja California and Diego would visit whenever he could get away from the border. After high school,

Esmeralda had decided to attend the Universidad Vizcaya de las Americas, also in Ensenada, to obtain a degree in nursing. Which she did.

Since Esmeralda missed her father dearly, after getting her degree she decided to go stay with him for a while and take care of him in Villa Ahumada now that it was deemed safe. To pay her way, she took a nursing position at the regional health center, the Centro de Salud Ahumada, while she was living with her father.

"That's all well and good, dad, but this doesn't explain how an old buddy of yours, who you don't see on a regular basis, would suggest that you take care of his daughter after she was apparently kidnapped," suggested Deacon.

"If you'd just hold your horses for a minute, I was going to get to that. Now shut up and let me finish!

"A few years back, while you were still in the service and I'd been here a few years, I got a call from Diego concerning a group of women who had been kidnapped in Cabo San Lucas. These women were not Mexican nationals but eastern Europeans and Brazilians who had been on vacation. They had been kidnapped to essentially fill orders from wealthy degenerates in the States and had been flown out of Baja California to a remote airstrip near Los Lamentos. They would refuel the plane and care for the women there. Keep in mind that the women were valuable merchandise and would have been treated firmly but fairly.

"Once the kidnappers had been assured that everything was in place to receive the merchandise on this side of the border, they would wait until darkness then fly the girls across the border to another dirt strip on this side where they would be collected and passed on.

"Diego had a mole in the trafficking organization and would be advised when the plane had landed at Los Lamentos, the problem was that he and his people were stretched thin at the time and he wanted those women back safe and sound, he really didn't care what happened to the plane or the traffickers, and he asked me if I could perhaps put together a team to 'meet & greet' the plane when it arrived on my side of the border?

"What could I say? Somebody had to go rescue those girls. The fact that the traffickers would likely be killed bothered me not at all, but cleaning up things afterwards might present a problem. When I put this to Diego, he simply said to stack the bodies in the old buildings at the airstrip and then burn the plane and the buildings along with the bodies. He would meet me on the US side of the border at the Riata Inn Presidio, a few miles north of the official border crossing at Presidio, where I would hand the girls over to Diego. He had the connections to get them back into Mexico and then back to their families."

Grady took a few pulls on his beer to wet his whistle before carrying on with his story.

"Well, I couldn't do this on my own and I needed to find some others who would be willing to kill a few assholes, and to torch an airplane and some old buildings while pulling off the rescue. Hank, the present sheriff of Brewster County came to mind, so I gave him a call and he was all in for a little excitement. Hank was a deputy sheriff at Fort Stockton, in Pecos County at the time, I asked him if he had suggestions for some other folks we could approach to help us out. This is where Benito Cabrera got involved. Benito at the time had been a junior deputy sheriff in Winkler County. Hank and Benito had worked together over the years and Hank knew that Benito was definitely a 'law & order' man who would be very upset if he wasn't included. I asked Hank to approach Benito and let me know if he was onboard or not.

"I was in difficult spot now. I had a team of three including myself, but I didn't know how many bad guys would be at the airstrip when the plane landed, or how many potential shooters would be on the plane. On the other hand, as they say, the only way for three people to keep a secret is if the two of them are dead. I did not want a bigger crew with the risk of what we were planning to do getting out before the big event, or especially after the event. I made the command decision to go with three if Benito decided to come onboard. I called Diego and let him know the situation and asked him to keep me up to date and let me know when the plane was headed to Los Lamentos so that I could round up my team and get to the airstrip on my side in plenty of time to get the welcoming committee set up.

"Two days later, Diego called and let me know that the plane was scheduled to land at the Los Lamentos strip in three days. If everything went to plan, it would fly into Texas that evening. We rehashed what to do with the girls once I had them in hand, and I let him know that I would call him after the festivities if I wasn't dead.

"I then called Hank and told him that he and Benito needed to be down at my place around noon two days from then and be kitted up and ready to go when they got here. With that done, I jumped in my truck and took a run over to the old airstrip that the cartel was planning to use. Diego had given me the GPS coordinates and I needed to do a recon before the other guys showed up.

"The strip was only about 40 miles as the crow flies from the house here, but I had to drive back through Fort Davis, then south to Marfa to get on I-90 and taking it back up towards Van Horn. Cutting off into the desert on County Road 2017, I took it as far southwest as it went before getting on the old Chispa dirt road. I followed this road for five or six miles until I came to the locked gate across the dirt road leading to the airfield and the old ranch house described by Diego. I couldn't see anything from the road, and since it was desert, there was no place to hide my truck. I backtracked about a quarter of a mile to an arroyo I'd seen earlier and drove my truck down through it to a dry riverbed. I stashed my truck there then walked back across Chispa Road and along a ridge until I found a spot that overlooked both the old ranch and the airstrip before taking out my binoculars and giving the whole set-up a good looking over.

"The strip had been built running almost directly northwest to southeast with the northwestern end about 500 yards from the dirt road leading to the old ranch. There was a dirt access road leading from the airstrip to the road leading to the ranch, which intersected the runway about a third of the way down its length from the northwestern end.

"The old ranch consisted of an old two-bedroom house in poor condition with the roof sagging in places. There was a weather-beaten barn behind the house with a lean-to built against the right-hand side of the barn when looking from the back of the house.

"This was about all of the intel I was going to get, so I made my way back to the truck and drove home to try and put a plan together with what I had. It was sketchy, but with a little luck and a lot of surprise, I figured we could pull it off."

"Benito and Hank showed up on time in a rented 10-person Chevy Express passenger van and we drug their duffle bags into the house to go through their kit later. Sitting down at the dining table I gave them a briefing on what I had seen on my little recon mission and then laid out my plan, such as it was.

"We'd drive over near the strip before dawn the day that the plane was supposed to arrive. We'd hide the passenger van in the same riverbed I'd hidden my truck in, and we'd saddle up with our rucksacks and hike into a spot with some mesquite trees for shade about 200 yards north of the old ranch and slightly above it. We'd keep an eye on the ranch all day long to see what we were going to have to deal with. If it looked like a go, I would circle back towards the airstrip after dark and get into my 'sniper's hide', about 200-250 yards northeast of where the airstrip access road intersected the airstrip. While I was doing this, Diego and Hank would cautiously make their way down to the back side of the old barn and enter it, making sure there were no bad guys inside it to ruin their fun later.

"When the plane had landed and had come to a stop, I'd call Hank on his cellphone and let him know that the party was about to begin. Once I'd popped any bad guys who were on the plane, I'd call him again and he and Benito would then move on the old ranch house and clean it out. While they were doing this, I'd have to corral the girls somehow. Hopefully, they'd sit tight and not scatter like quail all over the desert."

"I would be geared up with a ghillie suit I still had from my desert warfare training days, and my weapon of choice back then was a Sig Sauer 716i in .308 with a 2-16x28 Sightmark Wraith night vision scope on top. A 250-yard shot with this kit would be like shooting fish in a barrel. I'd have my old Colt 1911 .45 pistol on me for backup. Benito and Hank had gone with Mossberg 500 tactical shotguns and Glocks.

Since I would be the first one shooting down at the airstrip, and we really didn't want the guys in the house wondering what all the shooting was about, I'd also brought along a Dead Air Sandman suppressor to screw onto the end of my rifle to keep things as quiet as possible.

"Anyhow, to make a long story short, the plane arrived around 9:00 that evening. It was a Cessna 208 Caravan that made the downwind leg and final approach to the dirt runway and then landed northwest to southeast. Turning around at the end of the runway it taxied back to a spot where the access road intersected the runway and shut down. I called Hank to tell him the party was starting, which is when he informed me that a large van had just left the ranch headed to the strip, obviously to pick up the girls. My night was about to get interesting.

"Two men got out of the plane and helped the girls out and got them rounded up and sitting in a circle on the ground in front of the plane. About this time, the van had driven onto the access road and pulled up about ten yards in front of the aircraft, with the girls between the aircraft and the van. I desperately needed whoever was in the van to get out in the open so that I could shoot them. One guy got out of each side of the van and walked toward the two guys from the plane. All four men were now between the group of girls and the front of the van.

"The two guys in the plane obviously knew the guys in the van and they huddled up in front of the van to do the 'male bonding, check out the girls' thing. Which is when they all actually checked out.

"I had sighted in my rifle at 200 yards and my laser rangefinder told me they were about 237 yards away. I wasn't going to get fancy; I'd just hold an inch high and hope for the best. The pilot had his back to me and I shot him square between the shoulder blades and dropped him like a hot potato. This opened up a sightline to one of the guys from the van directly across from him that he'd been talking to, so I shot him in the center of his chest. Without waiting to see the result of my second shot, I swung onto the guy to the right that had that 'deer in the headlights' look on his face as I shot him in the left side of the head. The last fellow obviously knew what was happening, but not where it was coming from and took off running right at me. I got him in the chest as well.

"Luckily, the girls just went into shock and stayed grouped up where they were. I started walking over to them while I called Hank and told him that I was finished shooting at the airstrip and that it was his turn to get in on the action. I finally made it over to the girls, but I forgot that a guy in a ghillie suit limping along in the dark probably didn't look human and they started screaming. I finally got the suit off and they calmed down enough that I could talk to them. One spoke English and related what I told her to the others, basically that myself and some others were there to take them back to their families so just sit tight and relax until our van showed up. They really didn't have many options, so they did.

"Meanwhile, back at the ranch, Hank and Benito had moved on the ranch house as soon as the van disappeared toward the airstrip. Going in the back door into the kitchen area, they encountered one trafficker washing dishes at the kitchen sink. Benito shot him in the chest with his 12 gauge when he turned around to see who'd come in the back door. Meanwhile, Hank had continued walking through to the front room where two more traffickers were about to light a spliff, he shot both of them center-of-mass as they sat on an old couch that must have been part of the original furniture.

"After collecting the three spent shotgun shells, they piled the bodies in an old Dodge pickup that they had found parked in front of the house before liberally dousing the house and barn with gasoline they'd found in the barn. While Benito was busy setting the house and barn on fire before driving the bodies to the airstrip in the old Dodge, Hank hotfooted it back to the van which had been hidden in the riverbed, drove over to the locked gate on the road leading to the airstrip, shot the lock off the gate and drove over to where I was keeping the girls company. While we waited for Benito to bring the bodies from the house down to the airstrip, Hank and I prepped the plane and the trafficker's van for ignition. When Benito arrived, we threw the four dead guys that I'd shot into the van and tossed the other three in the plane before we torched the plane, the old Dodge pickup and the van.

"Needless to say, by this time the five girls were well and truly in a state of shock and docilely loaded up in our van with us. I drove us back here so that the girls could get cleaned up, fed and could get some sleep before I drove them to our meeting with Diego at the Riata Inn in Presidio the next day. Hank and Benito stayed at the house until I returned and we could get our stories straight.

"The meeting with Diego went off without a hitch and a few days later he called me to tell me that the girls had been reunited with their families and thanked me for a job well done.

"And now you know exactly why Diego feels that he can trust us with his daughter while he sorts out his business in Mexico. Obviously, he does not feel that she would be safe with him, so I guess we'll have a house guest until he does."

Deacon had to sit back for a second to absorb all that he'd just been told. "So essentially you, Hank and Benito dirt-napped seven traffickers, saved five women, smuggled them back across the border and have gotten off scot-free all these years."

"Yep, that's about it in a nutshell," confirmed Grady.

"Well, that explains your connection with not only Diego, but Hank and Benito as well. Does anyone else know about this little escapade?"

"I sincerely hope not. There is no statute of limitation for murder, even if they were shitbirds. To the best of my knowledge, nobody else is aware of what happened on that dirt airstrip years ago, and you should now keep it to yourself as well. There is no need for Lorna or anyone else to make the connection between an event which occurred long before she came into the area with Esmeralda's kidnapping and Diego getting in touch with us to safeguard his daughter. Until Diego lets us know the full story concerning Esmeralda's kidnapping, I think we should just keep all of this to ourselves and just say that Esmeralda's father is an old friend who is presently travelling and has asked us to look after his daughter while she convalesces until he gets back."

CHAPTER 13

THE MORNING AFTER GRADY HAD explained to Deacon why Diego would ask them to put his daughter up while she recovered and he sorted out his situation in Mexico, Sheriff Stims called Deacon into her office before he headed out on patrol for a summary of his interview with the Jane Doe in El Paso.

He ran through it as meticulously and accurately as possible, leaving nothing out, which caused Lorna to ask the same question that he had essentially asked his father.

"Why in the world would an Inspector for the Mexican National Guard ask for you and Grady to take care of his daughter while she convalesces?"

Deacon had to be careful here as he didn't want to get into the nuts and bolts of Grady and Diego's relationship. "It seems that Inspector Navarro and my father go way back and did some desert warfare training together out in California back when dad was in the Corp. From what I understand they also got together in Saudi Arabia during the buildup to the First Gulf War. They've stayed in touch, and I suppose they trust each other. Inspector Navarro, for whatever reason, does not want his daughter to come back to Mexico at the moment and dad said she could stay with us until Diego calls for her. You'd really need to ask my father if you want more details. I'm guessing that the kidnapping of his daughter may have something to do with it."

Deacon, although he didn't know it, had hit the nail on the head. Since the section of the border that Inspector Navarro was in charge of was essentially a disputed area between the Zeta and the Sinaloa cartels, regardless of the agreement between those cartels and Inspector Navarro, there was always some rogue splinter group trying to fill the void. This time it was the five Beltran Leyva brothers who had split off from the Sinaloa cartel. While trying to build a name for themselves, the brothers decided that they would relocate into the vacuum of the disputed area while they did so.

Needless to say, Inspector Navarro was not very pleased with this development and he and his crew began hitting them hard and were making life very challenging for them. This being the case, and cartels generally being peopled by unsavory individuals with little to no morals, the spin-off cartel, now known as the Gallos or the Roosters, depending on if your native tongue was Spanish or English, hatched a plan to kidnap Inspector Navarro's daughter, move her across the border and keep her in limbo and to hold here essentially for ransom until Inspector Navarro came to his senses and got off their case. The idea was to threaten Diego with selling his daughter to the sex traffickers if he would not reach an agreement with the Gallos.

One evening a car pulled into the emergency entrance to the Centro de Salud Ahumada, the medical center where Esmeralda worked, and one of three men got out of the car, walked into the emergency room and asked for Nurse Navarro. Esmeralda was called, and quickly made her way to the emergency receiving area to figure out what she was needed for. When she got to the receiving desk, the receiving nurse indicated that the man wanted to speak to her.

Once he was satisfied that the nurse who had shown up at the receiving area was in fact Nurse Navarro, he took a large, black, semi-automatic pistol out of his waistband at his back, grabbed Esmeralda by the arm and started walking her towards the automatic sliding doors which he had entered not too long in the past. By this time, the two sicarios, or gunmen, who had been waiting in the car got out armed with AK-47's to cover the emergency entrance and make sure that nobody did anything stupid while Esmeralda was thrown in the back seat and the lead sicario got in beside her. Once the rear door of the sedan was closed, the two other thugs got back in the car and they drove off.

The Roosters had severely underestimated the resolve of one Diego Navarro. Diego hunted far and wide across the desert to find the assholes who had kidnapped his daughter. He killed a few of the Roosters who stood in his way, but he couldn't locate Esmeralda. You can imagine his relief when Esmeralda finally called him from the hospital in Fort Bliss and explained the situation to him. Diego knew that Grady had a son who was now a deputy in Jeff Davis County, so when Esmeralda had handed the phone to Deacon, and Diego confirmed that Deacon was in fact the deputy who was Grady's son, Diego decided that it would be wise to have Esmeralda stay in Texas with the Allisons as opposed to returning to Villa Ahumada, until he could sort out the Gallos.

Sheriff Stims leaned back in her ergonomically designed chair while looking Deacon right in the eye. "Is that the whole truth, and nothing but the truth, so help you God?" just as if they were in court and Deacon was giving sworn testimony.

"I couldn't really say, but now you know as much about the situation as I do."

"Okay, you can go get this woman and bring her home whenever they say she is ready to travel, but I want to have a word with her when she gets here, is that understood?"

"Yes, Sheriff Stims, it is, and that should work out perfectly," said Deacon as he reached into his shirt pocket and pulled out the list that Esmeralda had made and passed to Major Williams, who then emailed it to Deacon.

Passing the shopping list to Lorna, Deacon asked, "Would you and Macy mind getting this stuff for Esmeralda? All she has at the moment is a hospital gown and nothing to wear on the way here."

"Why don't you get it?"

"Because it is a list of girl stuff and you guys would have a much better chance of getting it right than I would."

"I should have known. Your lack of knowledge concerning the female of the species is inexcusable at your age, but we'll help you out this once."

"Fantastic! I'll leave it to you guys and pick it up when it's ready."

"Deacon, before you go out and earn your keep, have you looked at this list?"

"Just a glance to tell me that it concerned things that I am unqualified to shop for. Why do you ask?"

"Well, judging by the sizes of the stuff listed here, this woman must have an amazing figure. I'd guess about a 34-24-32 if I'm reading this correctly. This wouldn't have anything to do with your apparent enthusiasm for a new housemate, would it?"

"Lorna, she was in an unflattering hospital gown, laying in a hospital bed with half her head shaved when I interviewed her. She could have been built like a pear for all I could tell. She's being put up at the house simply as a favor to Inspector Navarro," replied Deacon with trying to keep a straight face.

"You are so full of crap your eyes are brown! Get to work, I'll radio you when this stuff is ready, and you can pay me back later."

Deacon saluted Lorna, spun on his heel and marched out of her office and out to his truck to begin another day doing what deputies do. Getting into his truck, he considered that Lorna may have a point, Esmeralda would be rather attractive once the bruising disappeared, and the fact was that hospital gown could not entirely camouflage what was lurking underneath it. Having a houseguest might get interesting.

CHAPTER 14

WITH CHUCK COVERING FOR THEM, Lorna and Macy decided to take a few hours off and do the shopping required for Esmeralda in Fort Stockton. They hit Walmart for the required toiletry items and jeans before hitting Glitzy Trendz for some fashionable tops. They then stopped in at Hibbet Sports for some running shorts, t-shirts and a pair of Adidas sneakers, and then finally stopped in Cindie's on the way out of town for the required undergarments. Macy had a fun time selecting lingerie that was guaranteed to drive Deacon nuts if he ever actually got to see it.

Lorna called Deacon on the radio and told him that her and Macy had successfully completed the shopping for the list of "girl stuff" and that he should be prepared to fork over about $500 in cash. In the background, Macy let it slip that it was money well spent, and suggested that a modeling session for some of the items may be required.

Deacon took possession of the shopping spree articles while he wrote Lorna a check for what he considered an outrageous amount of money. Lorna winked at him and told him to thank them later. Before everyone called it a day, Deacon asked the girls to select an outfit for Esmeralda to dress in for the ride home from Fort Bliss. Sneakers, 501 Levis, and a t-shirt were laid out with a sexy black set of bra and panties. Deacon turned beet red as he put Esmeralda's traveling outfit in a separate shopping bag from the rest of the items.

Macy and Lorna's laughter followed Deacon out the door.

The following day Deacon was up bright and early again for another trip to the William Beaumont Army Medical Center and his date with destiny, although he didn't know it at the time. He carefully placed the shopping bags with the jeans and so forth on the passenger's seat before buckling up and heading down the road. Arriving at the medical Center, Deacon was once again met at reception by Major Williams who escorted him to Esmeralda's private room. While they made their way there, Major Williams explained to Deacon that although Esmeralda was healing rapidly, she should take it easy for a few weeks to ensure that there were no complications regarding the concussion and so that the laceration on her thigh could heal properly before and after the stitches were removed. Major Williams suggested that a daily application of vitamin E oil on both the head and thigh wounds would reduce the scarring. This wasn't much of concern for guys, but for young women it could be an issue.

When they arrived at the room, Major Williams said to just push the button to call the nurse when they were ready to leave, and an orderly would bring a wheelchair to the room so that Esmeralda could be discharged.

"Doctor, I can walk on my own and do not require a wheelchair."

"I have no doubt that you can, Ms. Navarro, but hospital rules state that the patient to be released must be brought to the entrance in a wheelchair. Also, I have suggested to Deacon that you take it easy for a few weeks to ensure there are no problems concerning your concussion and that if you apply some vitamin E oil to your wounds on a daily basis the scarring should be reduced," replied the doctor as he left the room.

"I think I should take responsibility for the vitamin E oil application. As the doctor suggested, you should not overtax yourself."

"Perhaps for the cut on my head, but if you ever touch my thigh without my permission, Mr. Allison, I will beat you like a drum. I assume that there are clothes in that bag you are carrying. If you could leave them on the foot of the bed and then wait in the hall until I call you, I will get dressed and we can be on our way."

"I don't think it is advisable to leave you alone while you dress. I should stay in the room in case you feel dizzy or need assistance," suggested Deacon. The more he looked at her, the more he realized that even bunged up and bruised, the woman was a diamond in the rough.

"Out!" demanded Esmeralda as she pointed at the door. Obviously, Lorna and Esmeralda were kindred spirits.

Deacon left the room and closed the door behind him and just loitered in the hall until Esmeralda called for him. When he went back into the room he jerked to a stop.

The bruised woman he's left in the room dressed in a hospital gown had transformed herself into an extremely attractive and sexy woman in an Adidas t-shirt, a pair of 501 Levis and sneakers. Okay, one side of her head was shaved, but that would grow back. As it was, she'd brushed out her long, black hair and had swept the hair on top of the wound on the left side of her head over the top and down the other side leaving the shaved side exposed. It was very alluring in a punk sort of way.

"Why are you staring at me, Mr. Allison?"

"Well, when I left the room there was a roughed-up woman lying in the bed with a hideous hospital gown on. She's now my responsibility and I demand to know what you've with her."

Esmeralda got a huge grin on her face, "Do you like the transformation?" asked Esmeralda as she pirouetted with her arms out at her side.

"Oh yeah, Ms. Navarro, you do clean up nicely," replied Deacon as he viewed the transformation.

"The black underwear was especially nice and feminine, did you happen to pick it out?" asked Esmeralda, acting as if this was just an innocent question instead of subtle interrogation.

Looking back on this moment months later, Deacon realized that this was probably the point where his life began to take a drastic turn, possibly for the better, but that would remain to be seen.

"Well, I guess I should buzz the nurse for the wheelchair so that we can get out of here," suggested Esmeralda.

"I suppose so. Hey, did you remember to put some vitamin E oil on your cuts? Maybe we should do that before the long ride home," there was an ulterior motive involved with Deacon's suggestion.

"No, I did not, and what is this 'we' thing. To put oil on the thigh wound, I would need to drop my pants."

"Exactly! Needless to say, I would be here to assist you if necessary," offered Deacon.

"As I told you during your last visit, don't even think about going where you are thinking about going, gringo. Let's hit the road.

On the drive back to Grady's house, Deacon let Esmeralda know that her father had filled them in on the situation down in Mexico that had resulted in her abduction, and Diego's request for her to remain with the Allisons for the time being.

"Fair is fair, Deacon, you seem to know much about me, perhaps you can let me know something about you."

Deacon realized with a start that this was the first time he could recall that she had addressed him by his given name and thought that things may be looking up. If he wanted to keep the ball rolling, he figured telling her a little about himself wasn't too much to ask.

"There's really not much to tell, Esmeralda. I grew up in Fort Davis. When I graduated, I wanted to see the world, so I enlisted in the Army. I got shot in Syria and came back here to figure out what I wanted to do with my life and became a sheriff just to stay busy and draw a paycheck."

"So, you do not intend on staying in the area long term?"

"I don't know yet. I really just plan to take it one day at a time and see how it goes."

"Very wise. You just never really know what twists and turns that life will take, do you," she replied cryptically while looking out the windshield.

The rest of the trip was spent just talking about what music they liked, movies they'd seen, and how their father's seemed to get into more trouble than would normally be expected of men their age.

Pulling into the graveled parking area in front of Grady's house, Deacon shut down his truck and went around to help Esmeralda get out of the vehicle and up the steps to the porch, her leg injury was still giving her problems. By the time they were up on the porch, Grady had come out and introduced himself before ushering Esmeralda into the house to show her the layout and the room that would be hers as long as she was his guest.

Grady's house was the quintessential ranch house. The covered porch, which extended all the way across the front of the old stone house was accessed by a set of three steps that breached the center of the balustrade which ran along the length of the porch. This set of steps was directly in front of a white oak Victorian style front door with two vertical stained-glass panels set into it.

The front door opened into a large, airy, high ceilinged living room with two large Mexican-style ceiling fans with palm leaf blades rotating just fast enough to keep the air moving. At the opposite side of the living room from the front door, a stone wall was inset with a large fireplace fronted by a hearth made out of a flat slab of black slate. A mantle built out of an old oak beam was above the fireplace.

To the left of the front door a wall built out of pine planking which extended almost down almost to the stone wall holding the fireplace, but ended in a doorway that opened in to a small anteroom that held three other doors: one to the left, one to the right and one straight ahead. The door to the left led to the guest bedroom which extended to the front of the house, and the door to the right led to Deacon's room which extended to the back of the house. The guestroom and Deacon's room shared the full bath between them, via interior doors. This bathroom could also be accessed by the visitors to the house via the door straight ahead in the small anteroom.

To the right of the living room, about midway along the wall, was another door which led to the master bedroom, Grady's room. This room extended about two thirds of the way from the front of the house and included an ensuite bathroom at the back end of the bedroom.

Walking through an arched opening to the right of the stone fireplace, you entered the dining area with the kitchen and pantry to the left and a laundry room to the right. The back of the pantry butted up to what was the wall of Deacon's room. The back door was between the kitchen and the dining room, and it led out onto a small, covered porch.

Since Deacon had already claimed the bedroom in the back, Esmeralda would be staying in the guest bedroom, which was toward the front of the house on the opposite side of the living room from Grady's master bedroom. As mentioned earlier, this meant that Esmeralda and Deacon would be sharing the bathroom located between their rooms. Each of the bedrooms had direct access to the bathroom, what could possibly go wrong with this setup?

Although Esmeralda was starting to grow on Deacon, he still had his day job as a Jeff Davis County deputy and couldn't hang out with her at Grady's ranch. Since it would be boring for her to be alone at the ranch house by herself during the day, Grady would take her along on his rounds of the ranch unless she expressed a desire to stay at home. Seeing a good-looking woman suddenly show up with the boss seemed to perk up the ranch hands staying in the various line shacks scattered around the ranch, and generated the usual gossip. She was a classic Mexican beauty with a body that could make a train jump the track to follow her down a dirt road. Although she wasn't voluptuous, everything was proportional on her slender and seductive frame. The package taken as a whole was simply outstanding.

Over the next few weeks, Deacon and Esmeralda got to know each other better just by sitting out on the porch and enjoying each other's company once they had cleaned up the kitchen after dinner. Two weeks after Esmeralda arrived at Grady's place, they held a barbeque on a Saturday afternoon so that everyone could meet Esmeralda and vice versa. An ulterior motive for the barbeque was to put a stop to the rumors that Macy was floating around the sheriff's office that Deacon was keeping a young woman at the ranch against her will.

Deacon and his father had taken that particular Saturday off to get everything ready for the fiesta. Grady's place, as you approached it coming up the long driveway leading up from Madera Canyon Road, consisted of the house to the right, a big pole barn directly in front of you as you entered the 'plaza', and a large three-car garage and workshop to the left facing the house. This set up created a courtyard of sorts in the middle of the buildings and a perfect parking lot and barbeque venue.

Deacon pulled the two barbeque pits fashioned out of split 50-gallon drums out of the pole barn, cleaned and scrubbed each before setting them up in the courtyard in front of the porch. He then loaded them up with charcoal and mesquite chips and they were ready to go. Grady and Esmeralda had spent the previous evening marinating and preparing the beef steaks, bratwursts and chorizo sausages, and were dusting them with some secret spice concoction when Deacon went in to see what they were up to.

The guests would be responsible for the supporting dishes: Macy was responsible for the salsa and chips, Lorna and Adrian for the green salad and dressings, Chuck was tasked with the potato salad, either purchased or handmade, and the three deputies had been asked to take care of the beverages and dessert.

At around 3:00 that afternoon, Deacon fired up the pits, and everyone went into the house to shower up and get ready for the party. Deacon heard the shower running in the bathroom he shared with Esmeralda, so he just sat in his room waiting his turn. Not being familiar with the duration required for women to utilize a bathroom in preparation for a proper shindig, he waited what he considered a reasonable amount of time after he heard the shower stop running, added five minutes just to be safe and walked into the bathroom from the door leading directly into it from his room.

The sequence of events that happened afterwards is debatable, but they seem to have occurred in the following sequence: Deacon opened the door and jerked to a stop as he was presented with the dorsal view of a butt naked Esmeralda leaning in to peer into the mirror while she primped. The sudden opening of the door to Deacon's room behind her, and his sudden appearance in the mirror in front of her, caused Esmeralda to spin around while putting one arm protectively over her breasts and utilizing the other hand to cover her nether regions in a futile effort to hide her nakedness. Deacon had now managed to view the entire naked backside and most of the salient features on the frontside of a naked Esmeralda and was understandably speechless for a moment.

"What are you doing in here!" demanded Esmeralda.

"I thought that you were finished in here, so I thought I'd grab a shower, now I'm just enjoying the vision which was graciously presented to me through no fault of my own," answered Deacon with a decidedly lecherous grin.

"You are not much of a gentleman. A real gentleman would avert his eyes, excuse himself, close the door behind him as he left, and forget what he had seen."

"I can only say that this real gentleman would be an idiot to do so while a vision such as yourself, in your present state of undress, burnt itself into his retinas."

"I hope that you and your retinas go blind. Now get out of here and let me finish getting ready. I will be sure to knock on the door when it is your turn in the bathroom, imbecíl," scolded Esmeralda.

An embarrassed Esmeralda studiously avoided Deacon while the guests showed up and the party got started. First to arrive were Lorna and Adrian with the salad and dressings, which Deacon helped carry to the kitchen and place on the island. Next up was Macy with the salsa and chips, which Esmeralda helped carry into the kitchen. Chuck was the next to arrive, and after parking next to Lorna's Dodge Durango, got out of his Impala with two one- gallon buckets of potato salad from the Riata Restaurant in Alpine. The final guests arrived in posse: Tito and Adelina, John and Susan, and Armando and Inez. Tito had a plastic garbage can with a pony keg of Tecate in it surrounded by bags of ice. He'd thoughtfully also brought a bottle of tequila as well as a bottle of Johnny Walker Blue. These were all carried up and onto the porch. John, Armando and their wives brought up the rear of the posse in John's Ford Explorer and provided the homemade guacamole, chips and enough churros to feed an army.

With Deacon and Grady doing duty at the barbeque pits, the rest of the menfolk made themselves comfortable on the ratty couches and chairs on the porch while they partook of their beverage of choice, while the women got everything laid out in the kitchen waiting for the main courses to be seared to perfection.

Needless to say, the rumors surrounding Esmeralda and her incarceration at the Allison place had run rampant. The women felt it was well within their bounds to analyze the situation, and the subtle interrogation began.

Esmeralda knew what was happening, and since she didn't have much to hide, she sailed as close to the truth as possible: Deacon had rescued her when she got thrown out of the van, she'd ended up in hospital at Fort Bliss, her father and Grady were old friends and her father had asked Grady to look after her while he was sorting out some business down in Mexico.

Eventually, what was bound to happen, happened. Young Macy, who was not well schooled in the matters of social decorum which were usually adhered to at these types of social events, simply asked what was on her mind.

"So, are you and Deacon going to hook up?"

The kitchen went deathly silent while Esmeralda did that Latina blushing/glowing thing.

"The young Mr. Allison and I are simply friends while I recover from my injuries, there will be no 'hooking up', as you put it, involved. Once my father calls for me, I will return to Mexico, continue with my nursing career, and that will be that."

Lorna, who had seen the way that Deacon was looking at Esmeralda, and the way Esmeralda was sneaking peeks at Deacon while the barbeque was getting set up, just laughed.

"Esmeralda, I was born at night, but it wasn't last night. I've seen how you've been eyeballing my deputy this afternoon, and I'd bet good money that before your daddy calls for you, you and 'the young Mr. Allison' will definitely be 'hooking up' as Macy says."

Some more of that Latina blushing or glowing thing occurred at this point.

The barbeque was a roaring success. Lorna and her crew had been working almost 24/7 for weeks on end and needed a break. Technically they were all still on call, but the county seemed to have decided to behave itself that day. Still, Lorna and Deacon just nursed beers throughout the afternoon and evening to allow Tito, John and Armando to cut loose, blow off some steam and just enjoy themselves.

Lorna kept pestering Deacon about his potential relationship with the alluring Esmeralda. He deflected this conversation every time it was brought up. Lorna, being wise beyond her years, just snickered.

Everyone had finally got to meet the mysterious houseguest at the Grady ranch, but the actual reason for her being there, and the relationship between Grady and Esmeralda's father, was still unclear.

Eventually it was time for everyone to pack up and go home. While the mildly inebriated deputies, excluding Deacon, lounged on the porch, the ladies cleaned up the kitchen and wrapped up the leftovers and put them in the refrigerator before getting their menfolk into the correct vehicles and driving them home.

Grady had somewhat overserved himself with the Johnny Walker Blue Label and after the last of the guests had headed down the driveway, he excused himself to Deacon and Esmeralda and went to his room to shower up, lay down and sleep it off. Which left Esmeralda and Deacon on one of the ratty couches on the porch with their feet kicked up on the handrail nursing their final beers.

"So, Mr. Allison, did you like what you saw when you so rudely barged in on me in the bathroom?" asked Esmeralda while looking straight ahead and trying desperately not to smile.

"Ms. Navarro, only a hormonally challenged, myopic, octogenarian eunuch would not have appreciated the view."

"Well, for your sake, I sincerely hope that the image has been burned into your retinas, as you alluded to earlier. The chances of you ever seeing me again in such a state are somewhere between slim and none," replied Esmeralda while continuing to look straight ahead and sipping her beer.

"Ms. Navarro, between slim and none there is still a bit of maneuvering room for a repeat performance, correct?"

Turning to Deacon and unable to hold it in any longer, Esmeralda laughed and replied, "And who said chivalry was dead? Generally I like a little optimism in my men, but in your case, I wouldn't hold my breath."

Polishing off her beer, Esmeralda informed Deacon that she was going to bed and that she would see him in the morning. Deacon watched her get up from the couch and depart with what he thought was just a little more sashay in her strut than was technically called for, although this could have simply been wishful thinking on his part.

While Deacon sat on the porch for another half hour or so to ensure that Esmeralda had enough time to finish up whatever she was doing in the shared bathroom, and to courteously avoid a repeat performance of what had occurred earlier in the day, he contemplated life in general, and a certain spicy Mexican girl with perhaps a little too much wiggle in her walk, in specific.

CHAPTER 15

GENERALLY, THINGS CARRIED ON AFTER the barbeque much as they had before, but more and more often Deacon would find himself stopping by on his rounds to have lunch with Esmeralda at home, or he would take her with him in the afternoon, with Sheriff Stims blessing, and they would grab a bite to eat in either Fort Davis, Alpine or Marfa.

Diego was keeping in touch with Grady concerning the situation in Mexico as well as calling Esmeralda every now and then just to see how she was getting along in her new surroundings. One thing that concerned Diego, was that lately his daughter did not seem to be in much of a hurry to return home. Diego queried Grady about this.

"Well, amigo, I think we may be suffering the unintended consequences of putting your daughter up in the same house as my son. They seem to be getting along much better than we anticipated," informed Grady.

"Is your son behaving himself as a gentleman?"

"He is behaving himself as well as can be expected while living in the same house with a girl who is hot enough to kill waist high corn simply by walking down the rows, Diego. Have you taken a good look at your daughter lately? She's hotter than a firecracker on the 4th of July and built like a bag full of wildcats, if you happen to like them slim, trim, and racy. My son apparently does. They are only a couple of years apart, I believe. How old is Esmeralda?"

"She was 27 on her last birthday."

"So, I'm correct, they are only two years apart."

"You have still not answered my question, Grady. Is your son acting alike a proper gentleman around my daughter?" reiterated Diego.

"Yes, he is. But how much longer they can keep their hormones in check is not something that neither you or I can control. For goodness sakes, Diego, they're adults!"

"Perhaps I should bring her back to Mexico before your son takes advantage of her," suggested Diego.

"Perhaps you should do it before your daughter corrupts my son," countered Grady.

"My hands are tied, amigo. The situation on this side of the border is still too dangerous for me to allow Esmeralda back. Could you put up with my daughter for another month or so?"

"I'll probably have to, if I tried to get her out of the house at this point my son would probably kick my ass."

"Okay, my friend. Thank you again. We'll cross that bridge later," laughed Diego before signing off.

CHAPTER 16

TOWARDS THE END OF THE summer, it was announced that there would be an 'end of summer' rodeo and barn dance to be held at the Brewster County Fairgrounds just outside of Alpine, in two weeks' time. Needless to say, this was the social event of the year, which provided every woman in the region with a good excuse to go shopping for suitable outfits so that they could look their best.

Lorna ordered Macy to take a weekend off to go shopping with her in El Paso, the closest city with the requisite shops for what they were after. Since it was a 5-hour drive one way to get there, they'd need both Saturday and Sunday to shop properly. All the deputies plus Chuck were ordered to man the fort until they got back. Being devious females who wanted more gossip where Esmeralda and Deacon were concerned, they invited Esmeralda to join them on their shopping spree.

Since Esmeralda was technically in the country illegally and had no money or visible means of support, she begged Deacon to let her use his credit card. This went on for a few days until Deacon finally relented and set a limit as to what she could charge on the card. If she failed to adhere to the limit, she would be sleeping in the pole barn for the foreseeable future. He also let her know that she owed him now, and that he would determine the method of repayment.

Esmeralda agreed to Deacons terms but had crossed her fingers behind her back while doing so. She'd heard that this particular gringo gesture made null and void any commitment she may have made verbally under duress. That said, she was sort of interested in what type of payment young Mr. Allison had in mind. She decided to worry about that later.

A few days later, Macy and Lorna showed up around 6:00 in the morning in Lorna's Dodge Durango to collect Esmeralda before heading off to El Paso for a girl's shopping weekend. They arrived at the La Quinta Inn in El Paso just after 11:00 that morning and checked into the rooms which Macy had booked for them the earlier in the week. Their hotel was strategically located within 500 yards of their first destination; the mall known as The Fountains at Farah. Esmeralda and Macy would share a room while the boss had a room of her own. Once they had rolled their suitcases and carried their backpacks to their respective rooms, they freshened up after the drive before scampering back to the Durango to begin their quest at The Fountain at Farah's.

The first store they entered was The Loft, which specialized in upmarket women's apparel. Since there is no sense shopping without buying, Macy bought a sequined cap sleeved top, Lorna purchased a V-neck layering cami, and Esmeralda charged Deacon's Visa for a paisley smocked tie neck media shell before they moved on to the Apricot Lane Boutique to spend more money.

The Apricot Lane Boutique was another upmarket women's clothing store, and again the girls were bound by convention to buy something; Lorna scored a joy dress, the name alone had Esmeralda and Macy in stitches, Macy scored a glam mini dress which was on sale, but Esmeralda struck out as nothing caught her fancy.

The next stop on the hit parade was Cavender's Western Outfitters where Esmeralda fell in love with a pair of Dingo primrose black with floral embroidery low-heeled booties that she just had to have while Macy scored a short sweatshirt dress, she obviously had plans extending past the barn dance and rodeo, while Lorna opted for a black, short tiered fringe skirt. She was likely looking past the rodeo as well.

As they were walking out of the mall to head back to their hotel, they just happened to pass the Cali Nails shop. The girls huddled up in the middle of the mall and it was a unanimous decision that they owed themselves a manicure and pedicure, but due to the ambiguous nature of Esmeralda's supposed relationship with Deacon, Macy's relationship with a guy from out of town still being in the early stages, and the fact that Lorna was married and it would only make Adrian laugh, the bikini waxing was put on hold.

That knocked the first shopping day in the head, so the girls packed up their loot and went back to their hotel. By this time they were famished, so they had dinner at the Andale Mexican Restaurant and Cantina across the street from the hotel as well as a couple of beers to knock the edge off. During dinner, the interrogation of Esmeralda continued, and she maintained the line that her and Deacon were just friends, and that the relationship was totally platonic, which technically speaking, it was at the time. Macy and Lorna just rolled their eyes.

Esmeralda managed to turn the tables on Macy and asked her what she was buying the short skirts for? It was now Macy's turn to blush, and she revealed that she'd met a young man in Stockton that she was now on the prowl for him.

After dinner, they walked back to the hotel and made plans to meet up at 0800 hours the following morning to grab breakfast at the hotel before continuing the shopping spree at the Cielo Vista Mall, which happened to be only about a mile from their hotel.

The next morning, they met up in the restaurant as planned for the free buffet breakfast to fortify themselves and to plan their day. At this point Esmeralda had not purchased suitable attire for a barn dance, which would also need to do double-duty not only attract the attention of young Mr. Allison, but to hold it for the foreseeable future. They finished their breakfast, then piled into the Durango again and drove over to the Cielo Vista Mall. This was a much bigger mall and had a larger selection.

The first shop they hit was Old Navy, where nothing caught their eye, so they moved on to Sephora where they all stocked up on makeup, skincare and hair products, and their preferred fragrances. Moving on, they went into Dillard's to see what they could find. By this time Esmeralda had totally forgotten about the scar on her thigh or the fact that she may not be mobile enough to trip the lights fantastic, but she was in shopping mode and those concerns were irrelevant at this point. She was conflicted as she liked a short little button front shirt dress in navy blue, but she also thought the Gianni Bini, satin cowled, halter necked, sleeveless, open backed mini sheath dress with the asymmetrical hem might do the trick even better. Eventually she decided on the Gianni Bini in black to match her new cowgirl booties.

As they were walking through the mall, lo and behold they spied a Victoria's Secret shop, which drew them in like moths to a flame. Now Lorna was happily married and was just looking for something to spice things up with Adrian, but Macy was actively on the prowl, and Esmeralda figured some lingerie might be nice to have in her toolbox concerning Deacon if the opportunity presented itself. Lorna finally settled on a chain strap, satin lace trim cami shorts set, and then had to wait for the others to make up their minds. Macy bought herself, actually she bought it for her young man in Stockton, which is how lingerie actually works, a demi lace teddy and a lace top satin slip.

Esmeralda had a more difficult task since she really had no idea where the thing with Deacon was headed, but she needed to be prepared. First off, she required something to wear in the bathroom to prevent being caught naked again. For that she got a mid-thigh sage colored cotton sleepshirt, subtle but sexy. Next, she needed panties and bras since she really didn't have enough of either for her extended stay. It is a topic of great debate among men as to what style of panties are the sexiest, and there are a lot of differing options. In Esmeralda's case they not only had to be sexy, but functional as well. You need something between yourself and your jeans when you are not actually wearing them under a skirt which may or may not accidentally creep up or fly up during an evening out. This being the case, there is really only one choice; bikini panties. Esmeralda bought six pairs in various prints. Next up were bras. God had only provided Esmeralda with a pert set of 34 B sized breasts, which were fine and fit the whole package rather nicely. Her breasts didn't really need any support, but any advantage in the possible quest for a certain young deputy's attention was appreciated. Esmeralda went with three of the lightly lined balconette bras in black and three of the lightly lined demi bras in coconut white rose, marzipan and white.

Everyone was good to go now, but as they walked out of the door back into the mall, a rangy looking Hispanic man about 5'11" tall, with salt and pepper hair worn short and some old acne scars on his cheeks, dressed in old jeans, a faded denim work shirt, a beat-up straw cowboy hat with matching boots approached them. He wasn't smiling and he looked like a thoroughly dangerous man, which he was. Lorna positioned herself between him and the other girls to see how things were going to go.

"It's okay, Lorna, that is my papá," informed Esmeralda as she ran to her father and gave him a hug that would have done a boa constrictor proud. Diego returned the hug with feeling.

"Papá, how did you know that we would be here today?"

"Grady let me know about the rodeo and that you ladies would be going shopping in El Paso this weekend. I reasoned that due to what you girls would likely be shopping for that eventually you would need to show up at this mall. You don't have many other options to choose from in El Paso. I simply staked out the mall. You passed me as you went into Dillard's."

Esmeralda then turned around and introduced Sheriff Stims and Macy to her father before they made their way to the Starbucks, which was back towards Dillard's, so that they could take a seat while Diego and Esmeralda got caught up.

Once they had their coffees in hand, Diego asked Esmeralda how she was healing up and how were thing's going out at Grady's ranch.

"I'm mending well, Papá. My ribs have healed, and the concussion has passed with no complications. The only problem is my leg. Although it has almost entirely healed, the scar on my thigh is ugly and will mark me for life."

"Is that so? I heard from a little bird that there is a certain young deputy that may not find that scar so unsightly," Diego said with a mischievous smile.

"If that little bird happens to be a sweet old cowboy who walks with a limp, I may need to have words with him for spreading rumors and gossiping like an old woman," replied Esmeralda trying unsuccessfully to appear upset at this revelation.

Lorna and Macy were not even subtle about it in the least as they laughed and high fived each other.

"Seriously, mi hija, are they taking care of you well? Do you need anything?"

"They treat me like one of the family and we owe them a debt of gratitude. That said, when will the difficulties in Mexico be resolved so that I can come home?"

"The problems across the border are still not resolved to my satisfaction and I need to ask you to stay with Grady for perhaps another month or two. I miss you as well, daughter, but it is simply too dangerous for you to come home right now," Diego explained before continuing. "Besides, what would young Mr. Allison say if you told him that you were leaving before he could court you properly?" Diego was grinning at his daughter when he said this.

Lorna leaned over at this point and told Esmeralda that Deacon's amateur courtship was obvious to everybody but her, she may as well accept the situation for what it was. Macy just laughed.

They chatted and joked with each other for a while, mostly at Esmeralda's expense. When they had finished their coffee, Diego told the ladies that he needed to get back across the border. After shaking hands with Lorna and Macy, he gave his daughter a hug and a kiss on the top of her head.

"If you need me, ask Grady to contact me and if I need to get a message to you, I'll go through Grady as well. Via con Dios, mi hija."

With that, Diego walked away in the direction of Dillard's and was gone.

"Your dad is a very exceptional person; I've heard about him in the briefs I get form the Border Patrol and ICE. He seems like a nice guy, but I'd hate to run into him in a dark alley if he was upset with me," Lorna told Esmeralda.

"He is the best papá, but I worry about him being down there with the cartels and all that mess. I think it is time for him to retire and just settle down and enjoy the rest of his days."

"Men like your father can never really retire; their job is who they are. I wonder if he would ever be safe in Mexico after the life he has lived and his sometimes, violent confrontations with the various cartels. Something for you both to think about," suggested Lorna.

CHAPTER 17

THE GIRLS ARRIVED BACK AT Grady's place around 7:00 that evening to find Deacon sitting on the porch. "Go get him, tiger!" Macy told Esmeralda as she got out of the rear seat and handed Esmeralda's shopping bags to her before climbing into the now vacated passenger's seat. Lorna pulled a U-turn in front of the pole barn and on the way back she stopped beside the porch and informed Deacon that she would see him at work bright and early the next day.

Esmeralda came up on the porch and was going to go straight to her room when Deacon spied the bag from Victoria's Secret. "Whoa! Hold on there. Is that what I think it is?"

"Depends, what do you think it is?" retorted an Esmeralda who was starting to glow again.

"Sexy underwear is what I think it is," said Deacon with a leer.

"The correct term would be lingerie."

"Same can, different wrapper. I think you should come over here and let me take a look at what you've got there, maybe you could model it for me later?"

"And I think that you need your head examined," replied Esmeralda as she made her way into the house with a smile on her face, leaving a discontented, but grinning, gringo in her wake.

At the Grady Ranch, the weeks before the rodeo and dance passed normally with Grady taking care of the ranch and Deacon doing his deputy's duties, but Esmeralda threw in some serious walking around the courtyard at the ranch house as well as daily hikes down and back along the mile long driveway from the ranch house to the dirt road that connected with County Road 116. She also began investing some time in yoga workouts she'd learned while attending the Universidad Vizcaya de las Americas. She was determined to present the best, sexiest, most alluring picture possible when she showed up at the dance in her black Gianni Bini mini dress, and she only had a few short weeks to get herself in shape. Her damaged leg was still a bit stiff and sore, so she figured that if she couldn't dance, she may as well present some eye candy to any single young men who may attend the dance. She finally had to ask herself who she was trying to fool, the sad fact was that she was on a quest to beguile, that is to lure and entrap by temptation, a certain sheriff's deputy.

With this in mind, she upped her game that evening on the porch when her and Deacon were sharing one of the ratty couches as the sun went down. They were just sitting there chatting about nothing of consequence. She had set the stage masterfully by wearing a pair of cut-off jeans and a t-shirt and sitting on Deacon's left, which had her scarred right thigh toward him.

While they were talking, Esmeralda reached into her front pocket and pulled out a little tube of vitamin E oil. After squirting a dab onto the index finger of her right hand, she continued chatting while massaging the oil into the scar. Keep in mind that this was not a case of an unsightly scar on a reasonably sexy leg, but by this time an incredibly sculptured, toned and sensually seductive leg that just happened to have a scar on it, which was not easy to overlook in the present setting. Deacon became tongue-tied as he watched the show.

Esmeralda noticed this and asked, "What do you think, Deacon, is this scar reducing or not?" as she grabbed his hand and ran his fingers over the 8" scar that sort of resembled a caterpillar with the small staple wounds on each side of it. They both felt that his touch was somewhat electrifying in a primally erotic sort of way, probably due to the endorphin and hormone overload present in both parties at this point.

Deacon, not one to let an opportunity go to waste, ran his hand over the scar a few times before telling Esmeralda that he thought she had missed a few spots and if she would put a dab of oil on his finger, he would touch it up. By this time, they both had some idea of what was, or what could be happening between them, but neither was confident enough yet to bring it up and possibly risk rejection.

The day before the dance, Esmeralda was at home alone looking in the mirror and came to the not so shocking conclusion that her hair looked like crap. It wasn't the hair itself, which was long, silky and wildly curly, but the fact that part of it over her left ear had been shaved to suture the wound there. Although the hair had grown out some to cover the scar, it had not grown out uniform and looked untidy. She called Macy to confer as to what could be done about the problem.

"I know exactly what needs to be done. I used to work at an upmarket salon in San Angelo after high school. I'll grab my clippers and scissors and come by Grady's after work. We'll decide on what you want when I get there."

Macy showed up just after dinner, while Deacon and Esmeralda were washing dishes. Esmeralda tossed her drying towel to Deacon and her and Macy hustled straight to Esmeralda's room to determine a suitable coiffure, under the present circumstances, for the upcoming dance. They were sitting on Esmeralda's bed and looking through a few fashion and salon magazines to come up with a suitable style, when Macy had a 'eureka' moment. She showed Esmeralda a picture in one of the magazines and Esmeralda simply asked Macy if she thought that she could pull it off. "No problem,", was the answer.

They carried the desk chair in Esmeralda's room into the bathroom and locked the connecting door to Deacon's room. Macy knew there was a backstory there and eventually Esmeralda told her how the rude, crude and socially unacceptable Deacon had walked in on her while she was in her birthday suit.

"How come that doesn't ever happen to me?" pouted Macy with a grin to match Esmeralda's before Macy had Esmeralda sit in the chair and covered her shoulders with a towel before the shearing commenced.

The hairstyle that they had decided on was sort of a retro-punk thing. Macy would trim the hair short, a number 3 in barber parlance, from the left side of Esmeralda's head, where the scar was, to a uniform length up to roughly the line where a proper side part would be. She would then continue this shear for the width of the clippers around and down behind the ear. Basically, the sheared area would extend from the sideburns up to the level of a low side part then back down, following the imaginary line of a side part to a point above and just behind the ear and then down to the neck. This would not hide the scar, in fact it would highlight it, but it would be intentional, and it would look as if Esmeralda did not even consider the scar to be an issue, which was the whole point of the exercise. The remaining mane above the part line on the left side of Esmeralda's head would be pulled in a 'comb over' to the other side of her head and either left loose or done up in a braid to hang over her right shoulder. Picture the actress and songstress Rhianna back in 2012.

When Macy had finished and brushed the hair into place as it would be worn the following evening, Esmeralda was ecstatic with the result. Macy suggested that she keep it under wraps until she was dressed to the 9's the following evening when Deacon would drive her to the dance, it would drive him nuts. Esmeralda agreed.

The following day, everyone was gearing up for the big fandango down in Alpine. Esmeralda had been running around with her hair in a turban since the previous evening to keep her new hairdo a secret. The menfolk were washing and cleaning their vehicles and generally getting ready for the big event.

Around noon on the day of the dance, Grady informed Deacon and Esmeralda that he'd need to leave soon as he needed to go down and pick up Hank before heading over to catch the bull riding at the Brewster County Fairgrounds, which just left Esmeralda and Deacon at the house.

Now the girls had all planned to just wear jeans, boots and blouses to the rodeo and then change into their fancy dress at the dance venue, which was essentially a large barn/meeting hall near the rodeo arena. This allowed them to kick back and watch the rodeo without getting their dancing attire messed up before showing it off. When Grady left to pick up Hank, Esmeralda said that she was going to shower up and get ready to go. Deacon told her to just beat on his door when she was ready for him to burst in again, she advised him that this was not going to happen.

About half an hour later Esmeralda walked out of the door into the living room to let Deacon know that it was his turn in the bathroom, and all Deacon could do was stare. Esmeralda was dressed simply in a pair of reasonably snug Levis, her old Justin boots and a black, fitted, floral embroidered long-sleeved pearl snap western shirt. You would not have expected this outfit to be really eye-catching, but on her it was remarkably appealing. The pseudo-punk hairstyle oddly complemented the western motif.

"What?" asked Esmeralda wondering why Deacon was looking like a rabbit caught in the headlights.

"N-nothing, I just haven't seen you all dolled up before," replied Deacon.

With a mischievous smile, Esmeralda said, "You ain't seen nothing yet, cowboy."

Deacon had to think about this while he stood up and went to his room to shower up and get ready for the rodeo. If he 'ain't seen nothing yet', then the rest of the evening was bound to be interesting.

Guys have it easy concerning these sorts of outings: a clean pair of jeans, any long-sleeved western shirt without the name Carhartt or Levis on the tag, a decent pair of cowboy boots and you were good to go to the rodeo, the dance or both. Deacon opted for a pair of 501 Levis topped off with a Cody James western shirt in the Himalaya southwestern stripe pattern and his 'dress pair' of Tecovas lizard skin cowboy boots. Dashing into Grady's bathroom, Deacon splashed on some of his Old Spice deodorant and aftershave to better his chances of seeing what he ain't seen yet.

Walking back out to the porch, Deacon collected Ms. Navarro and walked her and her little roll-on suitcase that contained her dancing attire out to his old Chevy stepside where he opened her door for her, and handed her inside before putting the suitcase in the bed of the truck and they got on the road to the rodeo and dance.

CHAPTER 18

IT WAS A GOOD 30-MILE drive to Fort Bliss, then another 25 from there to Alpine, which gave Esmeralda and Deacon about an hour of windshield time just to shoot the breeze and gossip. They were now comfortable with each other, but there was still a ways to go before they could be called 'an item'. This was fine with both of them, Rome wasn't built in a day, but it burnt down in one. Slow but steady wins the race was essentially what they both had in mind, although neither would put that into words.

Deacon pulled off State Road 67 and took a right onto Paso Del Norte Road for the quarter mile run to the parking lot in front of the large pole barn next to the rodeo arena where the dance was to be held. The rodeo had been going on all day, and it was now about 3:00 in the afternoon. The actual parking lot was full, and people were milling about everywhere, so Deacon was forced to park in the temporary dirt parking lot across Paso Del Norte Road from where the rodeo was being held.

They first walked into the pole barn dance venue, which at this time held the concession booths, and got themselves a chili dog and a Pepsi each before they wandered back out in the sun to the rodeo grounds and sat in the covered bleachers to enjoy their dogs and drink. They watched the calf roping competition, barrel racing and the saddle bronc events while waiting for the sun to go down and the dance to begin. While they were watching the rodeo,

Deacon noticed that many, if not all, of the men present were sneaking glances at Esmeralda. He couldn't really blame them. Since Esmeralda had been staying with the Allison's, she hadn't spent much time in any of the towns in the area and nobody could figure out who the exotic looking Mexican girl with the interesting hairstyle, hanging out with new deputy, was. In the small communities prevalent in the desert, everybody usually knew everybody else. Esmeralda seemed totally oblivious to the attention, or perhaps she just didn't care. In any event, the attention she was getting, and the fact that he was her date, flattered Deacon.

Eventually the sun went down, and things began to cool off. Deacon and Esmeralda had run into Lorna and Adrian as well as Macy and her date, Stuart, during the afternoon, and the girls decided that it was about time for them to get themselves ready for the dance.

The concessions had been moved out of the pole barn venue and tables and chairs now covered the first half of the pole barn as you walked in the front door. The remaining half was dedicated to dancing with the band being set up on a stage at the far end. Deacon walked out to the truck with Esmeralda so that she could retrieve her little suitcase, which had been locked in the cab. On the way back into the barn they met up with Lorna and Macy, who had gone to get their glad rags as well.

While the girls went into the ladies' room to change, the men commandeered a table just at the edge of the dance floor before going up to the bar, which had been set up along one wall, to get some beers to put them into the proper dancing frame of mind. No hard liquor was sold at the bar as the fairgrounds did not have a liquor license, but looking at the bottles sitting on some of the tables, it was obviously a BYOB night – Bring Your Own Booze.

The tables were filling up quickly when Lorna and Macy walked out of the changing room followed by Esmeralda, all towing little roll-on suitcases. There were the expected catcalls and whistles since both Lorna and Macy were attractive women who were dressed to the nines in short skirts. The girls laughed and curtsied, but then the hubbub and babble of the crowd noise suddenly died down before the room went silent. Lorna and Macy looked behind them and saw that Esmeralda had just emerged from the changing room.

It wasn't really Esmeralda's fault, and she by no means intended to upstage her friends, but she was an unknown quantity who was both exotic and alluring that evening in her short, black, halter necked, sleeveless, open-backed, asymmetrical hem dress, her primrose black cowgirl booties and her unique hair style. Esmeralda had an exceptional pair of long legs with slender, shapely calves that connected to a pair of nicely toned thighs that continued on up and made an exquisite derrière out of themselves. A significant portion of these phenomenal gams were on display that evening. Her slender, yet well-proportioned figure didn't hurt the picture either, and most people didn't even notice the scar peeking out from beneath the skirt on her right thigh. Deacon was almost hyperventilating at the sight.

Once Deacon got his breath back, he quickly stood up and walked over to where Esmeralda had halted due to the fact that everyone in the room was staring at her in spellbound silence. As he took her little suitcase and placed an arm around her waist to walk her over to their table, the crowd returned to its usual boisterous self.

While the crowd was getting lubed up, the older folks just to relax and the younger crowd to work up the courage to dance, the band, Heatstroke, was getting tuned up. Heatstroke was comprised of students at the Sul Ross University in Alpine. One reason they had been hired for the dance was to support the local musicians, and another was that they were actually pretty good. They played the larger towns in Texas during the summer break and their repertoire ran from classic country to modern country as well as from early 60's rock and roll up to the rock and roll of the 70's and 80's before metal, punk and rap became the flavor of the day.

A drum roll announced the beginning of the dance, and the band started with Ghost Riders in the Sky, the Marty Robbins version. The dance floor was quickly populated, Lorna, Adrian, Macy and Stuart were the first on it. Esmeralda was looking down at her beer and wouldn't look at Deacon.

"What's the problem, Esmeralda?"

"I can't dance, and I fear that I will ruin your evening if I do not," she finally answered looking up at him.

"You don't know how to dance, or you physically can't? In any case, I doubt you'll ruin my evening," Deacon said encouragingly.

She smiled at this. "I can probably dance circles around you, Mr. Allison, but at the moment my leg has not healed well enough to prove that to you. It's still a little sore and the scar is still tight, and I am afraid to tear it."

"So, if I'm reading you right, you could still manage a slow dance or two. Correct?"

"Will these be 'pity dances', or will they come with feeling?"

"I'll let you be the judge of that, Ms. Navarro. Now I suggest that you drink your beer and work up the courage to be seen on the dance floor with me."

"That might require more than one beer, Mr. Allison," Esmeralda informed him with a smile.

The band ran through a few old favorites such as Tulsa Time, A Country Boy Can Survive, Redneck Woman, Queen of Hearts, Friends in Low Places, and a few others to get the crowd in the mood, then changed tempo to some slow songs for those that wanted to get up close and personal. They started with He Stopped Loving Her Today, which was the signal for Esmeralda and Deacon to hit the dance floor. Esmeralda was about 5'8" tall while Deacon was 5'10", the difference in height was perfect for dancing slow. At first, given the fact that this was the first time that they had been this close to each other, it was a little awkward, but eventually Deacon just pulled her to him and she put her hands around his neck while he put his around her waist and that was that.

They really didn't dance so much as just swayed to the music, which was fine with Deacon as Esmeralda was firm, fit, warm to the touch, and she smelled like lavender and sandalwood. Deacon figured that he could do this all night long. Esmeralda, on the other hand, was wondering when Deacon would try to slide his hand from her waist to her butt and was debating whether she would remove if he did.

The band eventually moved into the southern rock genre such as ZZ Top, 38 Special, Lynyrd Skynyrd, Alabama and others to get the younger crowd on the floor. Deacon convinced Esmeralda to at least try to dance to ZZ Top's 'Gimme All Your Lovin', which she did, and she laughed the whole time she was dancing. Esmeralda was slowly coming out of her shell and didn't seem to realize that her skirt was occasionally riding high and exposing the scar which she was so concerned about earlier. It also tended to expose a lot more of her legs than intended, which concerned Deacon on an entirely different level. While Macy and Stuart remained on the floor, Lorna, Adrian, Esmeralda and Deacon sat back down and got another round of Tecate beers.

"Deputy Allison, you're looking a bit flushed. Are you feeling alright?" needled Lorna.

"I'm good, very good, thank you," replied Deacon with a wink.

"And, Esmeralda, you're looking a bit flushed as well. Are you ill?" Lorna needled again.

"I'm guessing that a few more dances with your deputy will set me right, as long as I can keep him from stepping on my toes. I think he needs the practice, so I will agree to keep dancing with him for instructional purposes."

"Good answer, Ms. Navarro. Has his hand inadvertently slipped to your butt yet?"

"Not yet, but I live in hope. Do these Texas boys need an instruction manual for everything?" Esmeralda queried Lorna with a wink.

"I'm not sure. Adrian is from Illinois, and they learn quick up there in Yankee land, so I've never had to deal with the romantically challenged."

Esmeralda looked over at Adrian who had been sitting there quietly enjoying the banter. "Mr. Stims, Lorna and I will be going to the bar in a moment, and I would be eternally grateful if you could impart some of your Yankee wisdom to my date there," she said as she pointed to a bashful looking Deacon.

Adrian said he'd try to impart some wisdom to Deacon, but Texans it seemed, in his opinion, were poor students.

Lorna and Esmeralda strolled over to the bar, with just about every set of male eyes in the place tracking them. Everyone knew that Lorna was the sheriff of Jeff Davis County, but she was looking very hot in the short yellow sleeveless racerback tank dress she had elected to wear that evening. The pair were mouthwateringly appealing.

While the girls were at the bar waiting to order, a Hispanic man who looked to be in his late 20's, and fairly well lubed up by this point, sidled up to Esmeralda and started making advances on her. Esmeralda politely declined his overtures, but this just seemed to agitate him, and he began to get loud and aggressive. Lorna asked him to leave her friend alone and go away, but this aggravated him even further.

By this point, everyone near the bar could see what was happening and were backing away from the confrontation. Adrian was in mid-lecture with Deacon when he saw what was happening at the bar. He pointed this out to Deacon, and they both hurriedly got to their feet and headed to bar. Once they arrived, as Deacon passed Lorna to put himself between Esmeralda and her unwanted admirer, she let him know that he could not assault the man unless he had to defend himself. He nodded his understanding then stepped between Esmeralda and her drunk devotee.

"Look, the lady is with me this evening. Why don't you go sleep it off and we'll all forget that this ever happened. What do you say, friend."

"I am not your friend, friend. I was having a discussion with this lady, and you have interfered," he slurred.

"All true, but as I said earlier, she is with me this evening, so it is my job to interfere."

"She is a Mexican, but has she no respect for La Raza? Why is she submitting herself to a gringo? Now that I think about it, she is probably just a whore."

The whole venue went deathly quiet at this point. "She is not a whore; she is my guest. That said, I think that you should choose you words more carefully in the future." Deacon now had menace in his voice.

But the man would not shut up. "While you were dancing, I saw that scar on her leg as her skirt rode up to her ass, it is hideous. Why would any man dance with such a disfigured woman? I am guessing that you cannot find a better woman to spend the evening with."

At this point, Esmeralda was totally embarrassed. Her shoulders were slumped, and she was staring at the floor in front of her Dingo booties. Her shame was obvious.

Deacon got a thoughtful look on his face, then faced the crowd which had gathered around them in front of the bar.

"Gentlemen, my friend here has suggested that no man besides myself would willingly dance with my lady friend here. Let me ask you, by show of hands, how many of you guys would dance with my lady friend here if you were given the chance?"

Instantly, almost every male hand in the room shot up. This was immediately followed by the sounds of many of the men getting elbowed in the ribs or slapped on the back of their heads by their dates or wives.

Esmeralda saw what was happening and a smile slowly emerged on her face. She curtsied to the crowd and mouthed the words 'thank you'.

Deacon turned back to the drunken jackass, "Well, I guess you're wrong, shitbird. Seems like nobody else in this room shares your thoughts or opinions concerning the lady. I'd highly suggest that you haul your mangy ass out of here and sleep it off. If I were to find out that you were hassling this lady in the future, things would get very interesting, very quickly. Do I make myself clear?"

The drunk slid off his stool and slunk out of the barn with a few of the old cowboys, both gringos and Mexicans, kicking him in the ass to help him on his way as he left. At this point, everybody got back in the swing of things and the dance continued as if it had never been interrupted.

Back at their table, Lorna told Deacon that he'd handled that well and that she thought that he may even have some sheriff material in him.

"I don't think that I have the figure for it," was his flattering reply.

After the altercation with the drunk, many of the people from around the area came by to shake Deacon's hand and to meet Esmeralda, more men did the latter as opposed to women.

"That was a very nice thing you did, Deacon. I was not sure what to do," Esmeralda told him when they had some time alone.

"It's my job, Ms. Navarro. I think you should consider keeping me close in the future."

"Speaking of keeping you close, did Adrian manage to impart any romantic secrets into that thick head of yours?"

"Perhaps a few, want to go try them out?"

"Oh yeah," replied Esmeralda as she took his hand and drug him out on the dance floor.

The final song of the evening was 'If Tomorrow Never Comes' by Garth Brooks, the ultimate couple's song at any barn dance. They stayed close and Deacon's hand did eventually slide down to Esmeralda's backside and Esmeralda didn't bother to remove it until the song ended.

Around midnight, Heatstroke finished their final set and began to pack up their instruments, which is the universal barn dance signal that the party is officially over. Esmeralda and Deacon said their goodbyes to Lorna and Adrian, and Macy and Stuart, before Deacon grabbed the handle on Esmeralda's roll-on suitcase and they made their way across Paso Del Norte Road to the old Chevy stepside. Once again, Deacon opened the door for Esmeralda and handed her into the truck before putting the suitcase in the bed and walking over to his side of the truck and firing it up.

"Well, Ms. Navarro, did you have a good rodeo and dance?"

"An excellent day and a fine dance, Mr. Allison. Thank you for the invitation. To be honest though, I haven't been out until midnight in years. I don't mean to be rude, but I may need to take a nap on the way home. Is that okay with you?"

"That's fine. Hold on a second," said Deacon as he opened the door and reached behind the bench seat for something. Getting back in the truck, Deacon handed Esmeralda a well-worn Carhartt fleece pullover.

"That's the best pillow in the house. If you roll it up and put it in your corner of the cab and stretch your legs out this way, you should be able to get comfortable. I'll wake you up when we get home."

"Aren't you the gentleman tonight? Do you treat all your ladies this way?" she queried as she cocked an eyebrow at him.

"Only the young, hot, Mexican ones. The rest don't get the pillow treatment."

Now Mexican girls are known to have fiery tempers, and Esmeralda was no exception. She sat straight up and swiveled toward Deacon.

"Is that so? How many young, hot, Mexican girls have you had in this truck and what is the pillow treatment?"

As they pulled onto Highway 67 heading back into Alpine, Deacon adopted a pensive look on his face as he stared out the windshield as he took his hands off the steering wheel and began counting on his fingers.

"Seven. I'm pretty sure that the number is seven young, hot, Mexican girls have graced this truck with their presence. As far as the pillow treatment, it comes in two flavors; the basic, which is what you are have been offered up to this point, and the deluxe version which includes a real pillow, in real pillow settings, if you know what I mean."

Esmeralda was preparing to go ballistic on Deacon, until he turned to her with a grin on his face and started laughing. "I had you going there for a minute, didn't I?"

Leaning back into the corner of the cab against the fleece, Esmeralda decided to play the game. "How can you be sure that it was only seven hot Mexican girls, isn't it easy to lose count?"

"Not really, I know for a fact that there are seven Latina cheerleaders attending the high school in Marathon, and when their bus broke down after a game with Alpine one evening, I found them stranded about halfway between Alpine and Marathon and had to cram them all over this truck so that I could take them back to their school for their parents to collect them. Those are the only hot, young, Hispanic-type girls to grace my old truck until now."

"Okay, fine. Now tell me about this two-tiered pillow treatment, it sounds interesting."

"Well, you are presently experiencing the first level or tier, which is just to make you comfortable while we drive home. The second tier requires much more commitment, more pillows, less clothes and a suitable environment within which to practice the recommended second tier activities," explained Deacon.

"You mean like a bedroom and a bed."

"That would fit the requirements nicely."

Thinking for a moment, Esmeralda asked, "And just how does a young, hot, Mexican girl qualify for the second-tier treatment?"

"There are two means of attaining second-tier status: the first is the young lady just requests the status, and the second is that I can guess the color and style of their dainty little underthings, and if I guess correctly, they allow me to confer second tier status on them."

Esmeralda had been leaning back against her corner of the cab with her knees angled towards Deacon with her feet in front of the stick shift, between the stick and the firewall. When Deacon defined the second method of obtaining second-tier status she quickly put her knees and thighs together and made sure that her short dress was not revealing anything that it shouldn't be revealing. Things remained quiet in the truck for a while until they were through Alpine and on 118 heading back toward Fort Davis.

"Okay, wise ass, what dainty little underthings do you assume that I am wearing this evening?" asked Esmeralda.

"Judging by your outfit and your demeanor this evening, I would have to guess that it would be a pair of black Victoria's Secret, stretch cotton bikini panties with the little black cherry polka dot motif. How'd I do?"

Esmeralda's eyes narrowed and her nostrils dilated as she said, "I am going to kill Lorna."

"Now, now, even if Lorna knew about the lingerie you bought in El Paso, how could she have told me which pair you would be wearing this evening?"

Esmeralda thought about this for a moment before replying, "True, so how did you know?"

Taking his iPhone out of his shirt pocket, Deacon tapped it on, hit a few buttons, swiped through a few photos and passed the phone to Esmeralda.

"While we were dancing to Garth Brooks ''Friends in Low Places', your little skirt was occasionally flying up perhaps more than you intended, and Lorna snapped a shot of it on her phone with the caption detailing the type of panty and the motif. I'd have never figured it out on my own. She thought that maybe I could wind you up with it later, which is where we are at now," replied Deacon with a twinkle in his eye.

Esmeralda thought about this for a while before asking, "So what did you think when you first saw the photo, be honest now."

"I was convinced that I had the most beautiful date in the building and that she had a phenomenal tush."

"Good answer. Wake me when we get home, I'm going to sleep."

They pulled in front of Grady's place about 2:30 in the morning and Deacon pinched Esmeralda's knee to wake her up and tell her that they were home. Grady's truck wasn't around so they figured that he was sleeping the evenings activities off at Hank's place in Alpine. Deacon handed her little suitcase to her while he opened the door and followed her inside. As they walked into the short hallway that separated their rooms, Deacon asked, "Earlier you said that I 'ain't seen nothing yet'. When do I get to see some of that nothing?"

Without saying a work, Esmeralda opened the door to her room and rolled her little suitcase inside before turning on her bedroom light and then turned to face Deacon. Walking slowly towards Deacon, she came to a stop in front of him and slowly turned around and asked if he would be kind enough to undo the little clasp on her halter style dress. Deacon, thinking that tonight was his lucky night, readily agreed and undid the clasp.

Esmeralda slowly walked back to a point just inside her room holding the front of the dress to her chest, she then turned around to face Deacon and let the dress drop to the floor around her booties. She kicked the dress off to the side leaving her attired in nothing more than those little black Victoria's Secret, stretch cotton bikini panties with the little black cherry polka dot motif and her Dingo booties. She did a slow pirouette to ensure that she had Deacon's complete attention, which she did.

"You just viewed a small part of the overall assembly on your phone earlier this evening, but I have decided that you should at least get a glimpse of the overall package before you retire simply to show you that the 'phenomenal tush' you mentioned earlier is just one of the outstanding items on the menu. Sadly, you will be going hungry this evening. Good night, Mr. Allison," Esmeralda said as she slowly closed her door. This vision had overtaken top billing on Deacon's retinas.

Deacon had a difficult time falling asleep that evening. To be honest, so did Esmeralda.

CHAPTER 19

THE FOLLOWING MORNING ESMERALDA WALKED into the kitchen, wearing a pair of cut-offs and a t-shirt, which was quite a change from the last time Deacon had seen her, and found Deacon already at the kitchen table having his morning coffee before heading off to work. Esmeralda poured herself a cup and sat down on the opposite side of the table. Neither knew just what to say after the previous evening's finale, so they just sat there enjoying their coffee in an uncomfortable silence waiting for something to break the impasse.

Fortunately, about this time a truck pulled up in front of the house, and shortly thereafter Grady walked in looking like he'd been ridden hard and put away wet the night before. Getting himself a cup of coffee as well, he leaned back against the counter and surveyed the scene.

"Judging by the lack of conversation, I'd say either you kids had a good time at the dance, or you didn't, which is it?"

"It was a somewhat revealing evening," Deacon said while winking at Esmeralda.

"We had a fine time, Mr. Allison," replied Esmeralda as she glared at Deacon across the table. "There was a very rude man at the bar who kept wanting to dance with me and would not take no for an answer, but your son handled the situation very diplomatically and no harm was done."

"Oh, you mean when that jackass asked why anyone would want to dance with you, and then Deacon took a poll to see who would? I saw that. I'd have raised my hand too, but I really can't dance anymore, and I would have probably spilled my beer if I tried to raise my hand," replied Grady with a grin.

"So why the lack of conversation at the breakfast table? You'd think that you two would have a lot to talk about after your first date," continued Grady, knowing exactly what was going on. He been in similar situations back in his youth.

Esmeralda looked over at Deacon and demanded, "Was that a first date?"

Grady interrupted at this point and said he was going to his room to take a shower and clean up after a night out with the guys.

When Grady had gone into his room, Esmeralda reiterated her question.

"Well, I thought that it sort of was, but even after all these weeks together I still can't get a read on you. You have to admit that you are somewhat standoffish at times."

Esmeralda thought about this for a moment before replying. "You are confusing standoffish with proper etiquette. I am not familiar with how you hayseed, red necked cowboys north of the border go about courting your women, but it is probably more of a chase than a romantic pursuit. I am not a trophy, Mr. Allison, I am a lady. Barn dances and rodeos are a nice way to break the ice but enquiring about a lady's undergarments is definitely off the table when you are considering romancing a lady properly. I suggest that you research this topic and get back to me," Esmeralda admonished.

Now it was Deacon's turn to take his time before responding. "Do ladies often drop their laundry and expose the previously mentioned undergarments while adhering to proper etiquette rules? That does not seem like it should be included in the courtship rules unless the lady follows through after the unveiling."

"I was simply showing you the rewards of a proper courtship. That said, if you don't take the bait and pursue a proper courtship, we may have to revert back to the rednecked romance thing. Besides, you already had photographic evidence of my underwear. Did you like the bait?"

"I'm going to work now; you are an extremely frustrating young woman. Do you want me to come by and pick you up for lunch?"

"Please do, and don't forget to let Lorna know that we had this conversation, she may be able to give you some tips."

On the way to the Jeff County Sheriff's Office, Deputy Allison ruminated on the events of the past 24 hours, he was definitely getting some mixed signals. On the one hand, Esmeralda seemed okay with dancing with him and allowing him to protect her honor at the dance, and even allowing him to view her in essentially an undressed state when they got back home. On the other hand, it was still hands off and apparently a proper courtship was required before things went any further.

After the morning briefing by Sheriff Stims, Deacon was heading out of the briefing room when Lorna called him back and said, "What's the problem, Deacon? You're looking a little discombobulated this morning. Anything to do with a certain spicy looking Mexican girl?"

"Discombobulated is a pretty big five-dollar word for a simple county sheriff, isn't it?"

"I could have used confused or upset, but I just like the way discombobulated rolls off the tongue. If I am not mistaken, that was an attempt at deflecting this conversation.

"If you tell any of the other guys I said this, I'll never forgive you. Esmeralda is driving me nuts. The rodeo and dance were nice, and we seem to be getting along, but that seems to be as far as things are going to go." Deacon then told her that he'd had a little fun with the photo of Esmeralda's knickers while on the way home, and then gave a brief synopsis of what had taken place in the hallway between their rooms, before giving Lorna the CliffsNotes version of the conversation they had that morning after Grady had gone to take a shower.

Lorna laughed, "The army didn't teach you much about serenading women, did they.

"Here's the deal. You are obviously attracted to her, and she seems to be attracted to you. I have no earthly idea why, but that discussion is for another day. Esmeralda is at that age where most of her friends are married, and at least half of them are miserable. I would say divorced, but I'm making the assumption that she's a Catholic and divorce is stigmatic to them. She doesn't want to make that same mistake and is going to be very selective as to who she decides to give her affections to. In Mexico, the customs are different than they are on this side of the border. Down there a woman wants to be courted properly. Courtship is not to be confused with dating. Courtship is more serious than dating. It involves getting to know your partner with an expectation that the relationship will continue to grow and mature, with the possibility of a marriage proposal at some point.

"She has apparently made the determination that you are worth pursuing, which again really makes me question her sanity, but if you're serious about Esmeralda, you'll need to get serious about taking it to the next level, to the point where she considers it courting. That said, it may be a while before you see those snug little black cherry butt huggers again. I'd be willing to bet that the wait will be worth it, if you play your cards right. With that said, don't you think that you should go to work now?" lectured Lorna.

"I'm not sure that I can be an effective deputy with visions of those black cherry knickers dancing in my head while out on patrol," said Deacon.

"Guess you'll have to fake it if you want a paycheck. Keep me informed on your romantic front and I'll try to steer you in the right direction."

"Did you put Adrian through this wringer before you got hitched?"

"Oh yeah, it was kind of fun for a while. Now get out of here and go to work!"

CHAPTER 20

AFTER PATROLLING FOR A FEW hours, Deacon hesitantly stopped by Grady's place around 11:30, none too sure of the reception he'd receive, and picked up Esmeralda to take her to lunch. She did a pair of faded jeans, a black t-shirt and a pair of sneakers justice, Deacon would say that for her. He just pulled up alongside the porch and she jumped in before they headed into Fort Davis to Mary Lou's Café out on 118.

They had obviously both decided to ignore the conversation which they had that morning over coffee, and things seemed to have reverted back to the way they were prior to the rodeo and dance. Deacon gave her a rundown on his uneventful morning, leaving out his personal conversation with Lorna, and Esmeralda told him some of the usual small-town gossip she'd heard while at the dance.

When they pulled into Mary Lou's, Deacon made sure that he got out and opened the door when Esmeralda got out of the truck, as well as when she entered the café. He was determined to be the proper gentleman after Lorna's words of wisdom that morning.

Once they were seated, Esmeralda ordered the beef fajitas asadas while Deacon went for the Mary Lou's Special, which was a little bit of everything: two cheese enchiladas topped with melted queso carne guisada, one crispy taco, one chalupa and rice.

During their lunch, Esmeralda asked Deacon if he'd by chance asked Lorna for some courtship advice. She asked this while paying attention to her plate so that she could keep a straight face. Deacon replied that he had, but left it at that. Obviously, either Lorna had called Esmeralda or vice versa, after the 'courtship' tutorial that morning.

While Deacon was driving back to Grady's place after lunch, Esmeralda's curiosity got the better of her. Apparently, Lorna had not shared the nuts and bolts of the tutorial with Esmeralda, simply that Deacon had been soliciting courtship advice.

"Okay, spill it! What did Lorna say to you after you asked her for some advice, you can't just leave me hanging."

"That was a conversation between two officers of the law, and I can't discuss the contents thereof with a civilian," informed Deacon.

"Really? Is that the way it is? I guess I may as well burn all of those expensive lingerie items that I bought in El Paso then. I don't believe those articles would be suitable for viewing by law enforcement personnel. Your choice."

"Okay, let's not do anything rash!" Deacon protested. "I'd probably have to arrest you for burning up perfectly good Victoria's Secret stuff, that has got to be a crime somewhere. If it isn't, it should be. Anyhow, that supposes that some lucky law enforcement person will be viewing those 'articles', as you call them, at some point in the future. Is that correct?"

"Much of that would depend on the conversation you had with Sheriff Stims this morning, the advice she gave you, and your ability to follow through on said advice. The ball is firmly in your court, Deputy Allison."

"In an effort to view those black cherry bikini briefs of yours again at some point in the future, I will swear you to secrecy concerning our legally protected discussion. Do you agree to be sworn to secrecy?"

Esmeralda was snickering at this point and trying to again keep a straight face. "I agree, now spit it out!"

"I was informed that my past efforts to woo and possibly seduce you were totally inadequate when the object of my affection was a hot Mexican chick of Catholic persuasion. I was further informed that I would need to up my game from a dating approach to a proper courtship strategy. How am I doing so far?" asked Deacon.

"Pretty good, but Lorna called me after she talked to you, and this is not news. I need to know specifics, such as how you intend to up your game?"

"That little snitch! I may have to arrest her for disseminating official law enforcement secrets to a civilian over the phone."

"You are deflecting yet again or perhaps buying time to figure out the specifics of your new approach, now answer my question."

"Well, the playing field, for lack of a better term, is not ideal for courting. First, we are both staying in my dad's house. Second, we live in a desert with nothing but small towns to amuse ourselves in, and finally, I think it would be wise to inform your father of the situation so that he does not come up here and shoot me for dallying with his daughter."

Esmeralda gave this some thought before replying. "Your father already thinks that we had our first date last night, so I think he'll give us the time and space to maneuver while we are staying with him. As far as living in a desert, I don't see where we need a lot to keep us amused, there are lots of things to do out in the desert," she replied with a lascivious grin.

"As to Papá, let's give him a call," Esmeralda suggested as she pulled her phone out of her hip pocket and started to dial. Deacon thought this was ill advised as it left him no time to prepare his defense, but Esmeralda was already dialing.

"Hello, Papá! Are you safe?"

He must have answered in the affirmative as the next words out of her mouth were, "You remember that discussion we had over the phone before the dance the other night? Well, I have someone here who would like to have a word with you," she said as she handed her phone to Deacon.

"Hello, Mr. Navarro. How are you this afternoon?" which sounded lame even to Deacon.

"I'm fine, you may not be. You need to shut your mouth and open your ears. For some unknown reason, my only daughter finds you attractive and interesting. How any spawn of Grady's could be either eludes me, but it is what it is. With that being said, I do not have much say in the matter, my daughter is a grown woman, and she will do whatever she wants. You, on the other hand, will not do whatever you want, or I'll come up there and shoot a bunch of holes in your ass. You will treat her like a lady, and you will do nothing that would bring shame to her, or cause people to gossip. If and when this situation gets serious, I expect you to inform me as to how you plan to provide for her, I will not have my daughter living in squalor in this miserable desert. Finally, I will have Esmeralda keep me up to date on your relationship and if anything inappropriate occurs during this courtship, you will be receiving a visit from me shortly thereafter and I guarantee that you do not want this to happen. Is this all understood?"

"Yes, Mr. Navarro. I read you loud and clear."

"Good. Now that that is over, I want to thank you for taking Esmeralda to the rodeo and dance the other night. It was good for her to get out and socialize with others after the accident and her convalescence. I know she was worried about her scar, both on her thigh and on her head. I would also like to thank you for defending her honor from that pedazo de mierda Mateo Molina, he is a piece of work and is of interest to me. You need to keep a watch on him, he lives in Sanderson, in Terrell County and works at Sanderson Towing and Truck Tires off West Oak Street. Let's talk tonight once you are back at Grady's."

"Okay," was all that Deacon could think of to say.

"Regarding my daughter, please behave yourself and do not do anything that would require me to come up there and shoot you repeatedly in the ass. That said, I'll say a prayer for you and light a candle, she can be a headache sometimes and a handful at all times," and with that, Diego hung up.

Deacon handed Esmeralda back her phone. After she had slid it back into the hip pocket of her jeans she asked, "So how did that go?"

"Apparently, I have his blessing to court you. If at any point in the courtship I misbehave or get out of line he will come up here and I paraphrase, 'shoot me in the ass'."

"As it should be. He is a good papá, and an even better shot."

"Before you get too cocky, he also said that he would say a prayer and light a candle for me, something about you being a headache and a handful at times. From what I've seen, he should probably join a monastery and light a bonfire."

"I have no idea what he is talking about, I am a good daughter and have never given him any cause for concern."

"Why do I find that hard to believe?" asked Deacon.

When they got back to the ranch, Esmeralda leaned over and gave Deacon a chaste kiss on the lips. "Just to hold your interest, Deputy Allison. We need to make haste slowly."

"If you really wanted to hold my interest, you'd drop your jeans and show me your choice of dainty little underthings for the day," suggested Deacon.

"I do not think that would be making haste slowly, Deputy. I think you need to go to work now, and I will see you later," replied Esmeralda with an innocent smile.

As Esmeralda turned to walk up onto the porch, she looked over her shoulder and said, "Since you asked, the panty du jour is a Jockey bikini in the watercolor poinsettia motif. Give that some thought as you do your rounds this afternoon."

Deacon was fairly certain that he would be getting a visit from Diego in the future.

CHAPTER 21

GRADY GOT BACK FROM DOING his ranch chores about 4:00 in the afternoon, and he and Esmeralda worked together in the kitchen preparing a spaghetti dinner for when Deacon returned home from another day of keeping the county safe. While they were working in the kitchen, Esmeralda happened to let slip the fact that she and Deacon were now officially courting, and that Deacon had even spoken to Diego over the phone and asked for his permission. She failed to mention that it had been she who had dialed her father and forced the conversation on young Deputy Allison.

"About time! I was starting to think that I may have raised a hormonally challenged idiot," was Grady's response, which got a laugh out of Esmeralda. Deacon arrived home and during a meal of spaghetti bolognaise, Italian bread with butter and garlic, and a green salad, Grady announced that he needed a word with them in the living room after the kitchen was cleaned up.

After Deacon and Esmeralda had washed the dishes and tidied up the kitchen, they went to the living room where Esmeralda took a seat on the leather couch, which faced the window looking out on the porch, beside Grady, while Deacon took a seat in the La-Z-Boy recliner off to their right.

"Okay, kids, here's the story. I had a call from Diego earlier today and it seems that the guy who accosted Esmeralda at the dance is a nasty piece of work named Mateo Molina. By day, this jackass works at the Sanderson

Towing & Truck Tires in Sanderson over in Terrell County, by night he freelances for the Gallo cartel over in Diego's neck of the woods to pick up illegal aliens and drive them to El Paso where they are passed on and moved further up the pipeline. Diego wanted me to give him a call after dinner when you kids were here to discuss some chatter his people have heard last night and earlier today. Esmeralda, would you mind ringing your father and putting your phone on speaker?"

Esmeralda did as she was asked and put her phone down on the coffee table as they all leaned forward to hear what Diego had to say.

When Diego picked up, Esmeralda said, "Papá, I am sitting here with Mr. Allison the Elder and Mr. Allison the Younger. What did you want to speak to us about?"

"First, has that miscreant Allison, the younger one, not the old fart, tried anything inappropriate with you yet?"

"No, Papá, but I live in hope," Esmeralda replied with a laugh.

"What is wrong with that boy? Not that you should allow him any leeway with your affections, but you would think that he would at least make an attempt."

"Maybe he doesn't want to be shot in the ass, have you ever thought about that?" Deacon offered in his defense.

"I realize that she is my daughter, and that I may be somewhat biased, but I would think that some things might be worth getting shot in the ass for," retorted Diego.

"I agree entirely, Diego. Back in the day we would have gladly taken a bullet in the backside for a chance at a girl such as your daughter," added Grady with a wink at Esmeralda, who by this time was trying not to blush, glow, or to burst out laughing.

"You guys do realize that I am sitting right here listening to you while you bust my chops, don't you," Deacon reminded them.

"Of course we do, it wouldn't be any fun if you were elsewhere," laughed Diego.

"Okay, I think we can get back to business now," said Diego. "As Grady may have already told you, our Mr. Molina is not really who he seems to be. Although he is a pedazo de mierda, except for his occasional drunkenness he appears to keep a low profile in Sanderson and seems to be fairly competent as a tow truck driver and with his truck tire work. At night, he moonlights for the Gallo cartel, or the Roosters as they are also called, as a pickup man where he collects illegal aliens who have successfully crossed the border and made it to various pick-up points along Highway 90, anywhere from Bryden to Lobo, and takes them to El Paso where they are dropped off and moved along further into the United States.

"Apparently our Mr. Molina recognized my daughter at the dance and made a call to his cartel connections letting them know that he had found the missing daughter of Inspector Navarro. It seems that the Gallos are the ones who originally kidnapped Esmeralda to have some leverage over me and force me to ease up on them.

"I have an informant in the Gallos camp at Los Lamentos, and it appears that Mateo has now been asked to assist in the re-kidnapping of my daughter. The Gallos are putting together a team to make this happen, but it will take them about a week to put the whole thing together. We have to think of a suitable plan of action, I would rather not have my daughter kidnapped again. Any ideas?"

Everyone at the Grady house gave this some thought, and Deacon finally suggested that they just let law enforcement know about the situation and let them take care of it.

"We could do that, but then we'd have to explain a variety of things which we probably do not want to, such as where did this information come from and why have the Allison's been harboring an illegal alien for a couple of months. Revealing where the information came from would put my confidential informer at risk, and although Sheriff Stims and the Sheriff's office already knows about Esmeralda's status and the fact that she is staying with the Allison's, if the Border Patrol or the Immigration and Customs Enforcement get involved this becomes a federal issue which will cause us all a lot of headaches."

"So, what do you suggest, Diego?" queried Grady.

"The issue is Mateo. Personally, I'd just kill them all and throw their bodies out in the desert for the coyotes, but the disappearance of Mateo, a US citizen would cause problems. Although we can't kill him, I would like to impress upon him that I am tired of the Gallos attempting to kidnap my daughter. Since both Esmeralda and the romantically dysfunctional Deacon are known to Mr. Molina at his point, you should just leave Mr. Molina to me. I will ensure that he is alive when I am finished with him, but I will ensure you that he will think twice before he considers getting involved in any further kidnapping schemes thought up by the Gallos.

"I seriously doubt that Mateo would be involved in the actual kidnapping event in any case, since he is still a valuable asset to the Gallos on your side of the border, and they would not want to risk him being apprehended by law enforcement if the kidnapping did not go as planned, which it will not.

"My informant will let me know how many men will be sent across the border and when. They will no doubt meet up with Mateo who will either tell them where to find Esmeralda or personally guide them to Grady's place. In any case, I will visit him that evening after the crew has met with him, or when he comes back from guiding them to your place, to show him the error of his ways.

"Your house is in a remote location with absolutely no neighbors for miles, a perfect place for an assault and kidnapping. I will let you know when the men cross the border, and I suggest that you have either a suitable offensive or defensive strategy in place to deal with them.

"I would firmly suggest an aggressive offensive plan since it would be best if the entire kidnapping team simply disappears. This would cause a lot of confusion in the Gallo camp, which would be of some use to me on this side of the border, and it would avoid a lot of annoying questions from law enforcement, no offense to Deacon. I'll leave the fate of the kidnappers to you, I'd suggest that some of those old, abandoned silver mines in the Davis Mountains might come in handy," proposed Diego before he told them that he would be in touch, said his goodbyes, and hung up.

Everybody just sat back where they were to digest everything that Diego had told them. Eventually Grady suggested that they sleep on it and come up with a plan sooner rather than later the following day. Everyone agreed and headed toward their respective bedrooms. When Esmeralda and Deacon were in the short hallway separating their rooms, Deacon suggested that he should remain close to Esmeralda until this situation was sorted out.

"And how close would that be?" asked Esmeralda.

"Like a second skin would probably be best," replied Deacon.

"I think that you are just trying to get another peek at my underwear."

"Well, I wouldn't say no to that, but I was hoping more for a view of the overall package again. A man needs to be reminded of what he is striving for during this courtship ritual thing."

Reaching up, Esmeralda caressed Deacon's cheek before giving Deacon a slightly less chaste kiss on the lips than the one he received when they had gotten home after the dance. "Good night, Deacon," Esmeralda said with a devilish grin before closing the door to her room and leaving him standing in the hall.

Deacon stood in the darkened hallway for a moment before slowly turning around and going to his room. Considering the caress and the kiss, perhaps he was making haste slowly, but it appeared that it was going to be a long, frustrating journey.

CHAPTER 22

THE NEXT MORNING, AFTER THEY'D had breakfast and Deacon had left for work, Grady and Esmeralda sat at the kitchen table to try and come up with a plan to prevent her next kidnapping. Grady had brought a notebook and a pen to the table to jot down the planning notes and to make a list of anything they may need.

"First off, Esmeralda, I don't want you anywhere near the action. We'll need a place to stash you for a while that does not involve the Jeff Davis County Sheriff's Department. The problem is that everyone who is aware of your situation here seems to be employed by that department," said Grady.

"That is an easy issue to resolve, Mr. Allison."

"How's that?" asked Grady.

"I am not going anywhere. This whole situation is because of me and my father, and I am not going to run off and let other people handle the problem for us. Please let me know if I need to repeat that?"

Grady took one look at the determination on Esmeralda's face and the fire in her coal black angry eyes and decided that her participation in the event, or lack thereof, was not a hill that he wanted to die on. "Okay, that's the first issue resolved then," said Grady as he crossed that item off the list in his notebook.

The next issue was how to prepare a proper reception for the kidnappers.

Since the Gallos would likely decide to do the deed in the middle of the night, the 'defenders' at the ranch would need some way to track the secuestradores, that's 'kidnappers' in Spanish, from the moment they came through the gate as they came off of Madera Canyon Road and turned onto Grady's driveway. The gate was located approximately 5-1/2 miles along Madera Canyon Road once you left County Road 118, and from the gate to the ranch was about a mile along a dirt road.

"Easy," said Esmeralda.

"That's twice you've answered 'easy' would you care to enlighten this old Marine as to why this is easy?"

"Down in Mexico, the people who hunt javelinas in the desert often set up cameras along the pig trails. These cameras are motion activated and I believe they will take photos day or night and send the pictures to your phone."

Grady sat back and looked at Esmeralda for a moment. "That is an excellent idea, assuming we can find these cameras on short notice. How did a nurse happen to know how pig hunters hunt pigs?"

"Well, your son is not the only man which has shown an interest in me, Mr. Allison."

"So, you've dated a pig hunter, have you?" Grady was getting into this now and was grinning at Esmeralda.

"He was a Lieutenant in my father's unit who just happened to hunt pigs. He was not simply a pig hunter," explained an exasperated Esmeralda.

Ignoring this dubious clarification, Grady continued, "Going from a pig hunter to my son is not necessarily a step up in the world, he's still a little rough around the edges. That said, a rodeo and barn dance date has got to beat a pig hunting date any day of the week."

Esmeralda looked at Grady like he was crazy before she burst out laughing. "Yes, a rodeo and a dance definitely beats hunting pigs. Don't you think that we should stop discussing my dating history and come up with a plan to keep me from getting kidnapped?"

There wasn't much that they could do to prepare a plan, they'd just have to try and 'prepare the battle space' as best they could: clean up around the garage, pole barn and house to deprive the secuestradores of any decent cover and just let the situation develop and try to be prepared for any eventuality.

Grady wanted to put these 'pig cams' as he was now calling them, at the turn off from 118 to of Madera Canyon Road, at the turn off from Madera Canyon Road onto his driveway, and behind the garage, pole barn, and the house. The plan that evolved was to simply barricade themselves in the house and let the bad guys come to them.

"Do you know how to shoot a gun?" Grady asked Esmeralda.

"Yes, Papá made sure that I knew how to handle firearms since I was a young girl."

"That's good to know. I'd hate to have to do all the shooting by myself."

"Believe you me, Mr. Allison, if those pendejos get anywhere close to me again, I will be on my worst behavior."

They then got on the internet with Grady's laptop and found that Muley Outfitters in Stockton had eight Moultrie Mobile XV7000i trail cameras in stock. Grady asked the guy on the phone to hold six of them for the Wassermann Ranch and that he would collect them the following day.

When Deacon showed up about 1:00 in the afternoon for lunch they told him the plan, such as it was, and he agreed that this was about all that they could do until game time. When he asked ask what weapons were going to be in play, Grady said that he'd be armed with the synthetic stocked Remington 870 7-shot tactical 12-gauge pump action shotgun with an 18.5" barrel that he kept in his bedroom as well as his old Colt .45 1911. He felt that this should be sufficient if the kidnappers tried to get in the house. They decided that Esmeralda would get the Mossberg 500 12-gauge tactical shotgun that Deacon kept in his room.

Deacon didn't bat an eye when he heard Esmeralda had decided to be in on the kidnapper's takedown, although he sort of batted an eye when he found out she was going to be packing a shotgun. He supposed that in her case the apple didn't fall far from the tree and that a shotgun was possibly de rigueur for Mexican vigilantes.

"So, what are you going to be shooting?" Esmeralda asked Deacon.

"I don't know. I can't use my M1A or the Beretta 92 that I carry on duty since we can't risk any ballistic signatures if things go sideways and Sheriff Stims gets involved. Maybe you guys can find something suitable at Muley's tomorrow. If you do, call and let me know. If not, I might need to go see either Sheriff Hicks or Sheriff Cabrera to get geared up. I really do not want to do that as it just brings more people into the loop. Anyhow, whatever you decide, make sure that we have enough ammo for whatever we'll be shooting."

At this point Grady said he was going to go take a nap, what he was actually doing was giving the kids some space. He sincerely hoped that his son would be able to out romance some pig hunter.

Esmeralda and Deacon just sat on the couch when his phone signaled that he had a message. He took a look at the message then turned to Esmeralda and asked, "So tell me about this pig hunter."

Esmeralda turned to the door to Grady's room and yelled, "Grady! I am going to beat you like a drum!"

Turning back to Deacon, "What would you like to know about the pig hunter, who, for your information was an officer as well as a hunter of pigs?" She was going to wind Deacon up as he tried to wind her up.

"What attributes did the pig hunter possess that drew you to him that I do not possess. I need to know my shortcomings in the courtship arena so that I can adjust my strategy."

"That list could be quite long, are you sure that your ego can take it?" another impish grin accompanied the question.

"My ego has the hide of an alligator, do your best."

"Okay, he was handsome and charming, knew how to treat a lady, was complimentary in all things, and he was not one of the enlisted riffraff who simply want to 'love them and leave them', I believe this is the correct phrase. What say you to that, Deputy Allison?"

"It seems that he has me beat in each and every category, but that begs two questions, Ms. Navarro. First, why are you even sitting on the couch with me having this discussion, and secondly, did he ever see you naked in the bathroom?"

"To answer your second question first, no, he never saw me naked in the bathroom or anywhere else. He never made it out of the dating phase and into the courtship phase, so him seeing me undressed was out of the question. The answer to the first question is simple, sometimes a girl might want to walk on the wild side and see what she might be missing. Any further questions?"

She had inadvertently set herself up. "I have two. Are we passed the dating phase and into the courtship phase?"

"I thought that I had made it abundantly clear in the kitchen the morning after the dance that we were moving on from the dating arena. Did you happen to miss those verbal and non-verbal clues?" Esmeralda said with a devious smile.

"No, I did not, I just wanted to get my facts straight. By your own admission a few minutes ago, the previously mentioned Lieutenant was not allowed to see you naked as you two had not entered the courtship phase. Since we are now courting, when can I see you naked again?"

Esmeralda had painted herself into a corner and now had to try and weasel her way out of the trap she had caught herself in. "Slow yourself down, Deputy. There are levels of courtship preceding the 'getting seen naked again' phase, I did not intend to lead you on and give you false expectations. I think that maybe we should…"

She never got any further in her attempt to prevent Deacon from misunderstanding the courtship and nakedness rules when Deacon just burst out laughing.

"Esmeralda, you walked right into that snare. Continuing our conversation, what was wrong with the esteemed officer that you didn't continue the romance with him?"

She laughed, "He was arrogant, predictable and not much fun, to be honest. Also, he smelled a lot like the pigs he hunted."

Deacon thought about this before replying. "Am I arrogant, predictable, boring, or smell like a javelina?"

"Perhaps somewhat arrogant, but predictable and boring no, and to date you have avoided smelling like a pig," answered Esmeralda.

"Good, I'll see you in the bathroom later this evening. Perhaps you can show me that little sage colored sleepshirt and some of those other bikini panties I saw in the laundry basket, and we'll take it from there." Glancing down at his watch, Deacon exclaimed, "Would you look at the time! I've got to get back on patrol. See you at dinner," as he jumped to his feet and scrambled out the door before Esmeralda could respond. She did sit on the couch a few minutes and fantasized about a bathroom rendezvous that evening though.

CHAPTER 23

DEACON HAD TO WORK LATE that evening due to a tractor trailer being blown over by high winds on State Highway 90 near the town of Valentine, and everyone was asleep when he got home. He quietly made his way to his room, shut the door and turned on the light. After getting out of his uniform, he made his way to his and Esmeralda's shared bathroom to get a shower before going to bed.

He turned on the bathroom light and had to grin at what was laid out on the counter beside the sink. There was a neatly folded sage colored sleep shirt, on top of this was an equally neatly folded pair of Victoria's Secret bikini panties in the midnight sea shimmer motif. Pinned to the panties was a note that simply said, "Use your imagination."

The following morning, Esmeralda was already in the kitchen having a cup of coffee while leaning against the kitchen counter when she heard the door leading from the small hallway between her and Deacon's bedrooms to the living room open. Shortly thereafter Deacon walked in dressed in his deputy's uniform and carrying Esmeralda's sleep shirt and panties. He gently laid them on the counter in front of Esmeralda who, with a quick glance towards Grady's room, snatched them up and hid them behind her back.

"I did use my imagination and I let it run wild. When it came back it told me to hold out for a thong and a cropped t-shirt. Think you can manage that? Imagination is all well and good for pig hunters and the like, but real men depend on their other senses as well: touch, taste, smell, as well as sight. I think you may need to work on your presentation a little more. I suggest that modeling your lingerie would be much a more effective strategy than simply leaving it folded on the counter beside the sink, although that was a good start. Afterwards we can get into the touching, tasting, smelling and all that this would entail," commented Deacon as he nonchalantly poured himself a cup of coffee.

At this point, the door to Grady's room swung open and Esmeralda quickly tossed her nightshirt and panties into the nearest kitchen cabinet that was available before she quickly closed the cabinet door and leaned back against the counter again as if she had nothing to hide. Deacon just grinned as he watched her panic.

Grady asked them if they'd slept well as he walked toward the cabinet that held the coffee cups, which this morning just happened to hold women's lingerie as well. Before Esmeralda could stop him, Grady opened the cabinet door, reached in and pulled out the nightshirt and panties and took a good look at them before putting them back in the cupboard and grabbing a coffee cup, turning back to a red-faced Esmeralda and a grinning Deacon he simply said, "I guess that answers my question."

While Grady was pouring coffee into the cup he'd taken from the recently repurposed coffee cup and lingerie cabinet, Esmeralda was trying to explain how her dainty underthings had made their way to the kitchen, and was failing miserably.

"This is not the way it looks, Grady! I forgot them in the bathroom this morning while I was getting dressed and Deacon just brought them to me now. I was simply embarrassed and didn't want you to see my sleepwear and just tossed them in there so that you wouldn't draw the wrong conclusion concerning my underwear being on display in front of your son."

Grady sat down at the dining table to sip his coffee before looking up at Esmeralda, who was still standing in the kitchen proper with Deacon, "It's okay, Esmeralda, that is as good of an excuse as any other you could have come up with, I'd stick with it."

Deacon was just leaning back against the kitchen counter beside Esmeralda by this time and was trying hard not to laugh.

"You two are impossible!" exclaimed Esmeralda as she grabbed the nightshirt and panties out of the cupboard and stormed out of the kitchen and back to her room.

"She's a feisty one," commented Grady.

"And I bet she looks good in that little get up as well," added Deacon wistfully.

"If you don't pull your head out of your butt and get in the game, you'll probably never know." Grady offered out of his abundance of wisdom and perhaps personal experience.

A few minutes later Esmeralda walked back into the kitchen as if nothing had happened and they finished their breakfasts of buttered toast and coffee. Deacon and Esmeralda cleaned up the kitchen before Deacon left for work. Shortly thereafter Grady and Esmeralda were in Grady's truck heading to the sporting goods store in Stockton.

On the way to the sporting goods store, Grady and Esmeralda avoided talking about the upcoming kidnapping attempt and just chatted about local events and personalities. After a lull in the conversation, Grady waxed philosophical, "I heard your comment concerning the enlisted riffraff last night, you do realize that I was part of that enlisted riffraff back in my younger days?" Grady asked while giving Esmeralda the side eye.

"You weren't supposed to hear that, and I was just trying to wind Deacon up," explained Esmeralda.

"You need to be careful, sometimes a lot of truth is said in jest, and although you may have said it playfully, Deacon might think that you consider him unworthy of your affections now. He may not show it much, but he has a lot of pride in what he has done in the past and what he is doing now."

Taking a short breather from imparting wisdom and knowledge to a stunning Mexican girl who just happened to be the daughter of a good friend of his and maybe his future daughter in law, Grady continued, "It is the enlisted grunts that do the vast majority of the heavy lifting in all services of the military. Granted, the officers lay out the strategy and tactics, but it is up to the grunts to execute the plan, whether it is a good plan or not. Deacon started at the bottom of the pile as a private, but he left the service as a First Sergeant, which is just a few rungs under the top of the enlisted ladder. He must have had some talent to get there in the time that he served. Why don't you give that some thought?" suggested Grady.

"I was just joking with the meathead!" Esmeralda said in her defense.

"He probably realizes that, and by no means is my son thin-skinned, but maybe it would be a good idea if you let him know that. I think he may have the hots for you, and I'd hate for you to put a damper on the heat with some silly little ill-advised comment made in the company of two enlisted meatheads."

"You think he has the hots for me? He doesn't go out of the way to show it."

"I think that knock to your head must have damaged your perceptive abilities. You'd have to be blind not to see how he looks at you, especially when you are walking away. No offense intended."

"None taken. Really? I guess I'd better improve my situational awareness in the future."

"That would probably be a wise idea." Thinking about the recent discussion, Grady added, "However you decide to play your cards, I'd appreciate it if you would show a certain amount of restraint. I'd rather not have your father get the wrong idea as to what is going on up here and shoot my son in the butt, which as you are aware, he has threatened to do if anything inappropriate were to occur between yourself and Deacon."

"That would assume that either you or papá would be privy to anything inappropriate if it were to actually occur. I am thinking that if Deacon and I decided to act inappropriately, that nobody would be the wiser," suggested Esmeralda.

"That's my girl!" said Grady with a grin.

Once they pulled into the parking lot of Muley Outfitters off East Dickinson Road in Stockton, they bailed out of Grady's old Dodge 1500 pickup and wandered into the shop. Needless to say, all the guys in the shop had the ill manners to drop what they were doing and stare at the old Marine Master Sergeant accompanied by what appeared to be an uncommonly attractive young Hispanic woman. In their sordid minds this sort of thing only happened in the movies.

Walking up to the counter Grady addressed the proprietor standing behind it, "When you are finished staring at my future daughter-in-law, I'd like some service." This was said in the speech pattern normally associated with a Marine Corp drill instructor and yielded immediate results. It also got him a poke in the ribs from the supposed future daughter-in-law.

"First off, I need to take a look at the trail cameras I ordered the other day. I then need two boxes of Federal 12-guage 3" magnum double ought buckshot loads. After that I need to take a look at that Ruger AR-556 MPR rifle on the wall behind you, and after that I'll need to look at some night sights. Think you can do that for me?"

The proprietor of the shop, after hearing the shopping list, was more than happy to accommodate Grady. He first brought out the six Moultrie Mobile XV7000i trail cameras and Grady had the man fire each one up to make sure that they worked as advertised. Next up were the two boxes of Federal 12-guage 3" magnum buckshot loads, which didn't require an inspection.

"Let's take a look at that Ruger 556 hanging on the wall there," Grady said while pointing at the wall behind the shopkeepers back. Ruger may not have made the fanciest AR-15 on the market, but they made good, solid, reliable firearms, and Deacon was infinitely familiar with the AR platform. The Ruger AR-556 MPR shot the 5.56 x 45 NATO round and had a 16.1" barrel, which would be fine for the distances that Deacon would be shooting at. It also had a flat top with a picatinny rail so that different optics and scopes could be attached easily. Grady looked it over, but before agreeing to purchase it he wanted a good day/night scope for it. The shopkeeper said he had just the thing and went back into the storeroom to get it. Coming back out to the counter he unboxed an AGM Neith LRF 2.5x20x32 night vision scope. This was not a top-of-the-line nightscope, but it would be good enough for shooting a couple of jackasses in the courtyard between the house, the garage, and the pole barn, plus it would mount to the Picatinny rail already on top of the Ruger.

"If you throw in a couple of boxes of Nosler 5.56 NATO in 77 grain boat tail hollow point ammo, I'll take the lot off your hands," Grady told the proprietor of the shop, who was only too happy to comply.

Getting back in Grady's old Dodge, Esmeralda asked how he could afford to just walk in there and buy a few thousand dollars' worth of stuff?

"Easy, to borrow your expression. I just charge it to the ranch and then write it off on taxes later. Everything I bought can easily be explained by saying I'm shooting varmints out at the ranch, which, in this case, will actually be the truth."

Before they got out of town, Esmeralda asked if they could stop by the Walmart Supercenter on the northeast side of town by the airport as she needed some women's things. Grady just got back on East Dickinson Boulevard and headed east before getting off on State Highway 285 and taking it northwest until the West 14th Street exit. Hanging a left it was only a few blocks until the Walmart store.

Before Esmeralda got out, she was embarrassed to ask Grady for some cash as she still did not have access to any, she told him that her father was good for it when he visited again. Grady grumbled, simply because it was expected of him, before handing over his debit card to her.

Since Esmeralda hadn't had a chance to shop except the time the girls had gone to El Paso, she needed toiletries, make-up, normal as opposed to Victoria's Secret underwear and some non-Victoria's Secret bras. A couple more pairs of Levis 501's wouldn't hurt either plus some shorts just to keep Deacon interested in her legs.

Once back in the truck with her loot, she handed Grady back his card and they decided that they were both hungry and that Pepito's Café was only a hop, skip and a jump from the Walmart store. While they ate their tacos al carbon and drank their iced teas, Grady thought he'd offer Esmeralda a few more words of wisdom concerning his son.

"You do realize that Deacon is not going to hang around the Chihuahuan desert forever, don't you? He only came here to harass me while he figures out what he wants to do with his life. I just can't see him spinning his wheels here much longer. He knows there is a whole world out there that he needs to explore. To be honest, if you hadn't come along, I think he'd be gone already."

"What, you think I'm holding him back?" she asked defensively.

"Absolutely, but you're looking at it from a negative perspective. If he didn't fancy you and didn't think you were worth it, he'd likely be in the wind already. Deacon is an old school type of man. He appreciates women who are ladies and act like one, which is not as common as it used to be. By the same token, he won't want to offer himself to any woman unless he knows that he can support and take care of her in proper fashion. The job as deputy sheriff in Jeff Davis County would not allow him to do that. This is all just to say, don't pigeonhole my son by what you are seeing now, there is more to him than that."

"I'm not disappointed in what I'm seeing now, to tell you the truth, but what am I supposed to do, just hang out at the ranch until he finds his way in the world?"

"I think that would is an excellent idea!" responded Grady with a smile. "I'm fairly certain that my son will find his niche in the world sooner than you think. If I was you, I'd bet on it."

Esmeralda thought about this for a moment, "You know something I don't, don't you?" giving Grady a scowl.

"I'm a few decades older than you, lass. There are probably volumes of stuff that I know that you don't."

"Is my father involved in any of this!" demanded Esmeralda.

"Of course he is! You don't actually believe that I could come up with such a nefarious plan on my own, do you? Us old codgers need to stick together."

"Well, I suppose I could hang around just to watch your nefarious plan fall flat on its face," responded Esmeralda. "But don't you two old codgers think that you can put a bit in my mouth and make me go where you want me to go. I have plans and considerations of my own. Do you understand me?"

"Your father said you'd say something like that. Are you finished? We need to start heading home."

Esmeralda actually thought that this whole train of thought was confusing, to say the least.

CHAPTER 24

GRADY AND ESMERALDA PULLED BACK into the ranch yard just before dinner time, so while Esmeralda put her shopping in her room and began to fix dinner, Grady hauled the loot from Muley Outfitters out of the truck and dumped it on the glass topped coffee table in the living room so that they could go over it with Deacon when he got back from work later that evening.

Deacon showed up about an hour after Grady and Esmeralda had gotten back from their shopping trip, and after cleaning up he joined them in at the dining room table for a dinner of beef fajitas and a green salad. Dinner conversation revolved around Deacon's day at work and the shopping trip Esmeralda and Grady had taken to Fort Stockton. After dinner and the kitchen had been cleaned up, they all went into the living room to take a look at the merchandise from Muley's.

First, they unboxed all the trail cameras and studied the enclosed instructions so that they were familiar with how they operated. They also downloaded the app so that they could receive the photos on their respective handphones. These cameras were triggered by detecting motion, so there would not be a continuous feed like a CCTV camera but would give them a 'snapshot' when activated that would at least tell them they had company and where that company was, which was better than nothing.

While the cameras were charging, Deacon took the Ruger rifle out of the box and inspected it before he unpacked the AGM night vision scope. He inspected it closely before he attached it to the Picatinny rail on the top of the Ruger rifle. He'd sight the combo in the following day.

After Grady had gone to bed, Esmeralda and Deacon were just sitting on the couch watching a re-run of 'Friends', when Esmeralda jokingly suggested that after the kidnapping issue was resolved that she might re-purpose one of the cameras as a 'bathroom cam'. She said fair was fair and that since Deacon had already barged into her in the bathroom while she was butt naked, she should be allowed to return the favor digitally. Deacon said that she was correct, and that fair was fair.

"Wait," said Esmeralda, "you are giving in way to easy." Then she had the eureka moment that she should have had earlier and punched Deacon in the shoulder.

"You have no shame whatsoever! You don't really care if I see you naked, but you could still get photos of me on your phone!" she exclaimed. "You are a voyeur and a shameful man to take advantage of a situation like that.

"It was your idea, as I recall," was Deacon's smug defense.

"That is immaterial! Just because it was my idea does not mean that you have to agree to it. A real gentleman would have offered to delete the trail cam app off his phone after this kidnapping situation is resolved."

"Okay, I'll delete it."

"You lie like a rug, Mr. Allison! I'd have a better chance of getting hit in the head by a meteorite than having you delete that app if I were to put one of these cameras in our bathroom."

"Just to be clear, I never said I was not a voyeur and when you opened the door by suggesting that we install a camera in the bathroom, you just fed my voyeuristic nature. This is your fault, not mine." Deacon was really trying hard to keep a straight face by this time.

"Okay, forget the camera in the bathroom idea. I don't want to see you naked anyhow," pouted Esmeralda.

"Keep telling yourself that if it makes you feel better. I need to get some shuteye since one of us has to go to work tomorrow, so I'll bid you a good night and I'll see you in the morning."

After Deacon had gone to his room, Esmeralda sat on the couch and decided that perhaps Deacon was right, and she wouldn't actually mind seeing him in his birthday suit.

Grady got back from his ranch chores the following day around noon, so after a lunch of grilled cheese sandwiches, he and Esmeralda grabbed the six trail cameras to go put them where they thought they'd do the most good and to test them out.

Since they only had six of the cellular trail cameras, they needed to be judicious in their placement. The first camera was strapped to a fencepost just where Grady's driveway cut off Madera Canyon Road. This would give them advanced warning that the bad guys were approaching. Since the cameras would only register motion out to about 100 feet, they couldn't aim one down the driveway at any point to follow the progress of the kidnappers, they'd need to put the other cameras around the courtyard in front of the ranch house formed by the house and the outbuildings.

Now these cartel secuestradores, or kidnappers, were likely not stupid people and probably had a few previous kidnappings under their belts down in Mexico, so it wouldn't be smart to underestimate them. On the other hand, they would be on the other side of the Rio Grande now and operating on foreign soil without the support and the fear of their cartel association to help them out.

The ranch house and outbuildings were three sides of a square with the garage on the north side, the pole barn on the east and the house itself on the south, with the driveway entering the square on the west side. The garage was about 30 yards from the front porch of the house and directly in front of it. The pole barn was to the east of both the house and garage and about 30 yards from each.

The plan was for Esmeralda and Grady to stay in the house and wait for the secuestradores to come to them with Deacon playing free safety and roaming around outside to check out the places where the cameras couldn't see. The ranch house and outbuildings were surrounded by pinyon pine and gray oak trees, plenty of cover for Deacon, plenty of cover for the kidnappers too.

They decided to place the first camera to cover the back of the ranch house. They strapped it to a tree back from the house a ways to give a clear view of the little porch at the back door and as much surrounding it as the camera would allow. The second and third camera were placed to cover both the left and the right sides of the pole barn which faced the house and camera five and six covered the sides of the garage in front of the house. These were assumed to be the best vantage places for the kidnappers to watch the front of the house and cover anyone coming out on the porch or coming into the courtyard via the driveway on the west side of the courtyard. The forced entry would likely take place at the back of the house. Much would depend on just how many kidnappers were going to be involved.

Once that was finished, Esmeralda remained outside to trigger the cameras while Grady retired to the couch inside the house and made sure that they had a decent connection to each camera. Some of them weren't aimed as well as they could have been so Esmeralda jumped into Grady's old Dodge pickup with her phone and drove down to the entrance to the driveway and adjusted the camera until Grady told her by phone that she had it right. Driving back to the house, Esmeralda parked the pickup in the garage and visited each of the other cameras and adjusted them until Grady was satisfied.

Deacon got home from work around 5:00, and while Grady cooked up some hamburgers and fries, Deacon and Esmeralda took the Ruger rifle out to sight it in. Deacon figured that considering the geometry of the courtyard, the longest shot that he would have to make would be less than 100 yards, so he had Esmeralda make one-inch black dots on the center of a few paper plates with a magic marker and nailed them to a tree 100 yards down the driveway from where it entered the courtyard. While Esmeralda was walking back to him, Deacon loaded up a magazine with the 77-grain Nosler ammo that Grady had bought. Once Esmeralda was back behind him, Deacon got down in the prone position he'd learned in the Army while in sniper school and rested the rifle on a rolled-up jacket laying on a cinder block he'd gotten from the garage. Once he was ready Esmeralda stuck her fingers in her ears and Deacon slow fired five rounds at the top paper plate. When they went down to take a look, Deacon had a nice tight grouping, but it was about an inch high and to the left. Going back to where the rifle was, Deacon made the necessary elevation and windage corrections on the scope and laid back down to do it again. The grouping was a little tighter, but still about 1/4" too high. Going back to the rifle a third time, Deacon dropped the crosshairs 1/4 MOA (minute of angle), which would be a quarter of an inch at 100 yards and laid back down. This time all five shots were grouped in the black dot that Esmeralda had inked onto the plates.

Esmeralda was impressed and asked if he'd mind if she gave it a try? Since he still had 15 rounds left in the magazine, he just handed her the rifle and watched in amazement as she acted like she'd handled AR platform rifles her entire life. Knowing a thing or two about Diego by this point, she may have.

Anyhow, she got down in the prone position and wiggled around a bit to get comfortable, which made Deacon forget for a moment why they were actually out there. Esmeralda's firm little posterior, squirming around on the ground in a pair of snug Levis, would have had most men forgetting all about the shooting and having thoughts of an altogether different nature instead. But Deacon managed to get his libido under control and just told her to fire at will at the lowest plate on the tree, the one that hadn't been shot up yet.

She took her time and slow fired five rounds before flipping the selector to 'safe' and handing Deacon the rifle before standing up and brushing herself off. When they looked at her plate, Deacon was impressed. Shooting a rifle which was new to her, on an improvised range, she had managed to put all five shots into 1-1/2" circle. She was shooting 1.5 MOA, which was damn good with an unfamiliar rifle, and he told her so.

"That's pretty good shooting with a rifle you've never handled before," he told her.

"You didn't do too bad yourself, for a white boy," she told him with a grin. You could tell that she was pleased with her performance, especially in front of Deacon. "Maybe we have more in common than we think."

"Well, let's give that some thought. So far, we have the love of shooting and the same taste in women's lingerie in common, I suppose that's a start."

"Really? I didn't think you would be the type to wear women's lingerie," teased Esmeralda.

"That is not what I meant, and you know it."

"One can never be too sure, there are a lot of strange people out there these days."

"I agree entirely, there are even people who suggest hanging a trail camera in the bathroom to spy on their housemates is a wholesome endeavor, if you can believe that."

"I thought it was a good idea at the time before you rained on my parade by saying you wouldn't delete the app and turned my good idea into your bad idea."

"Hey, if you can't stand the heat, get out of the kitchen," suggested Deacon.

"I am fairly certain that it would have been you getting uncomfortably hot and bothered. I have probably just saved you from many a sleepless night.

"Sad but true," Deacon said with a smile.

Reaching up behind Deacon's neck, Esmeralda pulled him to her and gave him a proper full-bodied kiss on the lips. "What was that for?" he asked.

"Well, with no camera in the bathroom to hold your interest, I figured that may help to keep you intrigued."

"Well, it's a start and we can work from there," agreed Deacon.

Getting back to the house they cleaned and lubed the rifle, loaded up the two magazines that came with it, then sat on the couch and watched 'The Dirty Dozen' with Grady until it was time for bed.

CHAPTER 25

ABOUT A WEEK LATER, ON a Tuesday, Diego showed up unannounced at the ranch house in an old, beat to crap Ford F-100 pickup that seemed to run exceptionally well for a vintage vehicle with its best years behind it. Esmeralda was the only one at home during the mid-afternoon, and when she saw her father pull up, she ran off the porch where she'd been relaxing with a book and flew into his outstretched arms.

"What are you doing here, Papá? Why didn't you call? Are you hungry?" Esmeralda was so happy to see Diego that she didn't know what to say or do.

"Easy, mi hija. I am here to see my daughter and to ensure that she is not kidnapped by cartel payasas. I didn't call because I wanted to surprise you, and I am starving. It is a long haul from Villa Ahumada to here by way of the crossing at Ojinaga."

Esmeralda led Diego into the house by the hand and sat him down at the dining table. Getting him an iced tea, she started making one of his favorite meals: scrambled eggs with cheese and bacon bits on toast. When it was ready, she put it on a plate and took it to her father.

"Gracias, mi ángel. Now tell me how your romance with Deacon is progressing while I eat. Do not try and tell me nothing is going on here, Grady has been keeping me informed in the event that things were getting out of hand."

So, while Diego ate his meal, Esmeralda gave him a rundown on the romance, such as it was, since the rodeo and dance down in Alpine. She decided to leave out her idea concerning the bathroom trail camera, and anything to do with Grady finding her panties in the kitchen cabinet. She felt her father really didn't need this level of detail.

After listening to his daughter, Diego sat back in his chair to sip his tea and said, "Well, he does seem to be somewhat confused in the romancing department, and as slow as cold molasses running uphill. On the one hand, it does not appear as if I will need to shoot him in the ass, but on the other hand I am not getting any younger. Isn't there something you can do to spur him on?"

"Papá, I am a grown woman, I can think of many ways to 'spur him on' as you say. The problem is that all of these strategies would embarrass me in front of you and would likely end up with a bullet in the butt of Deputy Allison," explained Esmeralda.

"Your concern for his safety and physical wellbeing is admirable, but it isn't getting you anywhere. You may need to adjust your tactics."

Esmeralda suddenly remembered her discussion with Grady while having lunch at Pepito's Café in Fort Stockton on their recent shopping expedition.

'Mr. Allison, the older one, told me that you and he have concocted some nefarious plan concerning Deacon and I once Deacon decides to move on from here. Is that true? Would you like to tell me about it?" asked Esmeralda as she looked her father right in the eye while leaning forward and resting her chin on her hands which she had clasped together with her elbows resting on the table. This posture, when adopted by a woman, usually means, 'I think you have something to tell me, and it would be wise for you to do so now.'

Sipping his tea, Diego got pensive for a moment before replying. "Yes, we do have a rudimentary plan in mind. It is still a work in progress, but it seems to be coming together nicely. No, I am not going to reveal this plan to you at this point as it is not the time to do so. That time will arrive once young Mr. Allison decides it is time to venture out of the Chihuahuan Desert again and make a life for himself, and hopefully you, elsewhere. This plan also includes both yourself and myself. I will let you know when it is time for you to know."

A highly frustrated Esmeralda replied, "If you were not my papá, I think I would kick you in the shin right now!"

"I almost wish you would, then I could ask Deacon to put you across his lap and paddle your behind in my place. I am fairly certain that handling your behind would help kick start this failing romance of yours," suggested Diego.

"It is not failing! It just hasn't progressed as quickly as it should have! Do you want me to fling myself on him?"

"Do you want to fling yourself on him?" retorted Diego while cocking an eyebrow at his daughter.

She had to pause here and form a mental picture of flinging herself on an unsuspecting Deacon before replying, "Perhaps."

"Well, if you do, please be discreet about it. You have the honor of the family name to uphold."

"Are you serious? Do you really think Deacon is the one for me?"

"Esmeralda, you are almost 30 years old and a grown woman, as you mentioned earlier. This decision is up to you. I have done everything I can do for you and will continue to help you in any way that I can, but this decision is yours and yours alone. I have known Grady for decades now and know that he is a fine and moral person and from what I have seen of Deacon, Grady has raised him to be the same, although if you ever tell anyone I said that, I will deny it."

Esmeralda had to give all of this some thought. Her father obviously had no problems with Deacon as a possible son-in law, Grady didn't seem to have a problem with her as a prospective daughter-in-law either, and so far, it seemed to be her leading Deacon on as opposed to the other way around. Deacon was the wild card in the deck, perhaps it was time to up the ante.

This would all have to wait until they had nipped this kidnapping attempt in the bud. Esmeralda and Diego were sitting out on the porch having a beer and catching up with each other when Grady pulled up in his old Dodge pickup. Seeing Diego on the porch, he got a big grin on his face and quickly grabbed a beer from the kitchen and sat on the porch with them.

At around 5:00, Esmeralda went into the kitchen to start making a mess of fajitas while the men sat on the porch telling lies to each other while waiting for Deacon to show up after work. He finally dragged in around 6:00. When he went into the kitchen to see if he could help with preparing dinner, Esmeralda handed him a beer and told him to go shoot the breeze with the boys and she'd call them when dinner was ready. As he turned to go outside, she grabbed him by the arm and turned him back toward her.

"Aren't you forgetting something, deputy?" she asked.

He looked around to see if there was something he forgot, but nothing stood out.

Esmeralda just sighed and rolled her eyes before grabbing him by the shirt and pulling him close for another full-bodied kiss, this time with just a hint of tongue play. When he managed to break free, he again asked her what that was for.

"Same as yesterday. It is just something to keep you in the game and to hold your interest. As you said, it's a start", she told him as she smacked him on the butt and shoved him towards the porch.

After dinner, everyone huddled up in the living room to hear what Diego had to say. He had studiously avoided mentioning anything to do with the kidnapping until then.

"Okay, my informer has told me that four secuestradores, kidnappers to you gringos, will be crossing the border at Ojinaga tomorrow afternoon in an older, dark green Toyota 4-runner. They will travel up to Mateo's place in Sanderson where they will stop to rest and prepare for the kidnapping. They will remain at Mateo's place until they decide to come over here and kidnap Esmeralda, likely very early on Thursday morning.

"Mateo lives in a slightly secluded, smaller house on the east end of Avenue B. I'll have eyes on the house from around noon tomorrow. I will call Grady when I see the old 4-Runner leave Mateo's place. This will probably be around midnight on Wednesday as they'll want to hit this place around 2:00 or 3:00 in the morning when you would normally be in an unsuspecting, deep sleep. These cartel assholes are not as stupid as people are led to believe, although they do have their moments.

"It's about 150 miles from Mateo's place to here. If they leave Sanderson at 11:00 o'clock Wednesday evening or at midnight, that should put them here around 2:00 to 3:00 in the morning on Thursday. You'll need to be ready for them then. I am assuming that you have a plan. You do, don't you?"

Deacon turned on his phone and sat down beside Diego on the couch. Tapping on the trail cam app, he flipped through the previously taken photos from the various cameras and explained what Diego was looking at. "We expect them to come in through the back door, which would be the obvious point of entry. My dad and your daughter will be in the house, and I'll be outside acting as a roving gun That's about the best we can do with the people we have; they also don't know that we know they're coming."

"Diego thought about this for a minute, then said, "Okay, that seems reasonable. How are you geared up to take these pendejos down?"

Grady took the floor now, "Esmeralda will be using Deacon's old Mossberg 500 12-gauge loaded with 3" magnum double ought buckshot loads. I'll be packing a Remington 870 7-shot tactical shotgun also loaded with 3" magnum double ought buckshot loads. I'll have my old 1911 Colt .45 with me as well just in case. Deacon will be out in the bushes with a Ruger AR-15 equipped with a nightscope to take out anybody they may leave outside for backup."

"Seems like you've thought this through, although I'd like Esmeralda to have a pistol as well just in case things do not work out as planned. Do you have a spare handgun around here?"

Deacon looked at Grady before he replied, "The only other handgun we have is my sheriff's department issued Beretta 92, but this would not be a good idea in the event that things went sideways, and people started matching bullets to guns."

"No problem," Diego said as he hiked up his pants leg and pulled a nice little subcompact automatic out of a boot holster that had been clipped inside the top of his boot where the shaft was loose enough for it to sit comfortably. "She can use my backup piece. It's a nice little Sig Sauer P365. Just over a pound with a 3.1" barrel and a 10-round magazine. It's loaded with hollow points and should do the job if necessary."

"The thing is, Diego, can she shoot it? I know she can shoot an AR, but a handgun is a different skill set entirely?" asked Deacon.

"Well, if we had any spare ammo for a 9mm I'd ask her to show you, but since we don't, and I don't want to waste these hollow points on a shooting exposition, let's just say she's been shooting these little 9mm's since she was a little girl, and I guarantee you she'll hit what she's shooting at."

Deacon looked over at Esmeralda, who just looked back him with a smug expression on her face.

"While we're here punching holes in these sicarios, what are you going to be up to?" asked Grady.

"Once the kidnapping crew leaves Mateo's house for the kidnapping business, I will go in and have a word with Mateo to ensure that he understands the error of his ways and that he is not to bother me or mine ever again."

"Are you going to kill him?" asked Esmeralda.

"I thought about it, but he is a US citizen and killing him would cause me nothing but grief. I'll think of something creative." The expression on Diego's face indicated that Mateo would not be enjoying Diego's creativity.

"Okay, we need to figure out what to do with the bodies and their vehicle after the fact," suggested Grady.

"If you can get the 4-Runner up to Balmorhea and just leave it in Kiko & Tina's RV Park, I'll have it taken care of," Diego said. "The bodies can just get tossed in the desert for the vultures as far as I'm concerned."

"There's an old abandoned silver mine out by Horn Spring that nobody ever goes to. I'll take them out there in their 4-Runner so that we don't get their DNA in any of our vehicles and dump them in the old mine. The coyotes will probably get to them anyhow, but at least they won't be left out in the open," suggested Deacon.

"Seems like we've covered all the bases except one then," postulated Diego.

"What would that be?" asked Deacon, as Diego knew he would.

"When are you two," Diego pointed at Deacon and his daughter, "going to stop this foolish game you've been playing and get on with this dating or courtship thing or whatever it is called these days? Grady and I could both die of old age before you two decide to even hold hands! You're really not fooling anybody except yourselves."

"To be honest, Mr. Navarro, I've been trying to avoid getting shot in the butt by doing anything 'inappropriate', I believe that is how you worded it," said Deacon in his defense.

"So, are you trying to tell me that my daughter is not worth a little bullet hole in your butt?"

"That is not what I meant to imply," replied an increasingly exasperated Deacon.

Before the conversation could devolve any further, Esmeralda cleared her throat to get everyone's attention before she calmly stated, "I'll take care of it, Papá," as her eyes bore holes into her father.

"That about covers it I suppose. Now we have a small logistical problem; there are four of us and there are only three bedrooms. I'm not giving up mine, so you guys need to sort that out," Grady announced.

Deacon saw an opening to get back at Diego for his remarks regarding his and Esmeralda's sluggish romance.

"The correct thing would be to offer my room to Diego as he is our guest," suggested Deacon.

"And then where would you sleep?" queried Diego.

With a mischievous grin on his face, Deacon responded, "Well, that would leave only one other bed in the house. Since you have expressed the opinion that your daughter and I need to kick start our romance, this seems to be a perfect opportunity to do just that."

"Do not throw my words back in my face, young man. I will take you up on the offer of your room, but I would highly suggest that you do not attempt to share my daughter's bed while I am under the same roof, it is just not done," replied Diego.

Esmeralda looked over at Deacon, "Well, it was worth a try. I'll get you a blanket and a pillow and you can sleep on the couch."

Later on, when everyone else had gone to their rooms, Deacon stripped down to his skivvies before laying the pillow that Esmeralda had brought him at one end of the couch. When he unrolled the duvet that she had brought him, a pair of those infamous Victoria's Secret bikini panties, in a previously unseen Lipstick Reindeer motif fell out with a note pinned to them, which read, 'If you have these, then obviously I don't. Give that some thought. Sweet dreams.'

THE NEXT MORNING, DEACON COVERTLY returned Esmeralda's butt-huggers to her and described, in vivid detail, his not-so-sweet dreams regarding her without them. After everyone had enjoyed a breakfast of pancakes and coffee, compliments of Grady: Deacon went to work at the sheriff's office, Diego went to keep an eye on Mateo and his guests, and Grady and Esmeralda refreshed the batteries in the trail cameras before parking Grady's truck in the garage to keep the courtyard clear and to deprive their Mexican visitors of any cover. After that, with nothing left to do, they just tried to relax until Diego called and told them that their visitors were on their way.

Deacon drove into the courtyard around 5:00 that evening and parked his truck at the far end of the courtyard in front of the pole barn to keep the courtyard free of cover before walking back to the house where Esmeralda had prepared spaghetti bolognaise for dinner. Once the kitchen was cleaned up after dinner, everyone double-checked their weapons and then sat in the living room waiting for Diego's call.

The call came at about 11:30, and it wasn't what they wanted to hear. Apparently, there were now five desperados that would need attention and from what Diego could see from where he was watching Mateo's house, the fifth man was someone higher up the totem pole than the four sicarios he'd arrived with since they seemed to differ to him.

This necessitated a change in plans out at the ranch. Deacon and Grady put their heads together and decided that five kidnappers attacking the house would be too much for Esmeralda and Grady to handle on their own. With five people, the bad guys could hit the front and the back of the house simultaneously overwhelming Esmeralda and Grady as they tried to cover the front and the back of the house at the same time. They needed to get the bad guys out in the open not only to give them a bigger playing field, but to keep from shooting the house up as well.

The plan now was for Esmeralda and Grady to hide in the garage across from the house with the bay door open and the lights out. Deacon would build himself a sniper's hide in the back of his truck, which was out by the pole barn with the bed facing the courtyard and the entrance into it. They would leave the doors to the house unlocked, which wasn't uncommon in the rural areas of the Chihuahuan Desert.

The thinking was that the sicarios would send some guys to the back of the house to effect entry while the others would enter through the front. Once inside, they'd quickly come to the conclusion that nobody was in the house and due diligence would force them to search the outbuildings, at which point they would have to get out in the open and could be taken down. Not the best of plans, but it was all they could come up with at the moment.

By 1:00 in the morning, everyone was in place; Grady was hidden in the far-left rear corner of the garage behind a few upright rolls of sheep wire fencing while Esmeralda was in the far-right rear corner behind a stack of old tires. Deacon had laid down the tailgate of his truck and was laying on an old tarp with a few old blankets pulled over him with the muzzle of the Ruger rifle resting on a sandbag and peeking out over the lowered tailgate. Now they just had to be patient and wait for their quarry to come to them.

At around 2:45 that morning, the old green 4-Runner tripped the camera strapped to the fencepost where Grady's driveway cut off Madera Canyon Road. This alerted Esmeralda, Deacon and Cody that their guests had arrived. The Toyota slowly drove into the courtyard with the lights out, rolling to a stop in the middle of the courtyard. All five desperados bailed out at the same time, with two going around to the back of the house while the other three moved swiftly to the front door. One of the kidnappers tried the doorknob, which turned in his hand and he slowly opened the door and entered with the other two following him into the house with guns drawn. Apparently, something similar had occurred at the back door. After about 15 minutes the house was filled with loud shouts and foul language in Spanish, which only Esmeralda could follow.

Eventually all five frustrated kidnappers appeared on the porch and the tallest one, apparently the leader, pointed toward the pole barn and ordered two of his men to check it out while he and the remaining two headed toward the garage.

The two who were selected to search the pole barn stopped by the 4-Runner before heading to the barn. Deacon was watching them and was baffled until they both shoved their pistols into their waistbands then reached into the vehicle and pulled out two AK-47 automatic rifles. By the time they started walking toward the pole barn, two of the others had entered the garage while their fearless leader remained outside beside the 4-Runner.

At this point, almost everything happened at once. Since Grady had parked his truck in the garage earlier, the two banditos had to split up to search the garage with one going down one side of Grady's truck while the other went down the other side. Straight into the barrels of the shotguns held by Grady and Esmeralda.

When the guys searching the garage came to the front of Grady's Dodge, they were no more than five yards from where Grady and Esmeralda were hiding. Grady fired first with Esmeralda instantly following his lead. They both jacked in another round and fired into their targets a second time before they could hit the ground.

Contrary to popular belief, the shot out of a shotgun does not spread out appreciably when it leaves the barrel. The old saying that the shot pattern spreads an inch per yard is a myth, especially when you are shooting buckshot. Both Grady and Esmeralda were shooting 12-guage shotguns with 18.5" barrels with full chokes. It is generally understood that at ten yards the spread of buckshot would have been about 8" in diameter. At five yards the spread would be roughly half that, which meant that each round fired by Esmeralda and Grady essentially put nine .33 caliber pellets in a 4" circle at essentially the same time. To put this in perspective, think about someone getting hit by nine .32 caliber pistol rounds simultaneously, in the same place. This made for a gaping bloody hole in each wannabee kidnapper every time they pulled the trigger. These guys were dead before they hit the concrete floor.

At roughly the same time, Deacon opened fire at the two guys walking toward him with the AK's. He double tapped each in the center of mass from about 20 yards. Those 77-grain boat tailed hollow points made little, tiny holes in their sternums when they went in, and golf ball sized holes when they came out. Small bullets travelling at high velocity don't always travel in a straight line through a body, especially if they hit a large bone, and these didn't either. These two clowns were pretty torn up internally when they hit the ground.

It was at this point that things went a little off the rails. First, the boss man kidnapper just froze at the sound of gunfire and the muzzle flashes lighting up the inside of the garage in front of him, as well as those off to his right near the pole barn. He adopted the 'deer in the headlights' posture.

It seems that as Esmeralda was attempting to jack a third shell into her Mossberg 500, when the action moving forward caught the tail of the previously fired shell being ejected and jammed the shotgun. By this time, Esmeralda was in berserker mode and dropped the shotgun while pulling the little Sig Sauer P365 that her papá had given her out of the back of her waistband and ran out of the garage to confront the guy who had been running the show to kidnap her.

When the boss man saw the target of his mission charging at him, he jolted back to reality and reached behind him to pull the 9mm Glock out of his waistband, and actually had it out and coming up on target when Esmeralda skidded to a stop, grabbed the little Sig in a perfect 'thumbs forward' two-handed grip and shot the boss man in the face five times just as fast as she could pull the trigger. She was kicking the crap out of the chief sequestrador and yelling at the body in what could rationally be assumed was very unladylike Spanish, when Grady limped up behind her and bear hugged her to get her to stop what she was doing. At about the same time, Deacon arrived and gently took the smoking pistol from her.

Once she had calmed down, Deacon asked her why she'd shot the guy five times in the face.

"That was the hijo de puta, the son of a bitch, that threw me out of the van! Give me back my pistol, I want to shoot him some more, the cabrón deserves it!" she replied.

"Maybe later, but right now we need to lay down the rear seat in that 4-Runner and get some plastic sheeting put down so that we can throw the dead guys in and take them out to that old mine by Horn Spring and dump them before the sun comes up," suggested Deacon.

While Deacon and Esmeralda started dragging the dead Mexicans over to the back of the 4-Runner, Grady called Diego and let him know that the deed had been done before he limped back into the garage to get some plastic sheeting. After laying down the back seat in the 4-Runner, he covered the entire area behind the front seats with the plastic and helped Deacon and Esmeralda stack the five dead guys inside like cordwood, which is easier said than done. They decided to keep the Mexican's pistols and AK-47's as you never knew when having an unregistered firearm, especially a fully automatic one, might come in handy. Grady would hide them somewhere else on the ranch in the next day or two.

While the kids were out getting rid of the bodies, Grady was cleaning up the blood pools and splatter in the garage, as well as raking over any evidence of the one-sided gun battle in the courtyard. The fact was that these guys had crossed the border illegally and nobody would be looking for them in the first place, but it was better to be safe than sorry.

The route to the old silver mine took Deacon and Esmeralda back down Grady's driveway to County Road 166 where they hung a left to skirt around the base of Sawtooth Mountain before taking a right on Moore Ranch Road and making their way into the desolate hills. Driving along a series of dirt roads trending to the north, they skirted the west side of the hills before coming to a dirt road going east into Phillips Canyon. After putting the old SUV into four-wheel-drive, they drove about another mile into the canyon before they came to a rocky outcrop, at the base of which was the old silver mine. Reversing the 4-Runner up to the entrance to the old mine, Deacon parked the SUV and they both got out and stretched their legs before opening the tailgate and grabbing the first ex-kidnapper by the legs and drug him up to the mine entrance. Deacon took a small prybar out of his back pocket and snapped the hasp of the padlock holding the old weathered wooden door closed. With a loud screeching of the unoiled hinges, Deacon managed to get the door opened enough to allow them to drag the body inside. Putting on a headlamp that he'd thoughtfully brought along, Deacon turned it on and they took a look around. The drift or tunnel they were in extended back into the outcrop about 40 feet and ended in a raise or shaft which dropped to the next level down, about 30 feet lower. They cleared any debris or obstructions out of their way before going back to the entrance. Dragging the first dead sicario to the lip of the raise, they pushed him over the edge. Over the next hour they managed to get the other four bodies over the edge and into the raise before they sat down at the entrance to the mine to take a break. Disposing of bodies in an old mine was tiring of work.

When they were rested, Deacon closed the door to the mine and replaced the broken padlock just for appearances sake. Deacon followed Esmeralda back to the SUV. While walking behind her, and while keeping an eye on his partner in crime's enchanting posterior, it occurred to Deacon that Esmeralda didn't seem particularly flustered by throwing dead sicarios down a mine shaft. Maybe this wasn't the first time that she'd had this sort of exercise and perhaps this was how Esmeralda had gotten such a nice, tight butt. This was not something that you would normally expect from a trim little Mexican cutie (to use a term from Jimmy Buffett's 'Margaritaville'), but then again, neither was shooting some guy in the face five times. Something to keep in mind for the future, thought Deacon.

The sun was just coming up when they pulled the 4-Runner around the far side of the house to hose out any residual blood which may have leaked off of the plastic sheeting. Grady had backed his old Dodge pickup out of the garage and cleaned up the mess inside. He'd also policed up all of the brass from either the shotguns, the Ruger rifle, or Esmeralda's little Sig Sauer pistol before he fired up his old John Deere tractor and drug a piece of old chain-link fence around the entire courtyard to cover up any blood, tire tracks or signs of the scuffle which had occurred there earlier.

After cleaning up the 4-Runner, Deacon pulled it into the garage and closed the door just to keep it out of sight. While he was doing this, Esmeralda had gone into the kitchen and fired up the coffee machine. When the coffee was ready, she brought the pot and three mugs out onto the porch, and they all just relaxed and drank their coffee while watching the sun come up.

CHAPTER 27

WHILE THE MAIN EVENT WAS taking place roughly 150 miles to the northwest, the sideshow had already begun back at Mateo's place in Sanderson.

Diego had arrived in Sanderson around 12:30 Wednesday afternoon and had taken a drive past Mateo's place after he'd gotten into town. Not seeing the green 4-Runner he'd been informed about, he drove over to the Ranch House Restaurant just off of Highway 90 and Avenue B to grab lunch and burn some daylight until making another pass. At 3:00 he drove past again. With still no sign of the green 4-Runner he drove back into town to a convenience store and gas station on the west end of town to grab a coffee and some snacks for the stakeout. Driving back to Mateo's neighborhood he pulled over in a vacant lot full of old cars and trailers on Ave B that kept him out of sight, while giving him a good view of the front of Mateo's house about two blocks away.

Around 5:30, the green SUV pulled in front of Mateo's place and stopped. Mateo came out to greet his visitor's, which is when Diego knew that the plan at Grady's would need to be revised. Instead of four desperados, there were now five, and judging by the way the others differed to him, the fifth man was a bit higher in pecking order than your standard cartel sicario kidnapping halfwit. Diego didn't call Grady at this point since there was no guarantee that the fifth man would actually join the other four for the big event. If he didn't, and he remained with Mateo, Diego's part of the plan would get infinitely more difficult while the plan could remain the same at the ranch.

It was around 11:15 when Diego felt the call of nature after finishing his coffee and sitting in his vehicle all evening. While buttoning himself back up after taking a walk behind his truck to relieve himself, the front door of Mateo's house opened. The light from inside shown like a beacon on a dark night. Quickly grabbing his binoculars, Diego trained them on the front door and watched as all five visitors came out of the house and got into the 4-Runner. Since they had to drive right past him on Avenue B to get to Highway 90 on the way to Alpine and then on to Grady's place, Diego took the opportunity to double check that there were five people in the SUV. This is when he called Grady and told him to expect five, not four, visitors and to plan accordingly.

With that done, Diego decided to just wait in the vacant lot until around 2:00 in the morning to ensure that Mateo was well into the Land of Nod before he paid him a visit. Just before 2:00, Diego fired up his old Ford pickup and slowly cruised past Mateo's house and parked in the back. Getting out, he pulled out a plastic bag with some purchases he'd made at the convenience store earlier and walked up to the back door. The outer screen door was latched on the inside, but Diego simply took out his Swiss Army knife and cut a slit in the screen and unhooked the latch. Oddly enough, the back door itself was not locked, so he just invited himself in.

Mateo woke up to a pungent liquid being splashed in his face. He roared and tried to get out of bed to figure out what was going on, when a fist smashed into the side of his head and knocked him back down onto the bed. While he was groggy and trying to figure out what was happening, his bedside lamp was switched on and he saw what he originally thought was the Grim Reaper standing beside his bed but revised this line of reasoning when the apparition spoke.

Pulling a chair up beside the bed and sitting down, Diego asked, "Mateo, do you know who I am?"

Mateo reached for his glasses on the nightstand and put them on to get a better look at the man, and then began to shake uncontrollably.

"Yes, you are Inspector Diego Navarro of the Mexican National Guard, but why are you on this side of the border? I have done nothing of interest to you."

"Mateo, that liquid which I have poured all over you and your bedclothes, and that stench, is an entire 12-ounce bottle of Ronsonal lighter fluid. In my hand I have a full box of kitchen matches. I assume you know what would happen if I decided that you are not paying attention to what I am saying, and I decided to strike a match and toss it onto your bed.

"Try not to bullshit me anymore this evening. I would like nothing more than to burn you down to a pile of ashes. I assume you are well aware of my reputation on the other side of the border."

Mateo was very aware of Inspector Navarro's reputation on the other side of the border. Many people who had crossed the Inspector had been found later with obvious signs of 'aggravated tactical interrogation', to put it mildly, or were simply never found at all. Mateo had no doubt in his mind that the Inspector would light him up in a heartbeat.

"Yes, Inspector. I am aware of your reputation."

"That is good, we can dispense with me having to convince you of the seriousness of the position you are in. Now, tell me, who were those five men who left your house earlier this evening, and what are they up to?"

"If I tell you, you will kill me," replied Mateo.

"If you don't, you will be burning long before you get to Hell. The choice is yours."

Mateo was sweating profusely now, and was somewhat conflicted as to how he should proceed. Diego thought that he should explain the situation which Mateo was in more succinctly so that he could make an informed decision.

"Mateo, I know certain things. For example, I know that you work for the Gallo cartel on the transportation side of things. I also know that they informed you that your visitors were coming today and that you were to shelter them until they went on their way. I also know that you disrespected my daughter at the rodeo, and for that alone I would like to kill you. You are very lucky that I am in a good mood this evening and that I will likely let you live if you simply answer my questions. So, I will ask you again, who were your visitors and what are they doing on this side of the border?"

"They are Gallo's sicarios. They are here to kidnap your daughter after the failed attempt a few months ago."

"I see. And how did they locate my daughter at the Allison place?"

Mateo knew he was boxed in now and was very close to being barbequed alive, but he thought he'd see just how much the Inspector really knew.

"I have no idea, Inspector. My job was simply to provide a safe house for these men this evening."

Diego sighed. Picking up the box of matches he'd put down on the nightstand, he took one out of the box and struck it on the friction strip on the side of the box and it flared to life.

"Are you sure that this is the way that you want to go out, Mateo? I am told that death by burning is very painful."

Mateo's eyes were glued on the burning match, "Wait! Yes, when I saw your daughter at the rodeo, I called the Gallos and told them that I had seen her and that she was with the deputy. I followed the deputy around for a while and he sometimes would go to his father's ranch to take your daughter out for lunch. It was obvious that she must be staying with him out at his father's ranch."

Blowing out the match, Diego said, "Thank you for your honesty, Mateo. Now what should we do with you? You have admitted to aiding and abetting Gallo sicarios who are at this moment are on their way to kidnap my daughter for a second time. I am leaning toward breaking my word and burning you and your house to a pile of cinders. Perhaps you can convince me otherwise."

"Inspector, I swear on my mother's grave that if you could see your way into not killing me tonight, that I will leave Texas tomorrow and make my way north and you will never see me again."

Diego ruminated on this for a few tense moments, well tense for Mateo anyhow. "Here is the deal that I will offer you. First, you pack up and leave Texas today. If I ever see you again south of I-70 I will kill you. If I hear that you are back in Texas, I will hunt you down and then kill you. If you ever get within a mile of my daughter again, I will kill you. If you do anything in the future that annoys me, I will get in touch with the Gallo's and tell them that you gave up this bunch of sicarios, who I should inform you are about to be shot to doll rags. For this alone, they would hunt you until the ends of the Earth. Do you accept my terms?"

"Yes, Señor Navarro! I will do exactly as you say. Thank you."

"You are welcome. Now I will sit here for a few hours while I wait for a phone call and to make sure that you do not do anything stupid such as try to contact our soon to be dead sicarios. I suggest that you lay back and try and get some sleep."

Mateo found it very difficult to get some sleep while soaked in lighter fluid.

Around 3:15 that morning Diego's phone rang. He answered it, listened for a moment then put the phone in his shirt pocket and stood up. Mateo, for the reason mentioned above, had not been able to sleep and watched this with trepidation. Diego looked down at Mateo and said, "Remember our deal. I expect you to be north of Lubbock by dinnertime. You'd better start packing."

Diego walked back out of the house and got in his old F-100 and fired it up. All in all, he felt that his conversation with Mateo had gone well and that his message had been received. If not, he'd have to kill the man, but he'd given him an option and the ball was now firmly in Mateo's court. Diego began the long drive to Grady's place.

CHAPTER 28

DIEGO DROVE INTO THE RANCH courtyard just after 6:30 that morning. Parking nose in to the porch, he got out of his old Ford pickup and wearily walked onto the porch where Esmeralda gave him a huge hug before going back into the kitchen to get Diego a cup for his coffee.

After he'd filled his cup from the pot sitting on the porch handrail, he took a seat beside his daughter on one of the ratty couches.

"So how did it go, amigos? I don't see the green 4-Runner or any of our five Mexican friends, so I am assuming that all went well."

Grady gave him the CliffsNotes version of the one-sided shootout that morning and let him know that the five sicarios were now cooling their heels at the bottom of an old mine out in the desert.

At this point Esmeralda asked him how he'd left things with Mateo. Diego related a paraphrased version of the discussion he'd had with Mateo, and that he doubted Mateo would be a problem in the future.

"So, he just gladly answered your questions and agreed to get out of Texas on his own free will, without any coercion or threats from you?" asked Deacon.

"To be honest, during the time we were having our conversation, Mateo was soaked with lighter fluid, and I had a box of kitchen matches."

"That would explain it," suggested Deacon.

At this point they all went inside where Grady got busy preparing a breakfast of scrambled eggs, toast and bacon while Deacon went back to his room to get ready for work. Esmeralda said that she needed to freshen up a bit herself, and shortly thereafter her and Deacon found themselves once again in the little bathroom separating their rooms.

Deacon had a leer on his face when he asked, "Do you want to freshen up together to save time?"

Without missing a beat Esmeralda faced him and started unbuttoning her jeans.

Startled, Deacon asked, "What are you doing!"

While making as if she was going to squirm out of her snug jeans right then and there, and had them down around hip level she replied, "Well, if we are going to 'freshen up' together I think that we should take off our clothes before we get in the shower, don't you?"

Esmeralda had called his bluff and Deacon started 'crawfishing', as they say in Louisiana. Since crawfish can only swim backwards, this was an excellent term for what Deacon was now doing, backing up.

"Are you mad! Your father is just out there in the kitchen!"

"I thought you wanted to 'freshen up' together, is that not so? I think it is time we just stop with this façade and let nature take its course. You do want to take me in the biblical sense don't you, or were you just leading me on?"

As Esmeralda squirmed back into her jeans and started buttoning them up, she grinned at Deacon. "You didn't know whether to sneeze or go blind just now. You need to stop writing cheques with your alligator mouth that you can't cash with your butterfly butt. At some point your actions will need to speak louder than your words, comprende?"

As Deacon retreated into his room in a state of confusion, Esmeralda walked out of the bathroom and back towards the kitchen laughing all the way.

When Deacon got to work, he was looking a bit flushed since he was still replaying the image of Esmeralda about to drop her jeans in his head. As he walked into the bullpen for the mornings briefing, Lorna told him that they had reports of gunshots out by Mount Livermore, which was just south of Grady's place.

"Yeah, we heard them as well. I think it was just some guys out there hunting javelinas," Deacon lied.

Taking a closer look at Deacon, Lorna smirked, "You seem a bit flustered this morning, deputy. Something to do with your budding romance with Ms. Navarro?"

"Lorna, she's moving at about twice my speed in this relationship. I may be lucky to survive."

"What the heck is wrong with you? If it is the woman who is driving the train in a relationship, it's about to go off the rails. Seems to me that she is ready for you to start working the throttle on this locomotive."

"You do know who her father is, correct?"

"Deputy Dumbass, if Diego Navarro has not blessed your courtship by this point, you'd probably be dead already. It's time for you to put your money where your mouth is."

Lorna was not one to beat around the bush.

When Deacon got home that evening, everyone ate dinner quickly before Diego and Esmeralda got into the 4-Runner while Deacon got into his old Chevy stepside and they convoyed up to Balmorhea to drop off the 4-Runner at Kiko & Tina's RV Park, where someone would collect it and dispose of it the following day. Leaving the keys in the exhaust pipe, Diego and Esmeralda climbed into Deacon's stepside and they headed back toward the ranch at around 9:00 in the evening.

On the way back, conversation was stilted as Deacon was still having recurring visions of the girl sitting in the middle of the bench seat of his truck, whose left thigh kept rubbing against his right one, wriggling out of her jeans that morning. While at the same time, he was acutely aware of her arguably psychopathic father sitting on her other side. Occasionally Esmeralda's hand would subtly rub his inner thigh, and just as occasionally, her father would pretend not to notice.

CHAPTER 29

AFTER BREAKFAST THE NEXT MORNING, Deacon and Esmeralda lounged on the porch with a cup of coffee before Deacon had to work, while Diego and Grady walked over to the pole barn to have a private discussion concerning the future of the Navarro and Allison clans. They obviously had some sort of devious plan in mind, but it may need some fine tuning after the recent kidnapping attempt and subsequent one-sided shootout in the courtyard.

While their elders were out putting the final touches on their fiendish plan, Esmeralda turned toward Deacon and suggested that they make use good use of this parentally unsupervised time and go back into the house and get intimate, she actually used the phrase 'knock off a quickie'.

"What happened to a proper courtship?" asked Deacon.

"Oh, those rules still apply, but I've got an itch that needs scratched, if you know what I mean," she explained with a randy grin.

While Deacon was pondering the pros and cons of scratching that itch, and his growing desire to do just that, read into that what you will, it became academic as Grady and Diego appeared out of the barn and were walking their way.

A very frustrated Deacon made his way to work shortly thereafter. Esmeralda, Diego and Grady just spent the day relaxing and making sure that the scene of the crime had been properly scoured and secured.

That evening after dinner, Grady called for a meeting in the living room to let everyone know the plan going forward.

"Okay guys and gal, we need to make a plan going forward. The threat to Esmeralda has hopefully been sorted out and she needs to get back to Mexico with Diego. I know you two kids have been getting along fairly well lately, but the fact is that Esmeralda is in the country illegally and has no papers, which means she hasn't been able to lead a normal life, go out unescorted, go shopping and has essentially depended on Deacon and I for all her needs. This is not a life for a young lady."

At this point, the writing was on the wall and Esmeralda turned to Deacon, who was sitting on the couch next to her, and whispered, "You should have taken me up on the offer of a quickie this morning." Deacon agreed and told her that hindsight is 20/20, which really didn't help either of them with their suddenly reoccurring itches.

The plan was for Esmeralda to return to Villa Ahumada the following day with her father, where Diego would continue his work with the National Guard and hopefully Esmeralda would get her old job back as a nurse at the medical center in town. Everyone would carry on as they did prior to Esmeralda getting tossed out of the van months ago which had resulted in the circumstances they now found themselves in. Once Diego was sure that the situation with the Gallo's was under control, they would look into getting Esmeralda a green card so that she could visit her apparently hormonally challenged boyfriend whenever she so desired.

"For the record, I am not hormonally challenged," interjected Deacon. "I am simply trying to court Esmeralda in the fashion dictated by Mexican tradition without getting a bullet in my ass."

"Bullshit!" declared Diego. "Any red-blooded male, Mexican or American, with a testosterone level greater than that of a gusano, a worm, would have already taken advantage of the situation that you found yourself in, that is, having a captive audience, and tried to take advantage of my daughter. You, on the other hand, are taking this courtship etiquette much to seriously and are wasting all of our time."

Esmeralda turned back toward Deacon and informed him that this was all true. Deacon just threw in the towel: he knew when he was outgunned and not likely to get anywhere by trying to defend his manhood.

That evening, Diego and Grady had gone into town to have a final night out and Deacon was propped up against the arm of the couch, which was his bed when Diego was in residence, reading a book when the door leading from the small hallway between the bedrooms swung open and Esmeralda sauntered in wearing only her little sage-colored nightshirt and whatever she may have had on underneath it. She walked up to the arm of the couch which would have been the foot of Deacon's bed, and by this point had attracted all of Deacon's attention.

"What are you doing?" asked Deacon.

"Well, this is the last night that you will have a chance to seduce me, or for me to seduce you. I wanted to give you something to remember me by while I am in Mexico getting my green card," she replied.

"I'm just curious, but do you have anything on under that nightshirt?"

"I would have thought that you would want to discover this for yourself. That said, if I do have something on under it then I am just a nice girl, and if I don't then I am a very naughty girl. Wouldn't you like to find out if I am naughty or nice?" asked Esmeralda.

Deacon threw off his blanket and stood up in his skivvies and Esmeralda took his hand and walked him back to her room and had him lie on the bed while she ensured that the door from her room to the shared bathroom and the door leading to the short hallway were securely locked. Walking back to the foot of the bed, she climbed onto the bed on her hands and knees, then slowly crawled up, over, and on top of Deacon until she was straddling his hips. During this maneuver, her nightshirt had ridden high up her thighs revealing that she was in fact a very nice girl who was on the brink of becoming very naughty.

Deacon, for his part, was understandably mesmerized by the sight of Esmeralda's lingerie covered loins positioned over his hips, a thin veneer of Lycra and lace separating him from nirvana. Although he was enjoying the show, he was also in somewhat of a hurry to remove them and get on with the program.

"Correct me if I am wrong, but those do not appear to be the usual Victoria's Secret style of underwear that I have become accustomed to seeing you wearing during the past few months."

"That is very observant of you Deputy Allison. The Victoria's Secret panties didn't seem to be getting me where I wanted to go, so I thought I'd try some Be Wicked, V-cut, low rise, lace panties to see if they would spice things up, and to be honest, from where I am sitting, things are definitely spicing up, no pun intended." Esmeralda grinned licentiously as she pulled her nightshirt over her head.

From this point, nature just took its course, and it could be said that Esmeralda's seduction was extremely successful from both their points of view.

Afterwards, they were just lying together savoring the moment when Esmeralda realized that if her father and Grady came home and Deacon wasn't on the couch, that they would have a pretty good idea where he was and what was going on. Explaining this to Deacon as she pushed him off the bed, she gave him a long and lusty kiss before shoving him out her door and towards the living room with the taunting comment that although the evening had been remarkable, there was still plenty of room for improvement. Practice makes perfect, she informed him.

CHAPTER 30

THE NEXT MORNING, GRADY AND Diego were in the kitchen having coffee when Deacon, and then Esmeralda, walked in looking a bit sheepish, but with smiles on their faces. Grady looked over at Diego and winked.

"You two seem to be in good spirits this morning," said Grady.

"Yes, but looking a bit flushed as well. Didn't you sleep soundly?" asked Diego with a straight face.

"Papá, it was the last night that we would be spending together, so we stayed up late reminiscing about our time together these past few months. We didn't get much sleep."

"Very understandable that you spent some quality time together. I am glad to hear it. Grady is making pancakes for breakfast and after that we need to get on the road. It is a long drive from here to Villa Ahumada and I believe that you still have to pack."

"I do not have many personal belongings here, Papá, and if I am going to be coming back occasionally, I can leave some things here."

"Fair enough, I want to be on the road by nine o'clock."

After breakfast, Esmeralda went to her room to pack up her things, which easily fit into one large old suitcase that Grady had in his room, and one old backpack that Deacon had out in his truck.

As Diego went out with Grady to check the fluids in Diego's old Ford pickup prior to making the long journey back into Mexico, Esmeralda and Deacon said their goodbyes in the living room with a newfound passion now that the ice had been broken, so to say. Esmeralda had tears in her eyes as she made Deacon swear to call her every evening and that if the green card was taking a long time to process, to come and visit her as often as possible. As Deacon grabbed her by her shapely backside and pulled her to him, she wrapped her arms around his neck and gave him a heartfelt, lingering kiss with just the right amount of tongue, Mexican style not French, to make sure he remembered it.

With that, they walked out to Diego's truck and Deacon opened her door and handed her in before placing her suitcase and backpack in the bed of the truck. Meanwhile, Grady was over on the driver's side telling Diego to stay in touch and they'd revisit their plan in the upcoming months to finalize it. Neither Deacon nor Esmeralda had any idea what they were talking about, and at the moment they really didn't care.

Things at Grady's ranch got back to normal with Deacon working his regular deputy sheriff's schedule and Grady getting back to managing his ranch properly. Needless to say, Deacon was now an extremely sexually frustrated deputy, which was noticed by the incredibly perceptive Sheriff Stims.

While at lunch one day, about two weeks after Diego and Esmeralda had hit the road to Mexico, Lorna decided to get to the bottom of it. "You seem to be a little out of sorts since Esmeralda went back to Mexico, Deputy Allison. I really didn't think it would affect you so much as, from what I have been able to put together, you botched the courtship thing about as much as any man could have," she was smiling as she said it to take the sting out of her comments. The fact was that after the dance and rodeo, she really hadn't seen much of Esmeralda so she really couldn't say if Deacon had fumbled the ball or not.

"Thank you for your concern, it is touching. To set the record straight, I was romantically assaulted by Esmeralda the last night that she was in the States, and I think I am suffering from PTSD. For such a sweet, young, innocent thing, she definitely has a very vivid imagination and the stamina of an ox. But, as you say, it was kind of a 'hit & run' since she is now back in Mexico, and I am unable to discipline her properly during a rematch."

"So, what's the plan then, big fella? You do have a plan, don't you?" asked Lorna.

"Funny you should ask. The plan at the moment is for Esmeralda to get her green card. After that, there is no plan as far as I can tell. That said, Grady and Diego were having a lot of private conversations for about a month prior to the Navarro's going back to Mexico and I would bet good money that they are hatching some sort of sinister plan, but dad isn't talking."

"Well, did you give her an engagement ring before she left? This is a common practice during the courtship phase."

Deacon looked thoughtful for a moment before answering. "No, I didn't, but I did use my handcuffs on her that last night though, does that count?" asked Deacon with a straight face.

"Too much information, deputy. Finish your burrito so we can get back to work."

About a week after the lunch where Deacon alluded to the possibility that he and Esmeralda had 'dipped their toes' into the bondage fetish the evening before she was repatriated to Mexico, Lorna called Deacon into her office after the morning briefing, she said that she had something to discuss with him.

After pestering her deputy for further juicy stories concerning Esmeralda and pseudo-bondage, she reverted back into her official sheriff mode.

"You remember that Mateo Molina character, the one who embarrassed Esmeralda at the dance?" queried Lorna.

"I do."

"Well, I received a report from Hank Gutersohn over in Brewster County a few days ago, and it seems that our Mr. Molina has disappeared. Apparently, he just packed up one evening and did a runner. Oddly enough, this was the same evening that those shots were reported out by Mount Livermore, which you suggested were just some people hunting wild pigs.

Thinking back on it now, if I remember correctly, you were looking a bit haggard that morning when you showed up for work. All these events wouldn't be somehow tied together, would they?" Lorna cocked her left eyebrow up when she asked this.

"As I told you before, Esmeralda had cornered me in the hallway the evening before I arrived at work looking haggard. During this encounter she teased me mercilessly by threatening to drop her laundry and seduce me then and there with her homicidal father mere yards away in the kitchen. I was very discombobulated, to use your own five-dollar word. This was why I looked knackered that morning," Deacon said in his defense.

"You don't seduce the willing, moron," informed Lorna. "Getting back on topic, not that I really give a hoot about the wellbeing of Mr. Molina, but I do need to concern myself with the reputation of the Jeff County Sheriff's Office, so I will ask you directly if you, or anyone you are related to, or Esmeralda or anyone she is related to, had anything to do with the sudden disappearance of Mateo Molina?"

Looking insulted, Deacon replied, "I can't believe you would even insinuate that any of us would have anything to do with the disappearance of Mateo! I haven't even seen the man since the dance."

"What about the others?"

"You'd have to ask them," suggested Deacon.

"I can't very well do that since half of them are in Mexico at the moment, which I somehow doubt is a coincidence."

"Law enforcement is often a game of chances, Sheriff. Better luck next time," offered Deacon with a smug smile.

"There will be no 'next time', Deputy Allison," Lorna scowled.

"Let us hope not. Crime is not good for tourism. That said, was there anything odd or out of place at Mateo's home? I'm assuming that Hank did a wellness check."

"That would be Sheriff Gutersohn to you, deputy. It looks as if Mateo just woke up very early one morning and decided to leave the area. Only his clothes and personal effects were missing. The curious thing is that his bed was still damp and reeked of lighter fluid, and there was an empty 12 ounce can of Ronsonol lighter fluid on the nightstand along with an almost full box of Diamond Strike kitchen matches. One match had been struck, allowed to burn halfway down, then blown out and dropped on the floor."

"How do you know it had been blown out?"

"Because a lot of that lighter fluid had dripped on the floor and if it had been dropped on the floor while lit Hank would not have been able to do a wellness check as the entire house would have burnt to the ground."

"Any fingerprints on that match?" queried Deacon.

"Why, are you worried?" queried Lorna.

"Not in the least, as I said, I have not seen Mateo since the rodeo."

"That still leaves the others."

"Do you have fingerprints on file for Mexican nationals?" asked Deacon.

"No," said Lorna wearily, "but if I find out that you or Grady somehow illegally got Mateo to do a runner, I am going to hand your asses over to Hank. You cowboys can't just do whatever you want to around here."

"Sheriff Stims, I will swear on a stack of Bibles that neither my dad or I have seen hide nor hair of Mateo since the rodeo. We had nothing to do with him disappearing."

"What about Esmeralda and her father?"

"The Mexican minx was either with me or my dad most of the time since the rodeo. When she was left by herself at the ranch, she wouldn't have had any transportation to get to Sanderson. I think that you can cross Esmeralda off of your list."

"How about Diego, he has motive, and since he seems to cross the border any time he feels like it, opportunity."

"I agree that Diego wasn't too happy with Mateo and his performance at the rodeo, but there is a big difference between being unhappy and running a guy out of the country. In any case, you'd have to ask him."

"Esmeralda would provide him with an alibi in any case, so I think Hank and I will just have to chalk this one up as a learning experience."

"That would probably be best for all concerned," intoned Deacon.

"You are a frustrating man, had anyone ever told you that?" asked Lorna.

"The list is long and distinguished. I should probably get out on patrol if you are finished with me."

Pointing at the door to her office, Lorna said, "Go." As Deacon was heading out the door, she added in a much friendlier tone, "If you have any sense at all you'll take a few days off and visit Esmeralda while she is getting her green card processed. Just a word to the wise."

On the way out to his truck, Deacon ran into Macy, who asked, "When are you going to make an honest woman out of Esmeralda?"

"Well, God has already made her a woman, I checked her out. As far as honest, I kind of like her dishonest and wanton. She is very creative when she is being naughty, and it keeps me limber."

Macy's mouth fell open as she tried to form a response, but eventually she just walked away shaking her head.

Chuck had witnessed the exchange from behind his reception desk and offered the opinion that if he was 30 years younger, he'd want Esmeralda to remain naughty as well.

"Yeah, it's all well and good until she causes me to have a stroke, but what a way to go," Deacon said with a grin as he went outside.

CHAPTER 31

WINTER HAD COME TO THE high desert, and the weather was mild to cool with occasional freezes. It hardly ever rained in the desert during the winter. This being the case, and as the residents were more accustomed and comfortable with the heat than the cold, the winter weather tended to keep people inside. Those that frequented the various drinking establishments during the cooler weather were more inclined to visit them immediately after getting off work or on the weekends. During the winter months, most people were usually at home by nine o'clock in the evening. This greatly reduced the workload on the Sheriff's Office since the vast majority of law enforcement issues in the county tended to be alcohol related and occurred just after closing time. In the winter, the hours around midnight were much less hectic.

After it became apparent that things in Jeff Davis County were settling down for the winter, and that most of the calls would simply be people whose cars had quit on them out on a remote road and needed assistance, hunters trespassing on private property or the occasional drunk and disorderly individual stumbling home from the bar after over-serving themselves, Deacon put in for a week's vacation so that he could go visit Esmeralda.

Deacon got up early one morning and loaded up his truck with the gear he would need for a week in the highly over-rated vacation hotspot of Villa Ahumada. Diego's home was also located in the Chihuahuan Desert, but about 85 miles on the other side of the border. He also had to load up a few suitcases of items requested by Esmeralda from shopping venues north of the border, which included a variety of blue jeans, Wrangler and Levis, as well as a variety of tops, sneakers, cosmetics and a mysterious package which had been delivered to Grady's porch from an outfit named Fleur of England, which when Deacon Googled it, turned out to be an upmarket lingerie establishment. As far as Deacon was concerned, this was the most important item he would be hauling into Mexico.

Deacon had decided to take the route through El Paso, so after leaving the ranch he drove through Fort Davis before getting on County Road 17, which took him south to Marfa. Taking State Highway 90 northwest out of Marfa, he just took his time on the 80-mile run through wide spots in the road known as Ryan, Valentine and Lobo before he reached the booming metropolis of Van Horn, population just over 2,000. From Van Horn it was a straight shot to El Paso on Interstate 10. Once in El Paso, Deacon waited his turn in line to cross the point of entry at the Bridge of Americas before crossing into Mexico.

Getting on Avenida Rafael Perez Serna, he followed it back south and east until it became Highway 45, which took him south out of Cuidad Juárez, which is the Mexican city directly across the border from El Paso. Staying on Highway 45 for about 80 or 85 miles brought him directly into Villa Ahumada.

Since he wasn't familiar with the town, the plan was for him to drive through the center of town until he saw the Centro de Salud on the left, the small medical facility where Esmeralda had been originally kidnapped and was now working at again. He'd just park in the lot, walk in and ask for Nurse Navarro.

When he walked into the hospital and up to the reception desk, he was drawing some appreciative looks from the other nurses. It wasn't often that a good-looking gringo came to their hospital, so they were taking advantage of the opportunity to inspect this one. He felt like a piece of meat as he asked for Nurse Navarro.

There was a shriek somewhere back in the little clinic before the doors to the right of the reception desk flew open and Esmeralda, dressed in a curiously sexy nurse's uniform that actually accentuated the positive, came flying out and wrapped herself around Deacon in a most unladylike manner. This seemed to annoy the other female medical personnel who had been eyeing him as a side of beef just a few minutes earlier.

After a few minutes of subtle groping and kissing in the French tradition, Esmeralda disentangled herself and asked Deacon to take a seat in the reception area while she changed into her street clothes so that he could take her for a late lunch at Mariscos Topolobampo a few blocks away on the other side of Highway 45.

When Esmeralda walked back out of the doors beside the reception desk that she had earlier blown through, she was dressed in snug jeans, cowboy boots and a split V-neck 3/4 ruffle sleeve blouse tucked into the front of the jeans. The V-neck really held Deacon's interest as it revealed just a hint of cleavage and was bringing back fond memories of their last night together. The snug keister-hugging jeans brought back fond memories as well, as Esmeralda knew they would.

They hopped into Deacon's truck and drove the across the highway and then the few blocks to the restaurant. On the way Deacon innocently asked her what was in the package from Fleur of England, although he had already done his research and had a fairly good idea as to what it contained.

"It will be easier to show you as opposed to tell you," Esmeralda replied with a sultry grin. Deacon figured Christmas might come early this year as he grinned back.

At the restaurant, Esmeralda ordered the tacos dorados while Deacon, being starved after the long drive, ordered gorditas and they both ordered Coke with ice and lime. Esmeralda was like a kid in a toy store and talked non-stop as she caught Deacon up with what she had been doing since she had left Grady's place. She was sitting across the table from him and held his hand tightly to ensure he was real and so that he could not escape. She only released his hand when their orders arrived so that they could eat.

While Esmeralda was enjoying her lunch, Deacon filled her in on what he'd been up to since she'd left the ranch. It was pretty boring, but the fact that they were together again more than made up for the poor subject matter. Deacon looked at his watch and asked Esmeralda when she had to go back to work. She replied that she was taking a few days off starting now, so her work would not get in their way.

After the late lunch, they got back in the truck and Esmeralda navigated Deacon back onto Highway 45 and they drove to the northern part of town where Diego had a nice, shaded three bedroom, two bath bungalow off Calle Jimenez. Since Diego was at his office on the other side of Highway 45, on the other side of town and wouldn't be back until dinner, Esmeralda and Deacon grabbed all of their stuff out of the truck and put it in the spare bedroom which had been prepared for Deacon's visit. Afterwards, they essentially ripped off each other's clothes and made up for lost time.

By the time Diego arrived home, Esmeralda and Deacon had showered up, together of course, and then re-attired themselves and had dinner prepared and waiting for Diego. Diego was much more relaxed now than he had been while at Grady's when he was preparing to sort out Mateo, he was even bordering on being friendly to Deacon, which Deacon found disconcerting. This was the man who threatened to put a bullet in his backside if he acted in the least bit inappropriately with his daughter, which he had now managed to do twice that afternoon. He had to have known that Deacon had been in his house, alone with his daughter, all afternoon and only a blind man would fail to see the rosy glow on Esmeralda's cheeks coupled with her radiant smile. Any Inspector worth his salt would have deduced that his daughter had likely been willingly engaged in dancing the horizontal mambo with Deacon earlier in the day.

Later that evening, once Diego had retired to bed, Deacon and Esmeralda sat out on the veranda having a beer and trying to come up with a plan that would allow them to repeat the afternoon's performance without getting caught by Diego, and the weeping and gnashing of teeth which that would surely result from the apprehension.

Diego's master bedroom took up the far-left corner at the back of the house. Esmeralda's room was on the far-right corner at the rear of the house while the guest room was located at the front right corner of the house. The rooms were adjacent to each other, but there was no connecting door. The kitchen and a breakfast nook were situated between Esmeralda's room and that of her father. A short hallway ran from the living room past the bedrooms on the right side of the house and into the kitchen, with a bathroom situated across the hall from the guest room. Since Esmeralda's room was fairly close to Diego's at the rear of the bungalow, it was ruled out as being a suitable place to make the beast with two backs. Deacon and Esmeralda devised a plan; they would go to their separate rooms later, as Diego would expect them to do, but Deacon would leave his door slightly ajar. Once enough time had elapse to put Diego's mind at ease, if he was in fact paying attention, Esmeralda would visit the bathroom across the hall from the guest room, wait the appropriate amount of time before flushing the toilet then go back to her door and without entering her room close the door with just enough force to suggest she had gone into her room. She would then tiptoe back to the guest room, where the door had been left ajar, and make her way in before closing the door very quietly. They would need to be very quiet while they were fooling around and engaging in amorous congress. Not a theoretical impossibility, but it would be difficult.

Around 2:00 in the morning, simply because she couldn't wait anymore, Esmeralda made her way to the bathroom and Deacon heard the toilet flush, so he prepared himself mentally for the upcoming, no pun intended, misbehavior.

Shortly thereafter, his door opened silently, and Esmeralda snuck in before silently closing the door. As she turned around, there was enough light in the room for Deacon to see that she had on her old sage-colored nightshirt.

"So, is this a repeat performance of our first night together?" asked Deacon.

"For it to be a repeat performance, I would be required to be wearing my Be Wicked, V-cut, low rise, lace panties."

"Are you?"

As she climbed into bed, she suggested that Deacon should find out for himself. The nightshirt came off after a few minutes to reveal the Be Wicked lingerie had disappeared and had been replace by a stimulating Fleur of England black balcony bra and a strap thong ensemble, which Deacon felt he could work with, and he did.

Around 4:00 in the morning, a smiling and an immensely satisfied Esmeralda stealthily made her way back to her room and closed her door as quietly as possible. Diego was a light sleeper and woke up when he heard his daughter's door close. Smiling himself, he muttered, "That's my girl," before falling back to sleep.

CHAPTER 32

THE NEXT MORNING, DIEGO WAS already awake and in the kitchen preparing scrambled eggs with chorizo, bacon and toast, when Deacon and then Esmeralda walked in looking quite pleased with themselves, although they were both trying to stifle yawns.

"What is wrong with you two, couldn't sleep?" asked Diego with his best poker face.

Deacon busied himself at the coffee machine while Diego's comment caught Esmeralda in mid-yawn causing her to catch her breath as she struggled to come up with a suitable response, when Deacon came to her rescue.

"I think it was just being in a strange house," suggested Deacon.

"Yes, I think that just having someone else in the house may have interfered with my sleep," proposed Esmeralda quickly.

Diego loaded up three plates and while Esmeralda and Deacon took their seats at the table, Diego set their breakfasts in front of them.

"I don't know, I slept well most of the night but around 3:00 this morning I swear I heard what I thought was moaning and groaning, but eventually it stopped, so I just went back to sleep. You didn't hear that?" said Diego while maintaining his deadpan expression.

Esmeralda just looked down at her plate while she ate her breakfast, afraid to meet her father's eyes. Deacon, on the other hand, suggested that it could have just been the wind.

"I suppose that is possible," agreed Diego, with a total lack of conviction. He was actually enjoying their discomfort, but decided to throw them a bone. "I have a few meetings today and will try to be home for dinner. If I cannot make it, I'll call. I am hoping that the wind will die down today and there won't be any more of that moaning and groaning noise in the house, but that is for God to decide. Don't you agree?" said Diego while he was looking directly at Deacon with a sly smile transforming his earlier deadpan expression.

Diego knew exactly what was going on between his daughter and the deputy and he was just letting Deacon know that although he could not outright condone his daughter getting frisky with his friend's son, he could at least turn a blind eye to it.

Once Diego had gone to work, Esmeralda and Deacon had a good laugh at what had been said in the kitchen and Diego's passive approval of their activities earlier that morning, but one thing led to another and second round of moaning and groaning took place about half an hour after Diego's departure. They obviously felt the need to make up for the slow start to their romance in Texas, and to reclaim the time lost since they had been apart.

Once they had again completed the bedroom gymnastics to their satisfaction, they showered up together before getting ready to go out. When they were back in Deacon's truck, with Deacon driving and Esmeralda navigating, Esmeralda gave Deacon a tour of Villa Ahumada and its surrounding environs.

Villa Ahumada never was, and never will be, a tourist destination, and it will likely never be featured on TripAdvisor. The town sits in the middle of the Chihuahuan Desert, about midway between the towns of Ciudad Juárez and Chihuahua, in a flat, arid plain without anything to entice someone to visit or to cause someone to stop on their way to either Ciudad Juárez or Chihuahua, depending on which way they were headed on Highway 45. The village is known for its cheese and its enchiladas, but these generally are not enough of an attraction to cause tourists to stop and explore Villa Ahumada.

The town's only claim to fame is that it was featured in the international news back in 2008 when it was terrorized and essentially taken over by an out-of-town gang. On the evening of May 19, 2008, dozens of men drove through the town firing assault rifles killing the chief of police, two police officers and three civilians, and abducting at least 10 people. Any of the police force that survived the initial onslaught ran away and the state and federal governments had to send in troops to restore order. Needless to say, this was just another example of the cartel violence that was rampant during that period.

With Esmeralda acting as tour guide, they drove the 5- or 6-mile perimeter of the truncated right triangle which delineated the perimeter of the town, with Esmeralda desperately trying to find things to impress Deacon but failing miserably.

After the short tour around the town, Esmeralda turned to Deacon and asked, "What do you think?"

Deacon just looked at her for a moment before answering, "I think we should have stayed in bed."

"You would have said that if I had just taken you on a tour of Disneyland," she said with a mischievous grin. "But you're right, the place kind of sucks, nothing but dirt, dust and desert. I wouldn't be here except for my father."

They then drove west out of town on Highway 19 to Carrizal to visit the Museum of the Battle of Carrizal, which effectively ended the American's Mexican Expedition in 1916. The real reason they went to Carrizal was to have lunch at a little hole-in-the-wall place called Café Rosy which was rumored to have the best chimichangas in Mexico. After having their lunch, they got a chimichanga plate to go, then drove back to Diego's office off Calle Argentina to drop off the chimichangas for him as a late lunch before heading back to the bungalow.

They sat on the veranda drinking a few beers before Deacon suggested that they go inside so that he could re-inspect the scar on her right thigh.

Esmeralda thought this sounded like an excellent idea since it required her to remove her jeans so that Deacon had access to the scar. During the following inspection, Deacon was required to remove more than her jeans, allowing access to more than just the scar. One thing led to another and before they knew it, they were both naked, which then led to a repeat of the morning's bedroom calisthenics. Although Villa Ahumada may not have been a tourist hotspot, Deacon was thoroughly enjoying his vacation so far.

The next few days began like the first, with some new creative workouts being thrown in the mix each morning to avoid getting in a rut. They would then venture further out in the countryside surrounding Villa Ahumada just for something to do. On the penultimate day of Deacons vacation, they dragged Diego along to the Dunas la Morita sand dunes up by Samalayuca to watch the sand rail races. It was a fairly big event, with drivers from all over Mexico and the southern US bringing in their rails, which are not to be confused with dune buggies, to race around a track laid out in the dunes.

Dune buggies generally have large tires designed for travelling over the sand, a fiberglass body and a rear engine. Sand rails, on the other hand, tend to be more bare-bones with a frame constructed from steel tubing. Sand rails come in a variety of shapes, sizes and horsepower, limited only by the imagination of the builder.

As the sun went down, they decided to drive up to the southern suburbs of Ciudad Juárez, since the Dunas la Morita were only about 30 miles to the south of the city and have dinner at Carnitas Don Epi just off Highway 2. On the way back home, Diego was lying up against the passenger door, with Esmeralda lying up against him, both snoring softly for most of the hour and a half trip back home.

On the morning of the last day of Deacon's vacation, while at the breakfast table, Diego indicated that he needed to go to Chihuahua for a meeting at the Guarda Nacional Coordinación y Estación Chihuahua offices in the city of Chihuahua that afternoon and that he wouldn't be home until the following day. Everyone knew that he was just getting out of the way so that Esmeralda and Deacon could have the final day and evening to themselves before Deacon had to return home. The gesture was much appreciated.

Deacon and Esmeralda walked Diego out to his truck with Deacon carrying his single suitcase. While Deacon put the suitcase in the passenger side of the old F-100's bench seat, Esmeralda was hugging her father and telling him to be careful. When Deacon got back to that side of the truck, Diego shook his hand and told him how much he'd enjoyed his visit and to feel free to come visit again anytime. With that, Diego, who hated long goodbyes, got in his truck and began the long drive to Chihuahua.

Esmeralda and Deacon took advantage of the time they had left together and mostly spent it studying each other's body geography in detail, with breaks for showering and eating to recharge for the next study session. Sadly, all good things must come to an end and the next morning, after a final, vigorous session of the horizontal bop, they showered up together for the last time, got dressed and had breakfast. After a long, lingering goodbye, Deacon got back in his old stepside Chevy and began his trip back across the border and home.

The last week had convinced Deacon that he was hopelessly enamored with Ms. Navarro. Besides the fact that she had a face that could launch a thousand ships, and a body that was so hot she could probably boil water by just walking by the pot, she was simply a very pleasant woman to be around and a lot of fun. She did have a temper, but this could be a lot of fun as well as long as you knew when to stop teasing to avoid the wrath or maybe even being shot in the face. Deacon had a lot of windshield time between Villa Ahumada and Fort Davis to think about a future with Esmeralda.

After Deacon had hit the road, Esmeralda got herself another cup of coffee and sat on the veranda to reminisce over the past week with Deacon. She would need to see what the future held after recollecting her conversation with Grady on the way back from Muley's in Fort Stockton when they had picked up the trail cameras. After the past week of debauchery, which was actually only the second time, actually the second through twelfth time by her count, that they had been intimate, she was convinced that they clicked on the physical level, but she would have to wait and see what Deacon had planned for their future, if there was to be one. She figured that she'd give it a year to see how things were working out. The problem she foresaw was that the 'long distance relationship' thing, from what she'd seen of others in similar situations, rarely survived more than a few months. That said, nothing ventured, nothing gained.

CHAPTER 33

DEACON GOT BACK TO THE ranch around 10:00 that Friday evening, and after parking his truck in the garage he carried his suitcase across the courtyard, up on the porch and into the house where he found Grady sitting on the couch reading a book.

"So how was your time down there with Diego and Esmeralda? Did you have fun?" asked Grady.

"Dad, that woman damn near killed me, and yes, I enjoyed every minute of it. I think Diego has thrown in the towel and has decided not to shoot me in the butt for courting his daughter."

"Go put your kit away, grab us a beer and tell me all about it."

Deacon gave his father the G-rated version of his holiday south of the border to keep him from having a heart attack. Truth be known, there were times during the past week where Deacon thought that he was the one in danger of having an aneurysm. Due to superior genetics and perhaps the fact that he stayed in pretty good shape, he hadn't flatlined during Esmeralda's energetic bedroom conditioning routines.

Getting serious, Grady asked his son just what his plans were for the near future. If he was going to get serious with Esmeralda, he'd need to put together a plan to get out of the desert and into an environment that would allow him and Esmeralda to enjoy life while raising a family if they decided to.

"You and Mom seemed to do okay here, and I didn't even know I was missing anything until I'd gone into the military and saw what was out there."

"This was the only life that your mom knew. When we got married, although I'd been out in the world, she had not, and she was comfortable here. I made the decision to stay here in the desert. You've seen what is on the other side of the curtain, and to some extent so has Esmeralda during the time that she was at university in Baja California. I'll tell you this right now, if you try to keep Esmeralda anywhere close to the border, you'll lose her eventually. Things would be rosy for a while, but eventually she'd want her chance to see what's on the other side of the curtain as well. Also, job opportunities here are few and far between. Yes, you have what is considered a good job with the Sheriff's Office, but if you really want to go out and make something of a life for you and Esmeralda, you need to figure out what you want to do with yourself, head north and make it happen. I also think that Esmeralda would want to keep up with her nursing credentials. To really do that she'll need to get out of here as well. Esmeralda, once she has her green card, could find work anywhere since nurses are in demand everywhere these days. I know you don't want to hear it, but she could keep you guys afloat while you are getting sorted out. Don't let that macho bullshit get in the way of common sense and practicality."

Deacon gave this some thought; Grady was right on every count. "The big issue I have dad, is that the only experience that I really have to offer anyone is my military experience and this short gig as a deputy. There just aren't that many people looking for ex-soldiers these days."

"You are looking at your skill set from the wrong perspective. Many employers like vets because they know how to take orders, they are focused, they are disciplined, and they are mission oriented. This has nothing to do with assaulting the beach or breaching the walls. The big question is what do you want to do? You need to figure that out first, then stay focused on making it happen. Do you have any idea as to what you'd like to do?" asked Grady.

"You'll laugh if I told you," replied Deacon.

"Probably, but why don't you try it out on me anyhow."

"I used to hang out with the guys in the motor pool back in the day and used to watch them rebuild motors, repair suspensions and just fix what was broken. I think in the long run I'd like to open my own machine shop somewhere."

"That's an honorable trade, why would I laugh at that? Do you have any experience with this sort of thing?"

"Not really. I've given it some thought, and I figure I'd need to go to a community college and get some training in welding, fabrication, design and just how to use the various machines out there to begin with.'

"That's a start. Have you spoken to Esmeralda about this? It seems to me that she'd have to be the bread winner of the family until you got yourself sorted out."

"We haven't really thought that far ahead yet, but I need to do that."

"Sooner rather than later. You don't want to lose that girl, and I don't think she wants to lose you, according to Diego anyhow."

Deacon perked up at this, but keeping a straight face, he asked, "Really, what did Diego have to say?"

"That's between us father figures. You've had a long day; you should go to bed. I'm headed that way myself so that you don't pester me all evening trying to find out what Diego had to say. Good night."

CHAPTER 34

FOR A WHILE, THINGS IN the desert, on both sides of the border, just became routine: Grady was finally giving the ranch his undivided attention, Deacon was going out on patrol, and Lorna was unsuccessfully trying to hire some more deputies to fill out the ranks and give her guys and gals a respite from the six-day work week. Diego was keeping his side of the border under control as well as could be expected with the cartel presence, and Esmeralda just kept working at the little hospital in Villa Ahumada.

One Saturday evening, Deacon and Grady were sitting on the porch after dinner having a beer when Grady's phone rang, and things once again got interesting.

"Yeah, Diego, what have you got?" answered Grady.

"Where are you at now and is Deacon with you?" asked Diego.

"We're sitting on the porch having a beer, why?"

"Put your phone on speaker and I'll tell you."

Grady put the phone on speaker and set it on the ratty couch between him and his son and told Diego to go ahead.

"The sons of bitches have tried it again!" Diego said as he tried to enlighten Deacon and Grady.

"Slow down, Diego. Which sons of bitches tried what again?"

"Esmeralda drove down to the supermercado this afternoon, the one at the end of Calle Revolución Alhumadenses near my house, and the Gallos must have been watching the house and followed her. They caught her as she was walking from her car to the shop."

"Did they grab her?" Deacon was getting a bit worked up by this point in the conversation.

"They did, but they wished that they hadn't. She'd tucked that little Sig P365 in her waistband under the tail of her shirt. Apparently three men got out of a pickup truck while she was walking toward the store and came up behind her. When one yelled at her, she turned around and quickly figured out what was happening. Before they could get to her, she had pulled out that little Sig and started shooting roosters."

"That's my girl!" Deacon exclaimed. "Did she hit any of them?"

"This is where I am not entirely sure what happened, she's asleep now after the excitement so I can't ask her for clarification, but it seems that when she yanked the pistol out of her waistband, the front sight hung up on some special English underwear she had on, something she had ordered when she was back in the States, and damaged the fabric somehow. Anyhow, this seemed to enrage her even further and she unloaded all 10 rounds at the pendejos. She blew the lungs out of one of the assholes, and from the CCTV camera at the supermercado, she got another one in the ass as he was running back to their truck, and it looks like she might have shot an ear off the last one. Two got away but one died on the spot."

"Those would be Fleur of England panties, not your run of the mill English knickers. From what I've been told they are the embodiment of empowering femininity and sophisticated elegance and apparently there is not much to them, and they are expensive," Deacon corrected Diego.

The phone went silent, and Grady was staring open mouthed at his son. "Sorry, I just thought I'd throw that in for accuracy, and it may explain why she emptied her pistol at these guys. We might want to consider getting her a gun with a higher capacity magazine in the future, but that would by necessity be a larger handgun and she may not be able to tuck it into her fancy panties. Just saying…"

"Deacon, if you could possible stop thinking about my daughter's underwear for a moment and get back on topic here, it would be greatly appreciated," suggested Diego.

Grady got things back on track, "Okay Diego, Esmeralda is fine for the moment, but I am guessing you have some sort of retribution in mind for the Gallo's, which is why you are phoning us now. Correct?"

"Correct. I am tired of these cabróns, that's assholes for you non-Spanish speakers, trying to kidnap my daughter to get at me. I think it is time to put an end to this. Could you guys meet me, Hank, and Benito at the Hotel Paisano in Marfa next Wednesday? I'll fill you in on the plan then, but I'm afraid it is somewhat outside the law as they say."

"If Deacon can get off work, we'll be there. If not, I'll be there and fill him in later," replied Grady.

Grady disconnected the call and looked over at his son. "I didn't know that you were such an expert on ladies' underwear," he said with a grin.

"I can't claim to be knowledgeable concerning all lady's underwear, but while I was down in Ahumada I got a crash course in one lady's preferred undergarments. She special ordered those Fleur of England butt-huggers and they were delivered here after her and Diego went back to Mexico. I hand carried them to her when I went down. They seem to be special so putting a run in one of them with the front sight of her pistol likely put her over the edge, much to the dismay of our Gallo buddies. Never mess with an armed woman sporting fancy English lingerie underneath her jeans is the takeaway lesson for the Gallo's I believe."

"Sounds reasonable, but to get back on topic again, I am fairly certain that whatever Diego has in mind in going to be highly illegal, violent and will likely involve gunplay. As an officer of the law, you may want to sit this one out," Grady suggested.

"Dad, If I were to sit this one out, seeing how it concerns Esmeralda, I'd never be able to look her in the eye again. I'm in, even if I have to resign as a deputy."

"All true. Okay, you go to work as usual on Wednesday and let me go down to Marfa on Wednesday to meet with Hank, Benito and Diego. I am guessing that the reason Diego has selected this crew is that this is the same bunch who rescued those eastern European and Brazilian girls years ago who had been kidnapped in Baja. We are all a lot older than we were back then, but Diego knows he can trust us, and since Hank and Benito are the sheriffs of Brewster County and Presidio County respectively, and both counties border Mexico, we'll likely be crossing the border illegally and coming back the same way. I hope Diego has a solid plan. I'm a little long in the tooth for a commando raid. My hip is starting to act up these days and I'm really not up for any long marches."

Deacon went to work each day as usual, while Grady drove down to the Hotel Paisano the following Wednesday to meet up with Hank, Benito and Diego. Everyone else was waiting in the lobby just inside the entrance off Highland Street when Diego walked in around 4:00 in the afternoon. Diego had booked a Mezzanine room on the second floor, so they went up to it to get some privacy while Diego threw out his nefarious plan for consideration. While Grady, Hank and Benito sat on the couch in the room, Diego pulled the lone armchair over in front of it so that he faced them.

"My friends, thanks for coming to meet me on such short notice. As you know, the Gallo's have now attempted to kidnap my daughter three times in the past year or so and I and very tired of this and also very annoyed. I have a plan in mind, but it will require some killing and will be highly illegal in all respects. I control the law enforcement institutions on my side of the border in this area, and between Hank and Benito, you control the law enforcement institutions on your side of the border. This gives us some wiggle room to operate outside the law, but if things go sideways, make no mistake we will be branded as criminals, and we may cause an international incident. If you feel that you cannot take this risk, I fully understand and no hard feelings."

Benito looked at his watch, "I'm hungry Diego, could you please get on with the program and skip the political correctness bullshit?"

Everyone else voiced their agreement, so Diego got into the meat and potatoes of his plan.

"I know for a fact that the Sinaloa cartel to the west, and the Zeta's to the east of the disputed territory that I am allowed to control, are getting very fed up with the Gallos and their constant efforts to create a new boutique cartel to handle all the narcotics and human trafficking trade in the disputed territory and essentially drive a wedge between them. This is bad for business and upsets the agreements which have been in place successfully for many years now. The Zeta's and the Sinaloa cartel will not interfere with an attack on the Gallos and would probably welcome it.

"A week from this Saturday, four of the top Gallo lieutenants, for lack of a better term, will be meeting at one of their properties in Las Varas, about 10 miles due west of El Navegante on Highway 45, at 2:00 in the afternoon. There is a large house or villa about a mile east of the village of Las Varas proper, which is where the meeting is to take place. The compound which the villa sits in is roughly two acres and the house is a 3,000 square foot ranch house in the middle of the compound. The compound is surrounded by an 8-foot-high cinderblock wall covered in stucco. There is only one gate in the wall, on the front side facing the main road to Las Varas. There is a covered parking area in the front righthand corner of the compound, inside of the wall. Roughly 150 yards to the south of the villa, to its front, is a high rocky outcrop just across the main road and about 45 to 50 feet above the level of the villa. A perfect spot to place a shooter covering the front of the villa. There is high ground about 200 yards to the rear of the villa, which would make a nice place for a man with a rifle to cover the back.

"The issue is that I do not know how many bodyguards these men will bring with them. Since they are driving in from other points in the area, and they assume that they are secure in Las Varas, and that they are not in competition with each other or fear each other, I assume that they will each arrive in their own up-armored SUV with only a driver and a single bodyguard. This would be the normal routine. If this is the case, we can assume that there will be eight sicarios plus the four principals in the compound for the meeting.

"Since this is in my backyard, I cannot be seen to be involved with what I am hoping is a massacre, and I feel ashamed about this. What I can do is provide you with whatever you need in regards to arms, equipment, and explosives. I have quite a stockpile that I have taken from various gangs over the years."

Diego walked over to the desk and grabbed four A3 sized manila envelopes and handed them out, two to Grady as one was for Deacon. Inside were topographical maps of the area around the house as well as several photos of the area and the villa itself, obviously taken from a drone.

Hank voiced what the others were thinking, "Diego, we'll have three old guys plus Deacon assaulting a compound with about 12 hostiles in it. The odds are stacked against us from the get-go. We need the element of surprise and some sort of force multiplier if we are going to do this without getting ourselves killed."

"Another thing," interjected Benito. "Will there be any innocent civilians at the villa, cooks, maids and so forth?"

Diego thought about this for a moment before answering, "I don't know. I can have someone watching the villa the day of the meeting, but that will not give us the time to alter any plan we have, or the equipment required."

"Can we take them before they get to the villa?" asked Grady.

"Only if they are traveling in convoy. Since they are coming from different areas, I do not think that this will be the case," responded Diego.

After a few minutes while everyone gave the problem some thought, Grady said, "What we need is a 'roof knocker' to get everyone out of the house."

"What the heck is a 'roof knocker'?" Hank asked.

Grady explained. "Roof knocking is a tactic employed by the Israeli Defense Force. Essentially, they drop non-explosive or low-yield devices on the roofs of targeted civilian homes or buildings being used by the bad guys as a warning of imminent bombing or missile attacks to give the civilians inside a chance to get out. If we could hit the roof of the house with some 'shock & awe', those inside should run out and we could then pick and choose our targets."

They brainstormed the idea of a 'roof knocker', but for a long time nobody could think of a suitable munition to get the job done, then Diego had a eureka moment.

"We use a drone," declared Diego. Everyone looked at him like he was joking, which he wasn't.

"Don't you guys ever watch the news? The Houthis have been hitting the Saudis with drones carrying explosives for years and in Ukraine, the Russians and the Ukrainians have turned it into a sport."

"Tell us what you've got in mind," suggested Hank.

"Okay, we need to somehow get anyone who is in the villa out of it so we can see if there are any innocent civilians at this meeting. Since Grady and Deacon are our two trained shooters, I suggest that we put Deacon up on the high ground behind the house and place Grady in the rocky outcrop across the road in front of the house, assuming the old coot can hobble about 100 yards once we drop him off out of sight of the house. Hank, you and Benito will be with Grady as the heavy weapons section.

"I'll rig up a drone with two M84 flashbang grenades and be up on the hill behind the villa with Deacon. Once the cartel goons are in the house and comfortable, I'll fly the drone into the back door if it is open, or through one of the rear windows if it isn't. Once you hear them go off, and you will definitely be able to hear them, the game is on.

"I would expect that everyone in the house who is still capable of doing so will run outside due to what they will assume is explosives going off inside the house. When they do, it should be easy to determine who is a cartel prick, and who isn't. Hank and Benito will fire two RPGs into the vehicles parked in the corner of the compound to add to the confusion and will then assist Grady in plugging any of the sicarios still alive and kicking. Any questions?"

Now everybody was convinced that Diego was nuts.

"Okay, that's all well and good Diego, but I can see some logistical issues with your plan," Hank replied. "First, we'll need a drone, a drone pilot and a couple of M84 stun grenades. Second, we'll need some rocket-propelled grenades and launchers. I'm not sure about Benito, but I have never fired an RPG in my life," Hank submitted.

"Anybody can figure out how to fire an RPG in about five minutes, they were designed with brain dead Russian conscripts in mind. Grady and Deacon will run you through the basics before game time. You'll be shooting at parked cars, not main battle tanks. As for the drone and operator, I confiscated a few Phantom 4 Pros with all the accessories about a year ago from some Sinaloa cowboys who were drunk and fixing to load them up with pig shit and drop it on some of the Zetas who were partying with girls that they considered their own. I've been playing with them and am pretty sure I can pilot them well enough for what we need. As far as M84 flashbangs, everybody down in my part of Mexico has a few, they, like RPGs, are a dime a dozen in Mexico nowadays, and are almost considered to be a fashion accessory."

Grady jumped in at this point, "How many drones did you confiscate, and how many do you have left?"

"I originally had three, but two were lost in training accidents. That said, I've become fairly adept at flying these things, it's actually a lot of fun."

"How are you going to rig up a couple of flashbangs to a drone so that they don't go off before they are inside the villa?", this from Benito.

"I've studied this problem for the past year or so, in the event that I'd have to use this sort of delivery system in my line of work. The most eloquent solution is to first pull the primary and secondary safety pins out of the grenade, then while holding the spoon or safety lever tight, you then slide the grenade into a 12-ounce Mason jar. The jar diameter is perfect for keeping the spoon engaged while the drone is in flight. When the drone crashes, the glass Mason jar shatters which releases the spoon and after 1 to 2.3 seconds, the grenade will explode."

"Diego, I think you actually enjoy your work way too much for your own good, but getting back to business, Deacon and I are going to need two solid sniper rifles with decent optics on them. Granted, these won't be long shots, about 200 yards at most, but we'll need to be sure that we hit what we are aiming for. We'll need semi-automatics with 20 or 30 round magazines, and they need to be chambered in a round definitely capable of putting a man down with one shot. What do you have in your inventory?" Grady asked.

Diego thought about it for a minute. "I've got two PTR-91FR rifles in 7.62 x 51 NATO, which are German G3 knock-offs and two Knights Armaments SR-25's also in 7.62 x 51 NATO. I also have a few Nightforce NXS 2.5x10 variable magnification scopes still in the box. The scopes will mate to the Picatinny rails on either rifle."

"Deacon and I will take the SR-25's, anything designed by Eugene Stoner is good enough for us. I'll pick up some match grade hollow points before we head south, but we'll need to sight these rifles in before game time," said Grady.

"I thought you had to stay out of this, Diego. Now you've decided to become a kamikaze drone pilot," asked Hank.

"Since it was my daughter who was disrespected and kidnapped, I feel that it is my duty to participate and defend her honor."

"Bullshit," laughed Benito." You just want to bust some caps on the Gallo's. Furthermore, I'm surprised that your daughter hasn't been the cause of more gunfights and other forms of civil unrest, that girl is just too much of a hot tamale for her own good."

From here on, they worked on the logistics and timing of their raid. It was decided that Hank, Benito, Grady and Deacon would trickle into Mexico during the following week and make their way to a friend of Diego's ranch in the hills to the east of Flores Magón, a village roughly 65 miles south-southwest of Villa Ahumada and roughly 60 miles north-northwest of Las Vara, where the raid would take place. All the players would be at the ranch no later than Thursday.

After having a nice dinner at Jett's Grill in the hotel, they all went their separate ways with the promise to meet up in Mexico the following week.

CHAPTER 35

GRADY ARRIVED HOME LATE THAT Wednesday evening after Deacon had already called it a day, so it was not until the next morning at breakfast, before Deacon had to go to work, that Grady could give him the CliffsNotes version of what was about to take place in Mexico the following week. He suggested that Deacon come up with some excuse to be away from Fort Davis for about a week.

"Lorna, I'll need to take next week off to take care of some business out of the county. I'll need to leave Thursday morning and should be back no later than the following Thursday afternoon." Deacon petitioned his boss later that day.

Leaning back in her office chair, Lorna commented, "That doesn't give you much time between the sheets, Deputy Allison. Are you sure you don't need more time to get the job done?"

"Sheriff Stims, this has nothing to do with Ms. Navarro. If it did, I would likely require a month off; two weeks to satisfy the wench and then two weeks to recover."

"Am I allowed to ask what it is that you need time off for? We are still short-handed around here even though it is the quiet time of year."

"It is related to my military service and my days in uniform." Which wasn't actually a lie considering he would be putting that training into action.

Lorna gave the request some thought, then agreed to it as long as Deacon kept his phone on him at all times just in case she needed him back in a hurry.

She then enquired seriously as to how Deacon's romance was progressing with the aforementioned Ms. Navarro. Deacon told her that they talked most evenings on the phone and that they were still waiting on her green card to be approved before they made any plans.

"Deacon, advice is usually worth exactly what you paid for it, but let me give you my two cents worth. If you are serious about Esmeralda, and it appears that you are, you need to make a future somewhere else besides this dry and dusty desert. You've been a good deputy, and we've had some fun, but you really need to start looking at the horizon. I'd give you a glowing referral if you decide to pursue a career in law enforcement, but I wouldn't recommend that. It doesn't pay enough and it's hard on a marriage. Maybe you could try apprenticing a trade or starting your own business. Anyhow, just my thoughts on the matter.

Deacon thought about this for a moment, "That sounds odd coming from you, Lorna. You actually came here from somewhere else, and you seem to have made a career out of law enforcement."

"All true, Deacon. The difference is that I had to get out of the male dominated, macho law enforcement environment which was prevalent in Chicago. I would never have had a shot at the top job in Chicago as a white woman. The planets just seemed to align with this job coming open and the teaching position for Adrian at Sul Ross at about the same time.

"We were, and both you and Esmeralda still are, young enough to set up shop elsewhere. Just between you and I, Adrian and I plan to leave here in a year or so depending on what opportunities arise elsewhere. You should start looking around as well."

When Deacon went back out on patrol that afternoon, he gave a lot of thought to what Lorna had said. It was almost chapter and verse of the advice his father had given him. He'd need to put a plan together and have it ready when Esmeralda finally got her green card sorted out.

Tuesday was spent with Grady and Deacon pulling together everything that they would need for the upcoming fandango down in Mexico. A couple of pair of jeans, underwear, socks, comfortable hiking boots as opposed to their normal cowboy boots, and earth toned shirts and jackets went into an old Army duffle bag and an old Marine sea bag.They had considered taking along the two AK-47's that they had taken off the sicarios during the last attempt to kidnap Esmeralda from US soil, but figured they didn't want to take the risk of crossing the border at the Ojinaga with assault rifles. For the same reason, they didn't pack their own handguns as well. They were fairly certain that Diego would have a good selection to choose from when they arrived at the ranch. One item they did not want to leave to chance was the specific 7.62 x 51 NATO ammunition they preferred for the SR-25 rifles that Diego was going to loan them. Since Grady would be heading out on Wednesday, and Deacon on Thursday, it was decided that Deacon would stop by D&B Enterprises in Marfa while on his way to Mexico and pick up 200 rounds of Black Hills 175-grain match grade boat-tail hollow points. Any reasonable 7.62 x 51 ammo would probably have worked at the distances they would be shooting at, but better safe than sorry and those 175-grain hollow points would make a nice sized hole in any sicario unlucky enough to be hit by one.

Grady loaded up his sea bag early on Wednesday, and after shaking his son's hand, climbed into his old Dodge pickup and started to make his way down to the ranch outside of Flores Magón, Mexico.

Deacon secured the garage and pole barn so that critters couldn't get in while they were away, then made himself a dinner of beans and sausage before carrying it out on the porch. Going back inside he grabbed a beer out of the refrigerator and took his phone off the coffee table before going back out on the porch to eat his dinner and to call Esmeralda.

"Hello, querida. Do you miss me?" Deacon asked when she answered the phone.

"Don't 'sweetheart' me! When were you going to tell me about what you and that geriatric posse plan to do down in Las Vara this Saturday? Why wasn't I invited? It seems to me that I am the one who has been the target of the kidnappings and that I should be there to help put a stop to it," said a very annoyed Esmeralda.

"Don't get your knickers in a twist! I am not the one running this show, perhaps you should ask your father these questions."

"You think that I haven't? Papá will not tell me anything except that you, he, and a bunch of over the hill vigilantes are planning to shoot up a Gallos meeting in Las Varas this Saturday to put an end to the Gallos trying to kidnap me all the time."

"Well, now you know as much as I do. What does Diego want you to do while we are in Las Varas?"

"I am to accompany him to his friend's ranch and then stay there while you men get to go out and shoot Roosters."

"That sounds like a good idea, it'll keep you out of harm's way while the geriatric posse and myself shoot up the countryside."

"Stop being flippant with me! Since I am the subject of the kidnappings, I feel it is my right to join you guys in shooting up the Gallos," she exclaimed.

"You'll need to discuss this with Diego, this is a family thing, and I don't want to get in the middle of it. That said, what are you wearing at the moment, I need some verbal stimulation to get me through the evening."

"I think that is referred to as phone sex, gringo."

"That would depend entirely on how far you want to take it. I just asked concerning your present state of dress, or undress as the case may be."

Getting into the spirit of things, Esmeralda described her attire. "At the moment I am lying on the couch in nothing but a cut-off pair of jeans and an old black Jose Cuervo t-shirt. Is that turning you on?"

"That depends. How short are the cut-offs and is there anything on under them or the t-shirt?"

"I just checked and under the t-shirt is a white demi bra courtesy of Victoria's Secret in El Paso, and the jeans were cut off just below where my butt starts."

"That's all good and my motor is starting to turn over. Next question, what do you have on under those Daisy Dukes to keep from chaffing your naughty bits?"

"Well, to be honest, in an effort to save on water and laundry soap I went commando today," snickered Esmeralda.

"I'm starting to get a good mental image now. Last question, are you still so hot that I could fry bacon on your butt?"

"That goes without saying, Mr. Allison, but just think about all the cracks and crevices that tasty bacon grease would end up finding its way into. It would take a lot of effort to clean me up after that bacon was fried," submitted Esmeralda for consideration. Before Deacon could utter a suitable riposte, Esmeralda told him to sleep well, and she would see him at the ranch on Thursday before she laughed impishly and hung up.

Deacon was conjuring up all the ways that he could think of to clean the grease off of Esmeralda's backside and out of the other various cracks and crevices where it may have accumulated. He could think of many, but several earned places of honor in his imagination.

CHAPTER 36

DIEGO AND ESMERALDA WERE THE first of the vigilantes to show up at the little rancho about two and a half miles outside of the little agricultural town of Flores Magón. The man that owned the rancho was Frederico Álvarez, an old friend of Diego's who had retired from Diego's unit in the National Guard several years earlier.

Frederico, who went by Fred, had a daughter who had left home some years ago as a headstrong teenager. She had gotten involved with some of the lower level Sinaloan dickheads in Nuevo Casas Grandes, about 85 miles west of Villa Ahumada. The cartel lifestyle seemed more attractive and exciting than life in Villa Ahumada, or so she thought. Eventually she realized that she was just a plaything for the cartel boys, but they wouldn't allow her to return home. She finally managed to call Frederico on a friend's phone and told him that she wanted to come home, but the degenerate cartel wannabees in Nueva Casas Grandes wouldn't let her go.

Fred got in touch with Diego and let him know what was going on. Since Diego had sort of a truce with both the Sinaloans and the Zetas, he made a few phone calls before he and Fred hopped into a black Guarda Nacional 4-door Ford pickup and they took a run over to Nueva Casa Grande to pick up Isabella, Fred's daughter.

The men in the Sinaloa cartel that Diego had spoken to apologized to him and told him that Fred's daughter would be waiting for them at the Church of the Latter-Day Saints on Avenida Victoria between Calle Ahumada and Calle Alvaro Obregón, at 2:00 that afternoon. They even suggested that perhaps a lesson should be taught to the aspiring sicarios that had prevented Isabella from returning home, simply to avoid a similar situation from occurring in the future.

Diego and Fred pulled into the parking lot behind the church around 2:15 to find a new black Ford Raptor pickup and a fairly new silver Dodge Grand Caravan waiting on them. When they pulled into the parking lot, the side door of the Caravan opened and Isabella jumped out and ran to her father, who had stepped out of the Garda Nacional pickup. While he was scooping her up and making sure that she was okay, Diego walked over to the Caravan and politely asked who was the boss of the crew. A very subdued guy in his mid- 20's got out of the Raptor and approached Diego.

"Señor Navarro, I truly apologize for the behavior of my crew and I. I was told to bring Señor Álvarez's daughter to him here at two o'clock and that I was to accept whatever punishment that you and Señor Álvarez felt was necessary. I would be very happy if you would decide not to kill us."

"How should I refer to you, young man?"

"My name is Pedro, Señor."

"Okay, Pedro, this is what we will do. I want all of your boys lined up in front of your vehicles. I will then ask Fred's daughter to point out any one of your crew who may have taken certain liberties with her without her consent. Once this is done, Señor Álvarez and I will discuss a suitable punishment. Is this understood?"

Pedro motioned to the passenger in the Raptor and the three men in the Caravan to get out and line up in front of the vehicles. Two of the young men were noticeably hesitant to do so.

Fred and Isabella started walking slowly in front of the line of young men, like a general and his commander inspecting the troops. Isabella stopped in front of each of the men who were hesitant to get out of the van and said something to her father, who then told them to take one step forward.

At this point, Diego and Fred had a quiet discussion. While Diego went to the rear of the Garda Nacional truck and lowered the tailgate, Fred ushered the two men over behind the truck and told them to sit on the tailgate with their legs dangling over the edge. This put their knees right on the edge of the lowered tailgate, with their feet hanging towards the ground. Fred then explained to them that they had abused his daughter, had shamed her and her family, and that this could not go unpunished. He reached behind him and pulled out a little semi-automatic Ruger SR22 chambered in .22 long rifle and handed it to Isabella and told her to 'go ahead'.

Isabella initially went over and placed the muzzle directly against the front of the first man's right kneecap, which was toward the outside of the bed of the pickup as he sat on the driver's side of the tailgate, but Fred explained to her that it would do much more damage if she shot into the knee from the side. Fred had done some research on this 'kneecapping' form of punishment which had been perfected by the Irish during the 'Troubles' over there.

Isabella repositioned the little pistol so that it would shoot through the knee joint from the outside in and pulled the trigger. The man howled like he had been shot, which was understandable since he had been. The other man made an attempt to run, but Fred pushed him back onto the tailgate and told him to act like a man. Isabella then repeated her performance on him, except on his left or outboard knee, with exactly the same result. Handing the pistol back to her father, Isabella got into the back seat of the Garda Nacional truck while Diego motioned to the other two men, who were still standing slack jawed in front of their vehicles staring at their two compadres, who were presently rolling on the ground howling in pain, and told them that there were always consequences for poor decisions and that they needed to get their friends to the hospital as soon as possible. With a wave, Diego and Fred got back in their truck and began the long drive back to Villa Ahumada with Isabella.

CHAPTER 37

GRADY AND HANK SHOWED UP at the rancho the next day, which was Wednesday. Benito was the next to arrive on Thursday morning with Deacon showing up on Thursday afternoon.

While Deacon was driving down on Thursday, Hank, Diego, Benito and Grady spent the day going over both of the Knights Armament SR-25 semi-automatic sniper rifles and attaching the Nightforce scopes to the Picatinny rails on the weapons. Once that was finished, Grady gave Hank and Benito a crash course in how to load and operate an RPG-7 rocket propelled grenade launcher while Diego practiced flying his drone, which was now carrying two 12-ounce Mason jars filled with enough old bolts, nuts and washers to simulate the weight of an M84 stun grenade in each. Needless to say, the flying characteristics of the drone with that payload were much different than that of the unarmed version, so Diego needed the practice.

Once Deacon arrived on Thursday, after he and Esmeralda snuck off for some personal time, the crew went over the plan looking for anything that they may have missed. Once the sun started going down and the place cooled off a bit, Deacon and his father carried an old 4' x 8" piece of 3/8" plywood out exactly 100 yards from the back porch of Fred's place and braced it standing up on the 4' side. Deacon then stapled four Birchwood splatter targets with a 2" bullseye in the center of each quadrant of the plywood, two up and two down.

Walking back to the porch, they each selected an SR-25 rifle and loaded one magazine with the Black Hills 175-grain match grade ammo that Deacon had picked up in Marfa. Once they each had a full magazine, they slotted it into their respective rifles and got ready to sight them in.

Since they did not expect to be shooting much over 200 yards, if that, and they would not be exactly sure of the distance until they got there and used their recently purchased Bushnell Tour V5 golf rangefinders to get an exact distance measurement, it only made sense to sight in at 100 yards and then tape the ballistics table for their specific ammo to the stock of the rifles so that they could adjust for the drop at any range. Most ballistics tables use a 100 yard zero, so they were easy to find on the internet and print them out.

Deacon took the splatter targets on the left and Grady took those on the right. Since the rifles were new and neither of them knew where the scopes were dialed into, it took them both about five shots to get the rifles printing on paper. Printing is a misnomer for splatter targets since a hit showed up as a florescent green 'splatter' on these reactive targets. With a decent pair of binoculars, they didn't need to walk out to the targets to see where they were hitting. By the end of their first 20 round magazines, both Deacon and Grady were shooting 1 MOA or minute-of-angle, which translates into a 1" circle at 100 yards. They both felt that this was sufficient for the task at hand, so they laid down the rifles, walked out and retrieved the sheet of plywood before cleaning and lubricating the rifles and putting them away until they were needed.

Hank and Benito were not allowed to sight in their RPGs, since the detonations of the warheads would have carried into Flores Magón causing the inhabitants to ask questions, which may have ended up in the Gallo's ears.

After a fine dinner of fajitas prepared by Isabella and Esmeralda, the men decided to get a good night's sleep before the big day on Saturday. If Murphy showed up at the party, they'd need it.

Diego, Benito, Hank, Grady and Deacon were all up at 4:00 the next morning, each one was preparing their specific backpacks and equipment loadouts while getting mentally ready for what was about to take place. Since they would be staying in touch with their cell phones, they needed to make sure that the batteries were topped up along with the spare powerpacks they carried for each. They wanted to get into position before the sun came up and be in position long before the meeting at 2:00 in the afternoon.

It was almost exactly a 60-mile trip from Fred's place to Las Varas, about an hour and 20 minutes on the road. Fred drove Grady, Hank and Benito in his 4-door Dodge Ram 1500, while Deacon and Diego climbed into Deacon's old stepside and followed them down to the turnoff to Las Varas off Highway 45.

Fred's truck was known in Las Varas, so he would drive into the town supposedly looking for some surplus sheep fencing for his rancho. On the way, while it was still dark, he would momentarily stop just out of sight of the villa behind a low rise and drop off Grady, Hank and Benito along with their kit before continuing on into the village and having breakfast prior to shopping around for the surplus fencing. This would leave Grady, Benito and Hank with about a 250-yard hike to get to the outcropping where they would set up their little sniper's hide and prep the RPG-7's. With Grady's limp, they figured that they would be in place about 20 minutes after being dropped off.

The last time any of them had done something like this was decades ago when Grady, Benito and Hank had plugged the guys at the dirt airstrip at Los Lamentos who had kidnapped the eastern European and Brazilian women from Cabo San Lucas. Diego had been the one to organize the Los Lamentos party as well, so it seemed that history was about to repeat itself and this lent a bit of déjà vu to the outing.

The effective range of an RPG-7 rocket propelled grenade launcher is 330 meters or about 360 yards. The outcrop that Hank, Benito and Grady were now hiding behind was, as measured with their golfing rangefinders, exactly 128.9 yards to the front gate of the compound. It was exactly 149.1 yards to the front door of the villa and 146.8 yards to the center of the covered parking area inside the compound in the southeast corner. All were well within range of the RPG's being fielded by Hank and Benito.

Diego and Deacon followed the same road in toward Las Varas but they turned off the road and headed north through the scrubland about 3/4 of a mile before they got to the villa. They slowly made their way cross-country into a shallow valley which ran behind a ridge that sat between the valley and the villa. Hiding the truck behind a clump of scrub oaks, they grabbed their gear and made their way on foot to the far edge of the ridge which looked down into the compound roughly 60' below them.

The drone itself only weighed about three pounds, but the Pelican case that Diego had packed the drone in, along with the controller, Mason jars, grenades and other drone-related kit was unwieldy and difficult for him to pack to the top of the ridge. Deacon traded Diego his rifle for the case, with the admonition not to drop it, and carried the Pelican case to the site they had selected for their hide after studying the ridge on Google Earth. The hide just happened to be between the only two clumps of scrub oak trees growing on that edge of the ridge.

Both teams were in place before sunrise, and the waiting began. This would be the most difficult part of the entire operation. With the sun coming up, both teams would need to remain as still as possible until their guests arrived around 2:00 in the afternoon. Even with the patience borne of age, most of the players were getting antsy long before noon. Also, the average winter temperature of the Chihuahuan Desert south of the border is about 60 degrees Fahrenheit, which is cool but comfortable, but the desert is also arid, and the guys had to remember to stay hydrated so that their performance didn't suffer when it was game time. Each man had hauled two liters of water to his position with him.

Back at the outcrop, which provided good concealment, Hank and Benito had opened their duffle bags and attached the optical sights to their launchers before loading a HEAT (high explosive anti-tank) round. This done, they found a place on each side of Grady's position to fire from and checked their backblast areas.

While they were doing this, Grady had placed a small sandbag in a notch formed between two large rocks with a good line of sight to the villa. Resting the forend of the rifle on the sandbag, Grady removed the rocks, pebbles and twigs in the area behind the rifle before spreading out an old horse blanket to lay on when he went prone and got ready to shoot. After making sure that a full magazine was in the rifle and there was a round in the chamber, he flipped the safety on and just settled down to wait. Again, waiting was the hard part. The adrenaline rush would get them through the actual engagement.

CHAPTER 38

AT AROUND 1:00 IN THE AFTERNOON, a late model, dusty white Chevrolet Tahoe drove through the compound gates and stopped at the front door of the villa. The man in the passenger's seat got out and opened the rear door on his side so that one of the lieutenants could exit the vehicle. While the driver pulled the Tahoe under the covered parking in the southeast corner of the compound, the other two men walked directly into the house through the front door, which had magically opened when the Tahoe had come to a stop. The driver walked over from the parking area and into the villa once he had parked the Tahoe under cover.

15 minutes later, two late model Ford Expeditions drove through the gates together, one agate black the other stone blue, and parked undercover in the parking area before all six men, two drivers, two bodyguards and two lieutenants, got out and again walked up to and through the front door which opened just as they arrived at it. The final lieutenant and his crew showed up in a late model 4-door Dodge 1500 TRX 4-wheel-drive truck in monotone black. It was a sinister looking ride as it also pulled up to the front door to discharge its bodyguard and lieutenant before the driver pulled it into the parking area before he also went into the villa.

Grady had been watching this through a set of Zeiss 10 x 42 binoculars and had been updating Deacon by cell phone as the targets arrived. They decided to give it another 15 minutes just to double check that nobody else had been invited to the meeting before Diego would launch his kamikaze drone to kick things off. No further discussion was necessary as the flash bangs detonating would obviously get the party started.

While Deacon was talking to Grady, Diego was busy getting the drone out of the case and getting it ready to fly. Once that was finished, he carefully removed both the primary and secondary safety pins out of a M84 stun grenade and while carefully holding down the spoon as he eased it into a Mason jar. Once he had both grenades safely in their Mason jars, he got out a roll of duct tape and attached one to each skid of the drone and prepared for the opening act.

At 1:45 exactly, Diego lifted the drone off and guided it towards the house. The access point, the back door which accessed the kitchen had been closed all morning and Diego was planning to fly the drone through a large window to the left of the door, but just as the drone flew over the compound wall at the rear of the villa, the driver of the Dodge 1500 TRX opened the door to come out on the patio and have a smoke. Three things happened almost simultaneously at this point: the driver froze as he saw the drone coming straight at him just as he was lighting up, Deacon shot him in the chest and dropped him which opened up a path so that the drone could fly unobstructed through the door and into the villa, and Diego readjusted to flight path so that the drone flew straight through the door at speed.

The drone made it through the open plan kitchen and into the villa proper before crashing into the first wall it came in contact with. The Mason jars shattered either then or when they hit the floor, and somewhere between 1 and 2.3 seconds later both M84 stun grenades exploded with thunderous 170 to 180 decibel bangs and blinding flashes. As luck would have it, when the drone hit the wall, it ricocheted into the living room at the front of the house where the lieutenants and their men, minus the now dead driver on the back patio, had congregated for drinks before it crashed to the floor shattering the Mason jars. They took the full effect of two stun grenades going off in an enclosed space.

The guy who had been acting as a doorman and the three ladies from Las Varas who had been preparing lunch were in the kitchen when the grenades went off. After recovering from their initial shock of seeing the driver who had gone out for a smoke getting smoked, the drone flying in the back door and the subsequent bangs and flashes in the living room, they all ran out the back door. Deacon called this in to Grady.

The front gate had been shut and secured after the last lieutenant had arrived, which meant that there was no way for any innocent people in the house to get out of the compound.

"Hank, hit the gates now!" instructed Grady.

Hank shouldered his RPG, stood up to clear the boulders in front of him and sighted in on the latch at the center of the gates and pulled the trigger. RPG launches create a tremendous back blast that would be deadly to anyone standing behind the shooter, it also kicks up a bunch of dust that would give away your position, if you were worried about that sort of thing. Hank, Benito and Grady couldn't have cared less.

After the initial 33' boost phase, where the rocket is propelled out of the launcher by a gunpowder booster charge before the rocket motor ignites, the rocket took just over a second to travel the remaining distance and blew both gates off their hinges and back into the compound toward the villa.

The rocket had impacted just as the innocent doorman and kitchen staff were turning the corner at the lefthand rear corner of the villa. When they reached the front corner of the house, they jerked to a stop at the sight of most of two gates laying between the villa and where they were supposed to be hung on the walls, but their flight response kicked in again and they went running out the open gate and hooked a right toward Las Varas.

At this point, and considering the dead guy on the back patio, there were still at least 11 men in the villa: four lieutenants, four bodyguards and the three remaining drivers plus any staff remaining after the four had left the grounds through the destroyed gate.

In an attempt to flush them out, Benito launched his RPG into the covered parking area, which blew the Tahoe to bits and set the other three vehicles on fire, but nobody else came out of the house. It was time to turn up the heat, literally. Grady asked Hank to fire his remaining RPG round into the tiled roof while Benito was tasked with taking out the 500-gallon propane tank situated up against the righthand side of the villa. They fired simultaneously and the result was spectacular. A 10' hole was blown in the roof, which must have been deafening to those inside, and caused a landslide of roof tiles into the house. When Benito's round hit the propane tank, the combined explosion of the warhead and whatever propane was in the tank blew the whole eastern facing wall of the villa inward and collapsed about a quarter of the roof. It also set that whole eastern half of the villa on fire, and it began burning fiercely.

At this point, the rats decided to leave their sinking ship with five men running out the back of the house to escape over the wall, which just happened to also be directly at Deacon, while the other six men ran out the front door toward the destroyed gate, directly toward Grady. For trained marksmen, even those who might have been a bit rusty, it was a turkey-shoot. Grady was not ready for the mass exodus and missed his first shot, but hit six out of six with his next six shots, all center of mass hits which dropped them in mid-stride. It is a Hollywood generated myth that people get blown off of their feet or fly through the air when hit by a rifle bullet, the application of basic physics would show that this is not possible. What actually occurs is that they just drop like a marionette whose strings have been cut. This being the case, there was a line of six dead Gallo's from the front door of the villa almost to the ruined gate. Being a Marine, Grady figured if a cartel asshole was worth shooting once, he was worth shooting twice, so he put a second 7.62 x 51 round into the head of each Gallo. They were much easier to shoot when they were laying on the ground and not moving.

Back at the rear of the villa, a similar scenario was unfolding as the five cartel flunkies ran out the back door on a straight line to the wall. Deacon, unlike Grady, had anticipated their rapid departure and dropped the whole lot before they even made it off the patio. Like Grady, Deacon felt that each lieutenant, driver and bodyguard deserved to be shot twice, likely due to the fact that it was his romantic interest they kept trying to kidnap, so he put another round into each as well. It was better to be safe than sorry concerning cartel perras, dogs in Spanish. You didn't want them coming after you later.

Deacon called Grady on his cellphone, and they did their sums and decided that they had killed everyone they had set out to kill and that it was time to go home. They made the decision to leave the weapons as a red herring since Diego had acquired them after battles with various cartels in the past. If they were traced, it would cause some confusion and maybe even some infighting among the various cartels, which would be a bonus. While Diego and Deacon were packing up the drone controller and the rest of the equipment they had brought with them, Grady called Fred, who was having a late lunch at the cantina in Las Varas, and asked him if it would be too much trouble for him to finish his lunch and come collect Hank, Benito and himself at the road in front of the villa before other Gallos decided to show up and see what all the noise was about. Fred said he'd be there shortly, after he had finished his cerveza.

Diego and Deacon made it back to where they had hidden Deacon's truck behind the clump of scrub oaks, and slowly made their way cross country back to the road from Highway 45 to Las Vara before driving as quickly as possible to get out of the area and back to Fred's place.

Fred finished his beer and drove casually out of Las Varas until he was opposite the nicely burning villa and stopped momentarily while Grady, Hank and Benito came out of the scrub oaks beside the road and jumped into the truck. Fred told them that they had made an impressive mess of the Gallo's villa before putting his truck into gear and following the same route that Diego and Deacon taken about 15 minutes previously and headed back to his rancho.

CHAPTER 39

ONCE BACK AT FRED'S PLACE the crew quickly packed up any and all of their personal belongings and headed back to their points of origin as quickly as possible. They needed to get out of the vicinity of the hit while confusion reigned and the Gallos tried to figure out what had actually happened and why.

Grady climbed into his old Dodge pickup and headed back to his place. Since he did not want to take the same way out that he took in, he went north out of Flores Magón on Highway 19 to Villa Ahumada, then north again on Highway 45 to Ciudad Juárez/El Paso where he crossed the border at the Bridge of the Americas. Getting on I-10 East, Grady drove for four hours, passed through Van Horn then took a right on County Road 118 which led him to his driveway and home.

Diego was driving an old, non-descript, white 1980 Ford pickup and he and Esmeralda just took the most direct route back to Villa Ahumada, which was identical to the first leg of Grady's trip home; Highway 19 north to Villa Ahumada.

Benito drove off in an old, originally red, but now faded to an ugly shade of orange, Isuzu Trooper. He took the southern route on Highway 10 to Chihuahua then northeast on Highway 16 to the official border crossing at Ojinaga before getting on US Highway 67 for a straight shot back to Marfa.

Hank followed Benito 30 minutes later. At Marfa, he took a right on Highway 90 for the 30-minute run to Alpine and home.

Deacon was the last to leave, but before he did, he got a call from Diego asking him to take a detour on the way home and to stop by his house in Villa Ahumada. Deacon had planned to follow Hank and Benito to avoid taking the same way out as he had taken in. Since this had the fringe benefit of touching base with Esmeralda before heading home, he gladly agreed to this.

When Deacon parked his old Chevy stepside on Calle Jiménez in front of Diego's house, Diego was waiting on the veranda with a beer, but there was no sign of Esmeralda.

"Where's Esmeralda?" Deacon asked.

"She'll be out here shortly, she busy packing at the moment."

"Packing for where?"

"She'll be going with you today. I think it would be wise for her to get out of town for a while until we see how the Gallo's respond to our little stunt today," Diego continued. "Deacon, the Gallos are a cartel, and while their members may not be the sharpest knives in the drawer, they aren't stupid either. At some point they'll figure out that prior to the attack on their villa today, the last act of violence in the region was when they tried to kidnap my daughter for the third time and one of them got shot dead in the process. They'll make the connection, but there is no proof. The weapons left at the scene belonged to other cartels, and I will have what they call 'plausible deniability'. As I mentioned earlier, they may ignore this deniability and try for Esmeralda again. I would feel better if she was across the border in your capable hands, in a manner of speaking."

"I won't say that this makes me unhappy, and it will save me the long drive to see her, but what about her green card? I thought this was the hold up on her coming north."

Diego laughed, "I was just pulling your chain, Deacon. I wanted her here with me for a while since she had been up with you guys for a few months after the first attempts to kidnap her had failed. Do you really think that I have any problem getting green cards?"

Deacon thought about this for a moment before asking, "What about you, Diego? You're getting a bit long in the tooth to be playing these silly games with the Gallos."

"I'll be retiring shortly. The way the game is played, once someone retires from either the National Guard or the cartel, they are allowed to go in peace. I will definitely get out of this dusty, forsaken town and find a better location to retire in, but that is a decision for later."

About half an hour later, Esmeralda came out of the house with three cervezas. Giving one to Diego, she sat on Deacon's lap and gave one to him while keeping one for herself.

"So, what are you boys discussing out here?" asked Esmeralda as she sipped her beer.

Before answering, Deacon took a swig of beer while looking directly into the eyes of Esmeralda with a lecherous grin, "Apparently Diego is placing you in my 'capable hands' for the foreseeable future. Do you think you are ready for that?"

Without missing a beat or breaking eye contact with Deacon, she replied, "I suppose that would depend entirely on how capable your hands really are."

"I have Roman hands and Russian fingers, I'll let you figure that one out. You have been warned."

Getting into the swing of the conversation, Esmeralda suggested that Deacon may be a typical Texan, all hat and no cattle, but she would be willing to give him the benefit of the doubt.

At this point, Diego cleared his throat just to let them know that he was listening to their verbal foreplay, then suggested that they should get on the road and out of Mexico. He would see them up at Grady's place soon, but they really needed to get on the road.

Deacon threw a pair of fairly large, fairly beat-up suitcases into the bed of his old Chevy stepside, followed by an old black Guarda Nacional duffle bag and a fairly new backpack. It looked like Esmeralda was planning to hang out with the Allison's for a while again.

Esmeralda gave her papá a big hug and a kiss before she climbed into

Deacon's truck. Deacon shook hands with Diego and said they'd see him soon. After Deacon was in the truck with Esmeralda, Diego asked Deacon to take good care of his daughter and asked him to have Grady give him a call in the next week or so.

Deacon said he would do that before he started his truck drove off. He and Esmeralda waved to Diego as they got back on Highway 450, Highway 45 becomes 450 south of Villa Ahumada, and drove to the city of Chihuahua. Before entering Chihuahua proper, 450 swings to the east just north of the city and intersects Highway 16 at the town of El Apache. While Esmeralda was snuggled up against him on the bench seat, Deacon took a left on Highway 16 and headed northeast toward Coyame and eventually the official border crossing at Ojinaga. Crossing the border without incident, they took US Highway 67 towards Marfa where they took Highway 17 north out of town to Fort Davis. Just north of Fort Davis they hung a left onto County Road 118 and followed it generally north and west until they came to turn-off for Madera Canyon Road, which took them to Grady's driveway.

When they pulled up to the porch around 9:00 that evening, Grady came out to give Esmeralda a big hug and to help Deacon carry her luggage into the house, and then into her old room. Afterwards, Deacon put his gear in his room before going into the kitchen where Grady had thoughtfully prepared a late dinner of 'make your own tacos', which is that he had soft corn taco shells warming in the oven and had browned some seasoned ground beef in a skillet. The chopped-up onions, tomatoes, cilantro, lettuce, salsa and shredded cheddar cheese were out on the kitchen counter. The diner then just made as many tacos as they felt were required, to their own specifications before joining the other diners at the kitchen table where beer or iced tea was available to wash down the tacos.

While they were having their late dinner, Deacon told Grady that Diego wanted him to call him during the week before they rehashed the one sided 'Battle of Las Varas' for Esmeralda's benefit.

Grady said he'd had a long day and bid the kids a good night. Esmeralda decided to shower up while Deacon cleaned up the kitchen.

Deacon retired to his room to unload his gear and pile up his dirty laundry to be washed the next day. When Esmeralda was finished in their shared bathroom, she knocked on the connecting door to Deacon's room and let him know that the bathroom was free. Why she didn't just open the door to tell him and let him gaze her near nakedness sort of annoyed him, but it had been a long day, and she was probably just looking forward to getting some sleep.

Deacon brushed his teeth before showering up, then turned off his light and got into bed. A few moments later the connecting door from the bathroom opened up and there stood Esmeralda in what appeared to be the old, now out-of-fashion but still sexy Victoria's Secrets panties and a cropped white t-shirt. She was a sultry vision that was backlit by the nightlight plugged in beside the sink.

"Okay, cowboy, don't get too comfortable just yet. I demand to experience those capable hands with the roaming hands and rushing fingers that you mentioned earlier. You will be graded later for imagination, technique and stamina," explained Esmeralda as she got on her knees at the foot of Deacon's bed and began to slowly crawl up the mattress toward him with an expression on her face similar to what you would generally expect to see on a mountain lion approaching a wounded, helpless deer. Deacon never stood a chance.

CHAPTER 40

THE NEXT FEW WEEKS WENT by quickly. Since Esmeralda now had a green card and Chuck had decided to retire, Lorna quickly hired her as the new receptionist at the Sheriff's office. This may have had something to do with her affirmative action quota, but more than likely it had to do with getting the latest gossip on her youngest deputy as well as interrogating her regarding the goings on out at Grady's ranch, the sudden disappearance of Mateo Molina, and the unconfirmed reports of a rifle and RPG battle that took place in her father's backyard down in Mexico. Esmeralda could gossip with the best, but she pled ignorance concerning Mateo and the battle south of Villa Ahumada. Esmeralda may have been a 'hot tamale' as Benito had once described her, but she had the brains to match her beauty and never divulged anything to Lorna which may have caused problems for her 'partners in crime'.

Tito, John and Armando, the other deputies in Lorna's band of misfits could not understand how a washed-out Army sergeant who lived with his father could have ever scored someone as sexy and entertaining as Esmeralda. They chalked it up to poor eyesight on Esmeralda's part and the overall lack of other suitable suitors in the area. They eventually accepted her as either Lorna's office spy or the office clown, depending on the situation and circumstances.

Macy and Esmeralda bonded well, and Macy eventually convinced

Esmeralda to go back to the partially shaved Rhianna hairstyle which she had worn to the rodeo and dance. Deacon was all for this as it really made Esmeralda stand out in a crowd, it was incredibly sexy in his opinion, and it just showcased the rest of the package.

Since Esmeralda had already spent a few months at Grady's place while she convalesced after getting tossed out of the van, her, Grady and Deacon settled in without any problems although Grady thought that there were some odd noises emanating from either Deacon's or Esmeralda's room late at night and the kids did not seem to be getting the seven or more hours sleep each night as recommended by the Mayo clinic.

About a month after the massacre at Las Varas, Deacon and Esmeralda returned home after work to find an old Ford pickup with the bed loaded down with cardboard boxes, duffle bags and the like parked in front of the porch, with Diego and Grady sitting on the porch sharing what looked like a bottle of Jack Daniel's Tennessee Honey whiskey, which appeared to be about half empty when they walked up on the porch.

Esmeralda ran over and hugged her slightly inebriated father tightly before she asked him what the occasion was.

"I have decided to retire, and I have decided to hang out with Grady while doing so. Once you kids are gone there will be plenty of room and Grady and I have a lot of catching up to do," informed Diego.

"What about a green card? You will have a difficult time this side of the border without one," queried Esmeralda.

"In my old line of work, getting green cards was easy. I got one for myself when I put in an order for yours with an old friend of mine. I'll have my pension from the Garda Nacional, and I'll find work up here once I get bored."

"Sounds like a plan," said Esmeralda, "but until 'you kids' hit the road' things may be a little cramped here. Deacon and I haven't really made any plans just yet."

Diego and Grady laughed. "Unless we are missing something," offered Grady indicating himself and Diego, "the sleeping arrangements seem to have recently been revised leaving Deacon's room spare most of the time. Diego can stay in Deacon's old room."

Esmeralda and Deacon were both suitably embarrassed at the revelation that their late-night romantic interludes had not gone unnoticed by Grady, but now that it was out in the open, they could quit sneaking around late at night. The shared bathroom would be an issue, but they could work around it.

"Concerning your plans, we'd have to wait until the next ice age for you two to come up with a reasonable plan for your future, but that is what fathers are for. Grady has an old acquaintance from his Marine Corp days up in San Angelo who has a thriving heavy equipment rental operation. He wants to take it easy now, he's as old as we are, and wants to hand the reins over to someone reliable, which is where Deacon comes in," explained Diego.

Deacon thought about this for a moment before asking, "What about family? Doesn't he have any family that could and should take over? This could cause some friction with an outsider just walking in and taking over."

"First, his wife passed a few years ago and his son and daughter want nothing to do with a heavy equipment rental operation, so this will not be an issue. Second, you would not be taking over, Scott will retain ownership and control of the business, but he needs someone to handle the business on a day-to-day basis, both with the rentals and equipment maintenance. Think you can handle that?" asked Grady while cocking an eye at Deacon.

"I'm no heavy equipment mechanic, but I'm sure I could pick it up quickly especially if the present crew stays on to show me the ropes. This Scott guy could probably get me up to speed on the business aspects. I think I could make it happen."

"Good, that's settled then. I feel assured that you will now have a real job and can support my daughter if she ever agrees to marry your mangy gringo butt."

"Not so fast, Señor Navarro. If we do go to San Angelo, we'd need to find an apartment and get started up there, which will take seed money that I don't have at the moment."

"Again, this is why you have fathers who can foresee these issues and resolve them ahead of time. If you would go to my truck, there is an old khaki colored duffle bag in the back near the tailgate. Could you grab it and bring it up here onto the porch?" asked Diego.

Deacon looked at Esmeralda, who just shrugged before he went out to Diego's old Ford pickup, found the specified duffle bag and carried it to the porch and dropped it in front of Diego.

"Unzip it and open it up," instructed Diego.

"What the...." said a startled Deacon with an equally startled Esmeralda looking over his shoulder.

"What you see is the ill-gotten gains of a group who used to run fentanyl over the border. They no longer needed it, so I thought I'd keep it for a rainy day."

The old duffle bag was filled to the brim with banded bundles of $20, $50 and $100 dollar bills.

"How much is in here?" asked Esmeralda.

"I've used some of it over the years, but at last count there was $497, 400 in there. That should get you started up nicely," suggested Diego.

Grady took over the narrative. "The job will pay you a salary equivalent to $100,000 per year for the first three months, which is the probation period that Scott, Diego and I decided on. After that, you'd be on the payroll for $195,000 a year."

"Any idea what it costs to rent an apartment in San Angelo?" Deacon was trying to get his head around the whole 'pack up and move' thing.

"I will not have my only daughter living in an apartment. Have you no sense of decency! To that end, when I relieved the aforementioned miscreants of their ill-gotten gains, I also found a deed to a house in what turns out to be a fairly nice neighborhood in San Angelo. I believe this was what they used as a 'counting house', a place to count their money, but I didn't see where they would be needing it any further either, so I had the same gentleman who makes my green cards prepare the necessary documentation indicating that the house been sold to a certain Esmeralda Navarro. The house is hers as long as she agrees to take over the mortgage. If you misbehave in any way you may find yourself out on the street. You'll need to take over the mortgage, but there are only a few years left on it so you should be okay."

"I've visited the house on several occasions, and it is a nice 2,300 square-foot ranch-style house with an attached garage. In my opinion it is suitable for starting a family. It has been rented out and well taken care of up until last month."

Deacon looked at Esmeralda and then back to Grady and Diego, "We don't know what to say. Thank you both very, very much."

"Don't thank us too much, we're both feeling the effects of Jack Daniel's Tennessee Honey firewater and need some dinner. Between the two of you, I'd think you'd be able to rustle us up some grub," suggested Grady.

As the kids went into the kitchen to prepare dinner and discuss their new windfall and plans, Grady poured Diego and himself another shot of Tennessee Honey before they grinned at each other, touched glasses and downed their shots. Grady commented that he loved it when a plan came together.

During a dinner of beef fajitas, Esmeralda asked when they needed to be in San Angelo. Without looking up from his meal, Grady informed her that Deacon needed to be at work a week from the following Monday at 0800 hours if he wanted the job.

CHAPTER 41

DEACON SPENT THE NEXT DAY convincing Lorna to let him resign from the Fort Davis Sheriff's Office immediately. His contract had a 30-day notice period, but when he explained that Grady had organized the job working heavy equipment with a friend of his in San Angelo, that he needed to be at work the following Monday at 0800 hours if he wanted the job, and that he needed to get Esmeralda settled in the house they were considering purchasing before he started working with the heavy equipment outfit, she relented. She had questions as to how this opportunity and a house had magically fallen into Deacon's lap, but when Diego was involved, she knew better than to ask too many questions.

Esmeralda had called the bank and agreed to take over the mortgage on the house if they would meet her there with keys on Saturday afternoon. Their final Friday at Grady's house was spent loading everything that they thought they would need to get started in their new life into Deacon's Chevy stepside, while Diego and Grady prepared their last supper.

After dinner and a few beers out on the porch, the kids bid the old crew good night and retired to Esmeralda's room for a good night's sleep before heading up to San Angelo early the following morning. Deacon was in bed waiting for Esmeralda to finish up in the bathroom and to join him, as she came out of the bathroom in her old sage colored night shirt, Deacon asked in all seriousness if she had remembered to pack her Victoria's Secret, La Perla, and Fleur of England lingerie.

"Those collections are safely stowed away in your truck," she said as she pulled up the bottom of her nightshirt to expose her nether regions, "but this has left me with only this old pair of Jockey No Panty Line lace bikini panties for the evening."

Taking a long look at the previously mentioned nether regions, Deacon replied, "I think those will do just fine for the next three to five minutes, after that they will be 'superfluous to requirements' as the British say."

The next morning, after breakfast and saying their goodbyes with a promise to call their fathers when they arrived in San Angelo and got settled in the house, Esmeralda and Deacon climbed into his truck and got on the road before the sun came up.

They arrived at the address given to them for the house, and they both had to just stop and stare. The ranch house sat on a large corner lot in an established suburban community just over a mile from Lake Nasworthy. The house was freshly painted, and the lawn was healthy and mown. The realtor who had been taking care of the property had parked her new Lexus at the curb and was waiting for them to pull into the driveway so that she could show them the house and pass them the keys and a 'Welcome to the Community' information package.

After a walk through the house, Lidia, the realtor, passed them the ring of keys to the property and waved as she drove off. Esmeralda and Deacon were still in a bit of shock and were acting like kids at Christmas. The house had come fully furnished so there was no need to rush out immediately to furnish it, but at the moment they needed to unload Deacon's truck and then find the nearest grocery store so that they could stock the cupboards and refrigerator with a few days' worth of supplies.

After getting the truck unloaded, they found a Safeway and loaded up with what they needed. On the way home they passed a Domino's Pizza and decided a pizza would go down well for their first evening in their new house. They took a drive past San Angelo Heavy Equipment Rental just off Highway

287 south of town just to make sure they knew where it was located, and since they only had one vehicle at the moment, that Esmeralda knew where to drop off Deacon on Monday morning and collect him in the evening. Esmeralda would need the truck while Deacon was at work to continue making their new house a home and setting up a few bank accounts so they could start laundering the cash from the duffle bag Diego had given them.

That evening, after their first dinner of pizza and beer in their new place, Esmeralda asked, "What's next?" A dangerous question to ask someone like Deacon with an over-active libido.

Standing up from the dining table, Deacon went into the bedroom without saying a word, which seemed odd and caused Esmeralda some concern. Deacon came back out to the kitchen with a sock shoved in each front pocket of his Levis so that they hung down beside his thighs.

"There is an old Indian ritual for braking in a new home. Have you ever kissed a rabbit between the ears?" Deacon asked with a straight face.

"No, I can't say that I have, but I'm willing to give it a shot if it could possibly lead to what is commonly referred to as the 'rabbit habit', which I think is a much more appropriate custom for breaking in a new house."

"You are wise beyond your years, please come with me," instructed Deacon as he headed back towards the master bedroom.

Esmeralda was laughing now. "Only if you take those ridiculous socks out of your pockets."

Without missing a beat, Deacon ripped the socks out of his pockets and threw them back over his shoulder at Esmeralda while he kept moving toward the bedroom.

During the next week, they finally got their new house sorted out, Deacon got comfortable in his new job, they started laundering their cash money, and Esmeralda purchased a new Toyota GT Supra so that she could get to her new job at the Shannon Medical Center in downtown San Angelo.

All in all, Esmeralda and Deacon had come a long way since they had become acquainted on the side of that dusty road in the Chihuahuan Desert southwest of Fort Davis.

CHAPTER 42

GRADY PUT DIEGO TO WORK almost as soon as the kids were on their way. Retirement, as most retirees will tell you, sucks. They go from doing something which they consider valuable every day, to doing nothing. Granted, it's fun for a week or so, but after that they feel that they are simply existing.

The Wassermann ranch that Grady's wife Mary had inherited when her parent's had passed away, and which Grady had inherited when Mary had passed away, encompassed over 47,000 acres or about 74 square miles of rough hilly terrain north of Mount Livermore and west of the Davis Mountains State Park. Most of the ranch was inaccessible by road, so it was necessary to have several line camps around the ranch to keep an eye on things, which meant Grady had to hire cowboys or vaqueros to man the camps.

Before Esmeralda had come along causing all the problems with the Gallo's and necessitating the attention of Diego, Deacon and others, Grady would hook up a horse trailer and load up his favorite grulla mare and drive out to the Davis Mountains Preserve, just off County Road 118, where he would unload his mare and ride to each of the line camps, of which there were seven, and hang out with the boys for a few days to inspect the range, check on the cattle and get a shopping list from the guys for items they needed. The day after Diego arrived, Grady loaded up two horses and took

Diego along to show him the ropes since they would be sharing the duty from here on out.

This went on for a month or so. One day they had gone out together to the Preserve to deliver supplies to the cowboys and were on their way home about dusk. To get to the Davis Mountain Preserve from Grady's place, you had to go down his driveway which intersected Madera Canyon Road, then take the canyon road north to County Road 118. Coming back the other way, just short of the entrance to his driveway, Grady pulled off the road and took out his phone to study something.

"What are you stopping for? I'm so hungry that my belly is bumping my backbone," Diego asked.

"Well, if you were actually a decent ex-inspector of the Garda Nacional, you would have noticed that there is another set of tracks on top of the tracks we left coming out of here this morning. Since you have no friends on this side of the border except myself and I am not expecting anyone this evening, I find this odd."

"So, let's go up and see who it is."

"With our recent history, I'd kind of like to know who I am rolling up on," explained Grady as he took out his phone and opened an app.

"What are you doing, gringo?"

"You remember those trail cameras we set up here before the Gallo's tried to kidnap Esmeralda the second time? The time she shot that one guy in the face? Well, I've never taken them down and I keep the batteries fresh. Let's see who's waiting for us."

With that, Grady started scrolling through the shots from each camera until he came to a clear shot of an old red 1970 Dodge 4-door Power Wagon just as it came into the courtyard between the garage and the house.

"You know any of these guys?" asked Grady showing the screen to Diego.

"I don't know the guys in the back, and I can't see the driver from this angle, but that guy in the passenger's seat looks very much like Augustine Chacón, but it looks like something has happened to his face."

"Forgive me Diego for not knowing every Mexican on the planet, but who the heck is Augustine Chacón, and why would he be visiting us?"

"Augustine Chacón, a.k.a. 'The Bulldog' is the jefe, the head honcho, of the Gallo cartel. I think it is fair to say that this is not a friendly visit and that he probably wants to kill us simply because we have been killing so many of his people over the past few months. I really do not think we should go up there without some guns. You don't happen to have any, do you?"

"Funny you should ask," said Grady as they got out of the truck and walked around to the toolbox mounted behind the cab. "You remember when Esmeralda and I shot those two pendejos in the garage and Deacon shot the two with AK-47's? Well, I just couldn't bear to get rid of their AK's, so I cleaned them, lubed them, and wrapped them in some old blankets before I put them and their magazines in the toolbox here for a rainy day."

"Kind of dumb, if you ask me. How would you explain two fully automatic AK-47's to the State Patrol if you had gotten pulled over."

"I'd have thought of something, now do you want one of these or not?" Grady asked Diego.

Diego decided that he would like to have an AK, so after they slotted a full magazine into their respective rifles, they got back in the truck and drove slowly along the driveway until they were about a quarter of a mile from the house. Shutting the truck off, they got out and put a couple of spare mags in their back pockets before jacking a round into the chamber of their AK's and started walking through the brush toward the house.

About 100 yards from the house itself, Grady browsed through the trail camera footage again. It seemed that things had changed since one of the bad guys had tripped the camera again. Now, one man with his own cuerno de chivo, which translates to 'horn of the goat', the cartelized slang for an AK-47, was hiding behind some old barrels on the front left corner of the garage when viewed from the house and another, similarly armed, was at the front right corner behind an old engine block. Augustine and another man, apparently only armed with pistols, were sitting on the pair of old ratty couches on the porch as if waiting for someone. Diego and Grady swiftly made a plan, and the old warriors set off into the coming night to execute it.

Augustine and his single surviving lieutenant were on the porch reminiscing about the old days when the signature sound of AK rifles sounded across the courtyard on either side of the garage. Grady and Diego had crawled up to within 30 feet of the sicarios at the front corners of the garage and drilled them with two rounds apiece from their AK-47's. They never even twitched as they died.

At this point Diego stood up and walked around the back end of the old Power Wagon. Augustine and his buddy had stood up as their associates were being gunned down, and had pulled their pistols and now had them aimed at Diego. This was according to plan as Grady wanted their attention on Diego as he came around his corner of the garage and carefully aimed at the lieutenant before he put a 7.62 x 39 AK round sideways through his chest from right to left as he was turning toward Diego. Granted, Grady could have switched the selector from single shot to rock and roll and killed them both, but Diego said he wanted to chat with Augustine for a minute before he killed him, and Grady didn't really want to shoot up his own house in any case.

At this point, Augustine wisely dropped the huge Smith and Wesson Model 29 in .44 magnum that he had been holding as Diego advanced on him with his AK-47 at his shoulder aimed directly at Augustine's center of mass. When the Smith and Wesson hit the porch planking, Diego lowered his weapon and waited for Grady to join him in front of the porch. When he arrived, they both walked up on the porch, kicked the .44 magnum off the edge and faced Augustine.

"What happened to you Bulldog? You look like you've been boiled in oil?" Diego asked.

"When you hit a cartel counsel gathering, you should actually go through the house and make sure everyone is dead. I lived, but you can see how close I came to burning to death in that villa."

"I will neither admit nor deny that I had anything to do with that hit. That said, I never saw you arrive, so after a head count, we decided to get away while the getting was good. When did you arrive?"

"I came the day before since I was already in the area."

"Okay, that explains it. If it makes you feel any better, we'd have come in and killed you too if we had known you were inside. We wouldn't want you to feel left out."

"You did all of what you did simply because of your daughter? Is she actually worth the trouble that you brought on yourself and will bring on yourself after you kill me?" asked Augustine.

"If you have to ask that question, then your soul has already rotted away. You, being Hispanic, should know that family is sacrosanct. To target a man's family is inexcusable, to do it repeatedly is unforgivable. As you sow, so shall you reap.

"Excuse me Diego, but I really don't think that you need to explain the error of his ways to this cartel piece of trash. Let's just get on with the show"

"Patience, Grady, what I am trying to explain to this pendejo is that as a Mexican man, he should have understood that when he tried to kidnap my daughter, not once, but three times, family honor would demand that I retaliate with the force of a whirlwind, the fury of a dust devil, and bury him in the sand."

At this point, Augustine became a little brave and suggested to Diego that if he killed him, the rest of the Gallo's would continue to hunt down his daughter and if she was lucky, she would just be given to them as a plaything and maybe they would not kill her when they were finished with her.

"Is that right?" said Diego as he reached into his jacket pocket for his phone, his back pockets still held an AK-47 magazine each. Handing his weapon to Grady, Diego dialed a number and once the phone on the other end had been picked up, he explained the situation to the person on the other end of the connection before he put the phone in speaker mode and laid it on the porch handrail so that Augustine and Grady could hear the person on the other end.

"Señor Chacón, do you recognize my voice?"

"Si, it is Señor Menéndez, correct?" asked a suddenly very attentive Bulldog.

"Correct, Augustine, I think that you should listen to me very carefully. As you know, Señor Navarro had an agreement with myself, as head of the Los Zetas in the state of Chihuahua, and with the Sinaloan cartel to the west. Since Señor Navarro has resigned from the Garda Nacional, this agreement is now null and void. The Sinaloans and the Zetas have decided that there is no room left in the disputed territory between us for the Gallos to operate in, which means that there is no longer a Gallo cartel. Your people will either be assimilated by either the Zetas or the Sinaloans, or they will be killed. Do you understand?"

"I understand. If I may ask, would I be allowed to return to Mexico safely?"

"I could not care less what you do, Augustine, but from what Diego has just told me concerning your threats to his daughter, I do not think it is I that you should be worried about at the moment."

With that out of the way, Señor Menéndez told Diego to call him at any time that he could be of assistance in the future before signing off.

Diego turned off the phone and put it in his jacket pocket before taking his rifle back from Grady and motioning Augustine off of the porch and out in the courtyard. When Augustine was in front of the Power Wagon Diego had him stand still while he walked on the other side of the man, about 10 yards past him. He then turned to face Augustine and in one fluid move brought his rifle up to his shoulder and fired two rounds into Augustine's chest, killing him instantly.

Grady had been standing on the porch watching the proceedings and asked Diego why he had positioned Augustine so precisely before killing him.

"Because, my friend, you are now going to call Sheriff Stims and tell her that she needs to get up here ASAP since there has been an attack on your place. A smart man would know that we need to have been seen shooting our assailants from the direction of the garage," explained Diego as if to a child.

"All true, smartass, but a smart man would also realize that we have just killed four men with completely illegal fully automatic weapons which will put us in jail for a long, long time"

"This is true, I had not thought of that. Everybody in Chihuahua has a cuerno de chivo in their house or vehicle. Any ideas?"

"Way ahead of you. Let's police up this AK-47 brass first and make sure that every round is accounted for. I have two Winchester Model 94 lever action rifles chambered for .30-30 in the house. A .30-30 bullet is slightly smaller than an AK bullet, but it has almost identical ballistics to the AK round. Since we were firing hardball full metal jacket rounds out of the AK's, all the wounds are through and through so no slugs were left in the bodies for forensic analysis. Although the Winchesters fire round nosed bullets and the AK's fire spire points, we should still be okay if they can't find any AK bullets to compare. We'll fire off the same number of .30-30 rounds and place the brass from them in exactly the places we found the AK brass. We should be fine, and the Winchesters will show that they have recently been fired. I'll need to go hide our AK's and our magazines before we call Lorna."

Lorna and Tito arrived about 45 minutes later to find Diego and Grady on the front porch waiting for them with a dead guy out in the courtyard and another one on the porch. Lorna and Tito would eventually be shown the two dead guys beside the garage. Lorna thought it was odd that the old guys didn't seem too worked up by the attack but put it down to them both being old soldiers and probably having been through things like this before.

Nobody could figure out just why the attack had occurred, but Diego told Lorna that the dead guy by the old Power Wagon looked strangely similar to the head of the Gallo cartel, but it was difficult to say for sure due to his severe burns. Lorna just stared at Diego, but that is all he had to say.

During the course of the investigation, Lorna asked how they knew to come in behind the garage to take out the shooters there first. Grady took out his phone and showed her the trail camera app and how it worked. He explained that when he and Diego came home and saw the second set of tracks overlaid on their tracks from that morning, he'd decided to check the app. Which was all the truth that Lorna was going to get out of Diego and Grady that evening.

Lorna thought for a moment before she asked, "So, what were you guys doing with two .30-30's in the truck at this time of year anyhow, there is nothing in season?" she asked.

Grady said they carried them in the truck for coyotes at about the same time Diego said they were for mountain lions.

Lorna just laughed. Winchester Model 94 lever action rifles were not your rifle of choice for varmints. There was something going on here, but she had no idea as to just what it was. "Okay, you clowns, I don't believe a word you are saying, but if the stiff out in the courtyard is actually a cartel jefe and this causes me any grief from south of the border, I am going to come back here and lock you two jokers up and throw away the key. Understood?

"Señora Stims," Diego had decided to nip this line of thinking in the bud, "I have been in touch with my old office in Mexico and I can guarantee you if the slightly overcooked dead man there is in fact Augustine Chacón, there will be no blowback from the other side of the border. According to my sources within both the Sinaloa and Zeta cartels, Señor Chacón was on borrowed time in any case, and we seem to have inadvertently saved them the effort of disappearing him themselves."

"Does this have anything to do with the repeated attempts to kidnap Esmeralda?"

"I don't see how, she is up in San Angelo living in sin with his son," answered Diego pointing at Grady.

Lorna just laughed. "How are the two love birds getting along anyhow. I haven't heard from Deacon in weeks."

CHAPTER 43

THE LOVEBIRDS WERE DOING FINE. They were both gainfully employed: Deacon working on heavy equipment and Esmeralda working as a nurse. They were slowly feeding Diego's ill-gotten cash into a variety of bank accounts, which they had set up in multiple banks just for that purpose, and the house was quickly becoming a home.

Without their fathers being in close proximity all the time, much time was spent in properly breaking in each and every room of the house. Deacon actually did experiment with chocolate syrup, as opposed to bacon grease, poured onto Esmeralda's backside to see exactly which cracks and crevices it would eventually find its way into, and how to get it out. In Deacon's mind, the results were inconclusive during the first three attempts, the fourth experiment finally yielded acceptable results. The cleanup after each attempt seemed to take hours.

Diego had called shortly after the demise of the Bulldog and let them know the story and the new situation concerning the cartels in the state of Chihuahua.

While lying entwined on the couch one evening watching the History Channel, Esmeralda turned to Deacon and asked him if he missed it.

"Missed what?"

"You know, the adventure and the excitement down in the desert."

"Not really. We finally got you out of there in one piece and we've got a pretty good thing going here." After a few minutes he asked, "Did you ever find that lingerie shop you were looking for?"

"The Intimate Love Shack? Yes, I did. Why do you ask?"

"Did you happen to purchase anything there, or did you just window shop?"

"I bought a few items which may be of interest you. They had a nice selection of teddys, chemises, and baby dolls, so I bought an assortment to keep you stimulated, lewd and lusty."

"My lustfulness would be alive and well if you were wearing a potato sack. Is there one particular item which may lead to say an hour or two of adventure and excitement in the comfort of our own home?"

Esmeralda was pensive for a moment before replying, "Yes, I believe that the Unwrap Me baby doll, or perhaps a black lace camisole paired with a matching set of Venus lace back bikini panties should do the trick."

Esmeralda stood up and said she would go prepare herself and give him a shout when the stage was set. 15 minutes later, from out of the bedroom, Esmeralda shouted, "Dinner is served, come get it while it's hot!"

The adventure continues.